W9-AJH-040

DATE DUE

DEC 1 5 2009	
JAN 0 5 2010	
MAR 2 3 2010	
APR 2 9 2010	
SEP 2 0 2010	
SEP 2 8 2010	
DEC 1 4 2010	
FEB 0 3 2011	
SEP 0 6 2011	
SEP 2 3 2011	

DEMCO, INC. 38-2931

Lake Zurich MS North
LIBRARY
95 Hubbard Lane
Hawthorn Woods, IL 60047

Lake Zurich MS North
LIBRARY
95 Hubbard Lane
Hawthorn Woods, IL 60047

Violet Wings

Lake Zurich MS North
LIBRARY
95 Hubbard Lane
Hawthorn Woods, IL 60047

Victoria Hanley

EGMONT
USA

New York

EGMONT

We bring stories to life

First published by Egmont USA, 2009
443 Park Avenue South, Suite 806
New York, NY 10016

Copyright © Victoria Hanley, 2009
All rights reserved

1 3 5 7 9 8 6 4 2

www.egmontusa.com
www.victoriahanley.com

Library of Congress Cataloging-in-Publication Data

Hanley, Victoria.
Violet wings / Victoria Hanley.
p. cm.
Summary: After learning that she is an extremely powerful fairy, fourteen-year-old
Zaria Tourmaline uses her magic to try to learn about her parents' and brother's
disappearance five years before, and to explore the human world—activities which
put her and all of Feyland at risk.
ISBN 978-1-60684-011-5 (hardcover) — ISBN 978-1-60684-039-9 (reinforced
library binding) [1. Fairies—Fiction. 2. Magic—Fiction. 3. Orphans—Fiction.]
I. Title.
PZ7.H196358Vio 2009
[Fic]—dc22
2009015876

Book design by SY Design

Printed in the United States of America

All rights reserved. No part of this publication may be reproduced, stored in
a retrieval system, or transmitted, in any form or by any means, electronic,
mechanical, photocopying, or otherwise, without the prior permission of the
publisher and copyright owner.

To FAIRIES, GENIES, LEPRECHAUNS,
AND THEIR HUMAN FRIENDS

Lake Zurich MS North
LIBRARY
95 Hubbard Lane
Hawthorn Woods, IL. 60047

No trees grow upon the world of Tirfeyne. There are many tall bushes and a great variety of flowers, most of which can also be found on Earth. Homes are built of stone and metal, not wood.

Fairies, genies, and leprechauns dwell upon Tirfeyne. So do pixies, trolls, and gremlins— but they do not live in Feyland, for they have their own countries.

—*Orville Gold, genie historian of Feyland*

𝓑ack when I was nine, my parents went missing.

At first it was easy to believe that each new day would bring them home. After all, they had only gone in search of my older brother, Jett. This was hardly unusual. Jett couldn't seem to stay out of trouble, though I was never certain exactly what sort of trouble he kept getting into. And of course, he never told *me* where he went, or why.

It wasn't the first time that my teacher, Beryl Danburite, had looked after me. My parents always called on her when they were going to be gone for more than a few hours. I didn't enjoy having my teacher take care of me at home, but no one asked my opinion. Once, she had stayed a week.

This time, she never left.

The day I learned that my parents would not return, I was sitting on a corner perch, studying the one book from Earth that my family owned. It was about trees. I liked to look at the glossy illustrations and memorize the shapes of the leaves.

Miss Danburite didn't approve. Whenever she saw me reading it, she would say that Earth was a dangerous place and humans were baffling creatures. But she never actually ordered me to close the book.

I was looking at a picture of a blue spruce when I heard a loud knock on our door. I put the book aside and flew to answer the knock, my wings trembling.

A stranger stood on the threshold, a wiry genie with eyes like garnet beads looking out over a bulbous nose. His skin was orange with gold blotches, his hair the color of tarnished brass. On his wrist he wore a large ruby.

"Good evening," he said in a raspy voice. "I am Councilor Wolframite. Are you Zaria Tourmaline?"

I nodded.

"May I come in?"

I thought for a moment of slamming the door. Maybe if I didn't let him in, the news he carried couldn't come in, either. I feared that only dire news would bring a councilor to our home.

"Zaria?" Miss Danburite called. "Who is there?"

I couldn't make myself speak his name, though I remembered it quite clearly.

A moment later, Miss Danburite hurried in. When she saw him, her orange wings shivered like those of a frightened child. I had never seen her lose control of her wings.

"Good evening," he said again.

"Good evening, Councilor."

"I am here to speak with you about Zaria." He looked down at me once, but after that he looked only at Miss Danburite. "I am sorry," he said, "but her parents have been declared *indeterminum detu.*"

Young as I was, I knew the meaning of that phrase from the ancient language. *Gone, never to return.* A window of night seemed to open in my heart. Dark, without stars, and filled with cold.

"We believe they were caught by humans," Councilor Wolframite continued. "The last anyone saw of them, they were taking a portal to Earth."

"But they—" she said.

"They have been gone a month. And we must make a decision about their daughter." He touched the ruby on his wrist. I noticed that the figure of a crown had been carved into it. "I must ask you, Miss Danburite. Are you willing to be her guardian?"

"I do not understand," she answered.

"Zaria's parents named you her guardian if they should die," he said.

I looked up at Miss Danburite and waited for her to say that there had been a mistake, that my parents were delayed, not dead. When she didn't speak, the window in my heart opened wider and let in more of the night.

The councilor frowned. "Miss Danburite?"

"Has she no relatives?" she asked.

"Zaria has no close kin," Councilor Wolframite answered. "Her family has been extraordinarily unlucky."

Miss Danburite's faded yellow eyes blazed up once and then watered over. For several moments she stood silent, her mouth twisting.

"Her parents named *you*," he said. "Perhaps because you have no children?"

She raised her voice a little, the way she did sometimes in the classroom. "I am two hundred eighteen years old," she said. "You expect me to move to Galena and raise an orphaned fairy?"

Orphaned fairy. Could that be me?

"She has no one else."

Miss Danburite swallowed and blinked and brought her wings under control. "Very well," she said.

"Thank you." Councilor Wolframite bowed to her. "I will come back tomorrow to ratify you as Zaria's guardian."

She didn't bow. She didn't tell him good-bye, and I didn't, either.

After he left, she looked at me. "Do you understand, Zaria? I will stay here with you until you are grown."

I wanted to speak, but I felt too cold.

"I am sorry," she said. "Your father and mother will not be coming back. Your brother is gone, too."

When she said those words, a wonderful thing happened. I felt as if a curtain appeared in my heart, a curtain woven out of something so heavy and strong, it could cover the window to the night.

She sighed. "I will try to be a good guardian to you. Try not to be a nuisance to me."

The curtain thickened. The tighter it closed, the less I had to think about my lost family. And I could look at Beryl Danburite and feel almost nothing at all.

Chapter One

FIVE YEARS LATER

FEY MAGIC IS MUCH MISUNDERSTOOD BY HUMANS; HUMANS SEEM TO BELIEVE THAT MAGIC CAN SOMEHOW TURN ASIDE PHYSICAL FORCE. IN FACT, FEY FOLK ARE JUST AS VULNERABLE TO PHYSICAL INJURIES AS HUMANS; MAGIC CANNOT SAVE US FROM BLADES, BULLETS, OR EXPLOSIONS. WE CAN USUALLY MOVE FAST ENOUGH TO DODGE KNIVES OR ARROWS, BUT ONLY THE VERY SWIFTEST AMONG US CAN AVOID A BULLET.

THE FIRST TIME A HUMAN FIRED A GUN UPON A FEY PERSONAGE, THE HIGH COUNCIL OF FEYLAND PROCLAIMED THE EDICT OF THE UNSEEN, ORDERING ALL FEY FOLK TO KEEP OUT OF SIGHT OF HUMANS.

—Orville Gold, genie historian of Feyland

*M*y friend Leona hardly ever flutters, but as she passed through the great Gateway of Galena for the first time, her silver wings quivered like a rippling mirror. Just behind her went Andalonus, unable to keep from bouncing up and down, the fronds of his blue hair waving around his head.

Meteor happened to be floating next to me, but at the gateway he stopped. "After you, Zaria," he said, his eyes shining like well-cut emeralds.

Gliding past the magic columns that guard Galena, I couldn't keep my wings from trembling: I was simply too delighted.

We had all been forced to wait until every member of our class reached the age of fourteen before a single one of us could go to Oberon City. Dreadful, stupid law, but like all the laws of Feyland, strictly enforced. We'd been stuck in Galena—the land of babies, toddlers, and children—until I, Zaria Tourmaline, youngest in our class of fifty, turned fourteen.

I was sorry to have caused forty-nine other fairies and genies to wait for my birthday. If I could have hurried it, I would have celebrated with Andalonus when he turned fourteen five weeks earlier.

Once through the gateway and inside Oberon City, our teacher, Mr. Bloodstone, ordered us to walk. *Walk!* As if we would cause accidents if we flew. It was total nonsense, because all of us had been flying since we were four years old.

Our feet found hard slabs of granite instead of the soft sand that is spread in Galena for safety. We had to crane our necks to see the buildings. Such buildings! In Galena, all structures are low to the ground, to prevent young fairies and genies from injuring themselves. But in Oberon City, great domes rose around us, gleaming silver, gold, platinum, and copper. Beyond the domes, I could see mighty towers studded with gemstones.

Squeaking with excitement, Portia Peridot soared five wingspans high before Mr. Bloodstone roared at her. "Stay on the ground, Portia, or I will bind your wings!"

Portia dropped so fast she must have bruised her heels on the hard walkway. She limped on, her green wings drooping. I glared at Bloodstone's back. Typical for him to treat us like infants, even in Oberon City!

He led the way through a marble arch into a viewing station filled with grown fairies and genies. Ignoring them, he ushered us into a room apart.

Like toddlers seeing colored smoke, we stared. Crystal booths, clear as the purest raindrops, projected out from the west wall. Each booth contained a scope, a magic instrument of silver that looked from our world onto Earth.

We were here to get our first glimpse of the fabled land of humans. We would also see a fairy godmother or genie godfather bestow a birth gift.

Meteor was ahead of me. I watched him step into a booth and put his eye to the scope while Bloodstone hovered approvingly. (Meteor is probably the one true scholar Bloodstone has ever taught, so Bloodstone thinks he's the greatest genie alive.)

When Bloodstone waved me forward, not even a flicker

of premonition warned me that in a moment my life would be forever changed.

I pressed my forehead gently against the fitting above the eyepiece on the viewing scope. For several moments all I saw were trees and sky. Looking at them, I felt the strangest yearning to jump out of the booth and find a portal to Earth. I wanted to float through that sky and brush those leaves with my fingertips.

"Find the baby you are here to observe, Zaria," Bloodstone said in my ear. Why couldn't he stay out of the booth?

I touched a switch that lit up a set of lines pointing to a human baby wrapped in a fluffy yellow blanket. Her skin was brown, a bit lighter than Meteor's, her hair a wispy thatch as plain as a gnome's. Apparently, humans do not have much variety when it comes to skin and hair color. I looked into the baby's beaming eyes and watched her kick her small feet and twine her tiny fingers together.

A bell chimed, signaling the event I had been brought here to see: the transmission of the baby's birth gift—my chance to see a fairy godmother in action.

I watched as a gift descended, streaming like mist, settling into the baby's skin. And though I wasn't asking to know, my magic told me what gift it was: to have *little curiosity*.

The baby's eyes dimmed.

I didn't understand. Why would a godmother hand out such a gift? It didn't seem like a *gift* at all, more like a curse that took away something good.

I squinted at the adjacent booth where the baby's godmother perched. Her sleek face turned away from her godchild without a backward glance. Before she left the booth I clearly saw her saffron-colored hair, braided with strands of morganite. Her thin nose turned down at the end, and her wings were white.

My elbow bumped the arm of the scope and I couldn't see the baby anymore. I tried to get her back. The scope jogged around, and the next thing I knew, I was looking at a human boy about my age. His coloring was so distinctive, he could have been a genie: hair red and gold like flames, hazel eyes filled with amber light. Somehow the scope caught him at a moment when he seemed to be looking back at me. I jumped, knocking the scope's arm all the way up.

The gray skin of Bloodstone's face creased into a familiar sneer. "You will get used to it," he said.

That's one of the biggest lies anyone has ever told me.

Chapter Two

SINCE THE EDICT OF THE UNSEEN WAS PUT INTO PLACE, HUMAN MISCONCEPTIONS ABOUT FEY FOLK HAVE BECOME MORE AND MORE COMMON. FOR EXAMPLE, WHEN HUMANS PORTRAY FAIRIES AND GENIES IN STORIES, THEY SHOW NOT ONLY FEMALE FAIRIES AND MALE GENIES, BUT ALSO MALE FAIRIES AND FEMALE GENIES. THIS IS AN ABSURDITY.

FAIRIES ARE THE FEMALE OF THE SPECIES; GENIES ARE THE MALE. FAIRIES HAVE WINGS, GENIES HAVE MAGIC FEET, BUT BOTH CAN FLY WITH EQUAL SPEED.

HUMANS APPEAR TO BELIEVE THAT FAIRIES ARE TINY AND GENIES ARE ENORMOUS. THIS IS NOT SO. ON AVERAGE, BOTH FAIRIES AND GENIES ARE BETWEEN FIVE AND SIX FEET TALL WHEN FULL GROWN, MUCH LIKE HUMANS.

—Orville Gold, genie historian of Feyland

After leaving the viewing booth, I tried to put the sinister godmother and her godchild out of my mind. All I wanted to think of was Earth. I still longed to be among the trees I had seen, really among them, instead of watching from another world through a diamond lens.

But according to law, I must be sixteen and registered with the High Council before making even one journey to Earth.

I couldn't imagine waiting another two years.

"Well?" I whispered to my friends.

"I thought it would be more exciting, but it was only a baby with no hair," Leona said. "Maybe it will be different, once I have my own godchild."

I wondered if my friends' magic had told them what gifts had been given while they were observing human infants. I opened my mouth to ask, but then Andalonus nudged me.

"I heard Bloodstone say you're Earth-struck."

"What?" I looked up and caught Bloodstone's eye on me and wished an evil fairy would stuff him into an old-fashioned genie bottle.

Leona stepped in front of me, blocking Bloodstone's view. She has never been afraid of him because she's a Bloodstone, too—his niece, in fact. He never reprimands her, no matter what she does. "Do human male babies have hair?" she asked Meteor and Andalonus.

As they talked, my mind drifted back to Earth. Was it possible I'd somehow been enchanted? How else could I explain what was wrong with me? How else could I be so drawn to the world that had killed my parents?

Chapter Three

THE MAGIC OF FAIRIES AND GENIES DOES NOT
FULLY RIPEN UNTIL AGE FOURTEEN. THERE ARE WIDE
DIFFERENCES IN LEVELS OF INBORN MAGIC FROM ONE
INDIVIDUAL TO ANOTHER.

LEVELS GIVE THE CAPACITY FOR PERFORMING SPELLS
FROM SIMPLE TO ADVANCED. FOR EXAMPLE, LEVEL 1
MAGIC ALLOWS THE CREATION OF LARGE SOAP BUBBLES
AND OTHER TRIVIAL ENCHANTMENTS. . . . LEVEL 3
ALLOWS A FAIRY OR GENIE TO BESTOW A SMALL,
RATHER USELESS GIFT ON A HUMAN GODCHILD (SUCH
AS A KNACK FOR STACKING SPOONS). . . . BUT LEVEL
75—WHICH IS EXCEEDINGLY RARE—IS REQUIRED FOR
THE CREATION OF PORTALS TO EARTH.

TO *TRAVEL* THROUGH THE PORTALS BETWEEN
TIRFEYNE AND EARTH, ONE MUST HAVE AT LEAST
LEVEL 5 MAGIC. IN AGES PAST, NEARLY ALL FAIRIES AND
GENIES COULD MAKE SUCH JOURNEYS WITH EASE; BUT
NOW, 89 PERCENT DO NOT HAVE ADEQUATE MAGIC TO
LEAVE TIRFEYNE AND ARE ABLE TO SEE EARTH ONLY
THROUGH VIEWING SCOPES.

—*Orville Gold, genie historian of Feyland*

When our class returned to Galena, everything looked babyish. Buildings seemed too close to the ground. The sand felt squishy.

The instant Bloodstone dismissed us, we all rose into the air. Meteor and Andalonus zoomed ahead and soon they were out of sight. Leona and I flew hard, too, racing to Galena Falls.

There's a place past the topmost rock west of the falls where we like to sit. Sheltered by rocks and plants, it's been our spot since we were little. When we were very small fairies, we'd play with diamonds, eat fresh sonnia flowers—and tell secrets.

In the years since, we've outgrown playing with diamonds, but we still tell secrets. I know that Leona despises her uncle Boris, that she rarely sees her father—who prefers Oberon City to Galena—and that she believes her mother will never understand her in the least. Leona knows I love sneaking out to Galena Falls at night, and that I don't like to talk about my dead family. She also knows I see way too much of Beryl Danburite, who shares teaching our class with Mr. Bloodstone.

We settled into our favorite spot, and I looked down to the pool under the falls. It was lined with gemstones— emeralds, rubies, diamonds, sapphires, topaz. Sunlight polished the colors and glinted off the spray. Lavish flowers were everywhere. It was truly beautiful, but all I could think of was Earth.

"Zaria," said Leona, so sharply she startled me.

"What?"

"You *are* Earth-struck."

I didn't try to argue. It would be useless; Leona knew me too well.

Her wings twitched, which meant she had a big secret. "I know where there's a portal to Earth," she said. "A portal we could take *today* and no one would know."

"Today?" I blinked in confusion.

She whispered, "This portal is in *Galena*."

"That's impossible!"

"Unlawful, not impossible," she said. "It's not far from here."

"How do you know?" I squeaked. "Have you been to Earth?"

"Not yet." She smiled and rose from the rock. "Let's go."

I sprang up. "Wait," I said. "What if we don't have enough magic to go through a portal?"

Leona sniffed. "Level Five?" She arched an eyebrow and turned, floating toward a boulder about twenty wingspans away. I flew jaggedly after her.

The boulder was plain sandstone, nothing special. No path beside it, just a jumble of wild zinnia flowers, orange and yellow. The nearer I got, the more I felt a strange urge to pass by the boulder and forget about it.

"This boulder is enchanted," Leona whispered, "so children won't want to play on it."

"A long-lasting spell?" I asked, impressed.

She nodded.

"How do you know?"

"I'll tell you once we get through." Leona glanced around, then stepped *into* the boulder and disappeared!

I hesitated only long enough to draw a deep breath. To be honest, even if someone had told me the portal would turn me into a troll or force me to live with fifteen gremlins for ten years, I still would have gone through it.

PORTALS ARE NEEDED TO TRAVEL BETWEEN TIRFEYNE AND EARTH.

THE MAIN HUB FOR TRAVEL IS THE GOLDEN STATION IN OBERON CITY. PORTALS LEADING TO AND FROM THIS STATION ARE USED FREQUENTLY BY THOSE WHO POSSESS LEVEL 5 MAGIC OR ABOVE.

OTHER PORTALS ARE OBSCURE, KNOWN TO ONLY A FEW, AND THEIR LOCATIONS ARE CLOSELY GUARDED. THEY HAVE BEEN MADE FOR THE SOLE PURPOSE OF SMUGGLING HUMAN GOODS INTO TIRFEYNE. SUCH PORTALS ARE UNLAWFUL.

—*Orville Gold, genie historian of Feyland*

*L*eona hovered in front of me, smirking. I looked back at the sandstone boulder. On the Earth side, it looked just as it had on Tirfeyne: dull stone in a tangle of bright zinnias. But here, it stood in the midst of an open field of golden grass on a hillside.

I spun in a circle, my wings open to the sky.

Leona watched me. "Your wings are shining."

It was good of her to mention my one beauty—my violet

wings. The rest of my coloring is so drab, I've often heard it whispered that I stand out no more than a shadow. My skin is an ashy lavender, and my hair an even paler version of the same pitiful color. It's very unusual for a fairy to be so plain; my dull appearance sometimes seems to act like a spell that makes others forget me. Well, at least my eyes match my wings, though a friend of my mother's once remarked that it was startling to see such bright violet eyes staring out of such a wan little face. (My mother sounded very cold when she responded that it was certainly odd how perceptions could differ from fairy to fairy.)

No one disagreed about Leona's appearance, though. *She is beautiful.* . . .

I gazed around. To the west, foothills traced a scalloped line against the sky. In the other direction, the long grass of the field met a row of trees. Behind them, I could see the buildings of a human town.

"Let's explore," said Leona.

"You said you'd tell me how you know about the portal."

She lifted her chin. "I've followed my mother at night."

"You've seen her use it?"

Leona nodded. "I think she made it herself. She must have a godchild nearby."

"Godchild?" But why would Leona's mother, Doreen Bloodstone, create an unlawful portal from Galena? Any godmother could use the scopes in Oberon City to watch over a godchild. Wasn't it a terrible risk to break the laws of Feyland just to have quick access to a human?

Leona shrugged. "Why else would she make a portal?"

I didn't know. I had always thought Doreen Bloodstone was proud of her status as a powerful fairy. Too proud. And although I concealed it, I didn't like her. She laughed too much. After my parents disappeared, she would giggle nervously when mentioning them, a raspy little cackle that put me on edge.

Leona spread her wings. "Let's explore," she said again.

We knew fairies weren't supposed to fly when visiting Earth, but how wonderful it felt to take to the air! How I loved gliding over the great sweep of land, with sunlit breezes filling my wings.

Chapter Five

THE HUMAN LIFESPAN IS QUITE SHORT COMPARED
TO THAT OF FAIRIES AND GENIES, WHO USUALLY LIVE
TWO HUNDRED YEARS OR LONGER. THE OCCASIONAL
LONG-LIVED PERSONAGE AMONG THE FEY WILL ATTAIN
TWO HUNDRED FIFTY YEARS. HOWEVER, FAIRIES AND
GENIES REACH PHYSICAL MATURITY AT A RATE SIMILAR
TO HUMANS, ALLOWING US MANY MORE DECADES TO
ATTAIN WISDOM.

LEPRECHAUNS LIVE SOMEWHERE AROUND ONE
HUNDRED TWENTY-THREE YEARS, IF THEY DO NOT
ABBREVIATE THEIR LIVES BY TAKING SILLY CHANCES.

—*Orville Gold, genie historian of Feyland*

When Leona and I got closer to the human town, we
stopped flying to walk a footpath that went winding through
the wild grass toward the trees. Entranced though I was with
Earth, I was also feeling a little afraid.

"What's wrong?" Leona asked.

"Nothing." I didn't want to bring up my parents or
my lost brother. Five years is a long time. To Leona, it must

seem like I had always been an orphan. After all, I never talked about my family.

I brightened as the path entered the woods. I stopped to put my arms around a tree trunk. Each leaf on the overarching branches looked as if an artist had spent hours cutting it into a pattern. I recognized the pattern—this was a maple tree. I lay my cheek against its bark and inhaled. The wood smelled spicy. "You're lovely," I murmured.

Leona laughed. "Trees can't talk."

"I know."

"Trees are harmless, but beware of humans," she said, talking in her best imitation of Mr. Bloodstone. "They can be very dangerous, worse than trolls, thoroughly unpredictable." Her eyes sparkled, and I wondered if she even remembered that my family had died on Earth.

I drifted through the trees and thought about my mother, something I almost never did. Unlike me, she had been a colorful fairy. Soft white hair, lavender skin, and dark yellow wings that were nearly gold. Her eyes had been deep and wild, like a storm.

Why had the humans killed her?

The woods ended at a walkway that ran in a circle around a clearing covered with bright green grass, clipped short. In the center was a playground. Sand lay under blue-and-red climbing towers, reminding me of Galena. Human children ran and leaped on the towers, as if they wished they could grow wings.

Transfixed by the sight, Leona and I stood in the shade of a tall cottonwood.

"A little early for Halloween, aren't you, girls?" said a voice at my left shoulder.

Startled, I turned to see a woman in a wide-brimmed beige hat and green clothes. Her arms rested on the handle of a small carriage in which a human toddler slept. "I love your costumes," she said, "and your makeup is out of this world."

I blinked at her. Whatever I had imagined a human to be, it was not this.

"What amazing fabric," she continued, brushing my sleeve. "I've never seen anything like it. It looks as if it should be sheer, but it isn't. Where did you get it?"

Then she touched one of my wings. "Wow," she went on, carelessly rubbing the margin. "Where did you find this material?" She lifted part of my wing close to her face. "So fine and delicate, but it looks strong. And the veins! What a nice touch. You look like a giant butterfly."

She didn't seem to notice that I wasn't answering her questions.

"I like to sew," the woman continued. "Did you send away for your costume?"

"Uh," I mumbled.

"Are you girls going to be in a play?" she asked next.

I shook my head.

Who knows what would have happened then, but the child in the carriage woke and began to cry.

"It's okay, Pumpkin," the woman crooned, letting go of my wing and crouching down to pat the toddler's head.

Pumpkin howled.

"All right, let's go home," the woman said, straightening. "Bye, girls. Beautiful costumes!" As soon as she started moving, the child's cries died down.

Watching her go, I saw a tall boy with light hair and skin striding down the walkway toward us. His eyes lit on Leona, and he flashed her a grin.

My first sight of Jason Court should not have been frightening. He looked like a healthy and handsome human specimen. I had no reason to feel uneasy, and yet, that's the way it was—as if I recognized from the first moment all the trouble he would cause.

I scooted back into the trees, hoping Leona would join me and we could leave. Instead, she seemed fascinated by the boy. He stopped beside her and introduced himself. She swayed on her toes, her skirts floating around her ankles.

We shouldn't have come. Not now, not during the day and in the open. Earth at night would be safer. Two humans had already seen us—three, if the toddler counted. What if word got back to Feyland somehow?

Uneasy, I looked out across the playground to the group of children twenty wingspans away. A small girl with red braids teetered high on the edge of a platform. A black-haired little boy behind her swung his arm, hitting her on the shoulder. She fell forward.

Without thinking, I flew, faster than I've ever flown, and caught the girl just before she hit the ground. I set her on her feet before realizing what I'd done.

She stared at me with round blue eyes. "How did you *do* that?" she cried. She waved at someone behind me. "Sam!" she yelled. *"Saaamm!"*

The rest of the children on the playground began screeching, "A fairy!" They swarmed over one another, scrambling to reach me.

The black-haired child slid down a pole and grabbed my right wing with both hands, twisting. "It's a real fairy!" he yelled. "Let's catch it!"

I tried to back away, but the small human gritted his teeth, holding tight.

"Hey!" a voice behind me shouted. "Let go of her!"

An older boy pushed through the children surrounding me and made the child release his grip on my wing.

This new human had red hair and gold-toned eyes. It was the same boy I had seen through the scope!

"Are you okay?" he asked.

I couldn't seem to speak.

He turned to the little girl with the braids. "What happened, Jenna?"

"The fairy saved me," she answered.

I can't explain what I did next. Instead of thanking the

boy, I rose into the air. I hovered for a moment, trying to get a view of Leona while the children screamed and hopped up and down, pointing.

"Sam," the little girl cried, "make her stay."

I didn't see Leona—or her new friend. Had they moved into the trees?

I turned and flew. My breath came in gasps and my wing-beats felt ragged. What had just happened?

I looked back once and saw the boy named Sam running along the ground, holding something small and red in front of his face.

Chapter Six

ALL FAIRIES AND GENIES HAVE INBORN RESERVES OF
MAGIC, WHICH ARE MEASURED IN UNITS CALLED RADIA.
THESE UNITS HAVE TO DO WITH AMOUNTS OF MAGIC,
WHICH ARE NOT THE SAME AS LEVELS.

A SINGLE JOURNEY TO EARTH AND BACK AGAIN USES
HALF OF ONE RADIA.

A UNIT OF RADIA, ONCE USED, IS GONE FOREVER.
        —*Orville Gold, genie historian of Feyland*

I flew blindly over the human town. It was several
minutes before I turned back to look for Leona. The sun was
sinking low; I had to squint against the glare in order to see
her, not far behind me, her wings like silver streaks in the sky.
I waited for her, hovering nervously.

When she caught up, Leona was beaming. "I wonder how
many laws we've broken?" she said breathlessly. "I thought
you were the *good* fairy. Who would believe you'd fly in front
of humans? Not that anyone will hear about it from *me*. And
what else could you have done, with that pack of children
attacking you?" She skimmed beside me, laughing.

Maybe the Earth air was affecting her.

"We'll come back soon, Zaree," Leona said. "I met a boy named Jason Court, and I'd like to visit him again."

"You would? But, Leona—"

She stopped smiling. "It's not as if I plan to become *good friends* with a human," she said.

It reminded me of the time she had said, *"It's not as if I would search for my mother's spellbook."* But then she had found the book and read it, even though it was forbidden for a young fairy to do so. And once she had said, *"It's not as if I would try to go through the Gateway of Galena."* But she had gone so close to it, she had set off the alarms.

There had been many more times when Leona had gone against the rules. But could she really want to be friends with a human boy? At our age, forming any relationship at all with a human was strictly forbidden.

Trying to calm myself, I drifted downward and landed in a cornfield on the edge of town.

We had studied cornfields, so I knew corn was an important source of human food and fuel. But being in an actual cornfield was nothing like studying it in a book. I stood among the green plants topped with silky spires and twined my fingers around a stalk. A warm, sweet scent rose from the corn.

Leona cruised down beside me. "We should go back. Miss Danburite will be looking for you."

I envied Leona. Her parents wouldn't fuss the way Beryl would; for all their faults they understood that Leona was growing up. But Beryl seemed to believe I was still the same nine-year-old who had become her charge five years ago. And now, thanks to my headlong flight, we were far away from the portal that led to Galena. I had flown in the wrong direction, and we must be miles east of where we had arrived on Earth.

How long had we been gone? The setting sun was lighting the sky like magical fire. Soon it would be dark.

Gazing at the flaming horizon, I saw an odd flicker at the edges of the cornfield. I glided toward the spot.

Cornstalks had been flattened into a perfect circle that glistened as if each stalk had been given an extra dose of light. Footprints led out of the circle and then stopped.

I waved Leona over. "Fey folk have been here."

Leona's eyes widened. "Zaree, you've found another portal?"

"Maybe. But why would this one be obvious when the one your mother made looks like a plain boulder?"

Leona frowned. "I doubt if humans can see this for what it is; you probably need magic. And my mother's portal is unlawful, so when she opened it, she must have done something to hide it." She nudged one of the footprints on the ground. "This looks like an official portal. We should take it so we don't have to fly all the way back to where we started."

As usual, she didn't waste time. She walked straight into the circle of flattened corn and disappeared.

Chapter Seven

FAIRIES AND GENIES RECEIVE A CRYSTAL WATCH WHEN ALL MEMBERS OF THEIR CLASS REACH THE AGE OF FOURTEEN. THESE WATCHES WERE DESIGNED BY THE ANCIENTS. NOT ONLY DO THEY TELL TIME, BUT THEY ALSO REGISTER INBORN MAGIC.

IN THE CIRCLE OF THE CRYSTAL WATCH FACE, THERE ARE SIX DIVISIONS, EACH MARKED WITH A DIFFERENT COLOR: RED, ORANGE, YELLOW, GREEN, BLUE, AND VIOLET. WHEN A CRYSTAL WATCH IS FASTENED UPON THE WRIST, A SMALL THIRD WATCH HAND WILL POINT TO THE AMOUNT OF RADIA RESERVES THE OWNER POSSESSES.

IN THE CENTER OF THE WATCH FACE, THE NUMBER THAT INDICATES LEVEL OF MAGIC WILL APPEAR.

—Orville Gold, genie historian of Feyland

he quiet cornfield portal on Earth led into a short empty hallway filled with racket, as though hordes of trolls in tin boots were clattering past on the other side of the wall. Ahead of me, Leona hovered next to a dull copper door at the end of the hallway. "I think this is the Golden Station," she said. She straightened her wings and pulled the door open.

The din increased. Thousands of fairies and genies, all talking at once, were flying in a hundred directions through a vast room, while dozens of doors banged open and shut. Marching gnomes seemed to be trying to keep order. We were inside Oberon City, in the Golden Station, a structure of marble and granite decorated with gold.

Leona aimed herself toward an archway at the end of the room. I dodged behind a wide-backed gnome and followed. Leona passed gracefully through the crowds, but my wings kept buffeting broad-shouldered genies. I mumbled apologies, grateful to be a drabs forgettable fairy.

Once outside, we instantly took to the air. Leona seemed to know where she was going. She led the way, and we flew high and fast.

When we reached the Gateway of Galena, we crept through quietly.

"Safe!" Leona cried.

Something cold struck me in the chest. I suddenly felt so weak, I fell to the ground. Leona sprawled next to me.

"Safe indeed," said Beryl's voice. She stood beside one of the pillars near the gateway, clutching a staff that had a blackened knob of iron on one end.

Leona glared at Beryl. "You used an iron fist on *me*?"

Beryl raised her staff. "You deserve far worse."

"But why?" Leona cried. "By *tomorrow* we'll have our

crystal watches. We'll be allowed to go back and forth through the gateway alone."

"Tomorrow is not today," Beryl answered grimly.

I could see Leona beginning to think up a lie. "We're sorry," she said, "that we stayed behind, but we wanted to explore Oberon City."

Beryl always claimed to be able to sniff out a liar—she said her many decades of teaching had given her a nose for the truth. Oh, how I hoped she wouldn't smell Leona's lie this time.

Silence rang around us before Beryl answered. "I *know* where you have been."

My wings trembled and ached. A spot of pain in my chest spread down my arms.

Beryl glided closer to us. "A godmother used the viewing scope to look in on one of her godchildren today." She jabbed the air with her staff. "Imagine her shock: two young fairies, on an unauthorized trip to Earth. Two fairies, showing themselves to humans in daylight. Flying in full view."

Leona picked herself up. "I don't understand why we can't allow *any* humans to see us."

Beryl folded her wings but didn't lower her staff. "It has been policy for over three hundred years not to show ourselves on Earth—as you know perfectly well."

"They weren't carrying weapons," Leona protested.

"It has taken centuries to convince humans that fey folk do not exist," Beryl hissed. "It would take only a few sightings now for them to become interested in catching us again."

I wished Leona would stop arguing, but she kept going. "How could they catch us?" she cried. "They can't even fly!"

"Humans can be unexpectedly ingenious—and cruel," Beryl told her.

Leona shook her head defiantly, but before she could say anything more, Beryl turned to me. "And what is *your* opinion, Zaria?" she asked in her coldest tone. "Is the human world dangerous to fey folk?"

Leona looked from Beryl to me. Her face changed, and she closed her mouth.

Beryl didn't wait for my answer. "After what happened to your family, Zaria, I would not have expected this from *you*."

My wings felt weak. I wanted to get up, but I stayed where I was.

Chapter Eight

To perform magic of Level 7 or beyond, a wand is required. Fairies and genies receive their wands at the same time as their crystal watches. Some have argued that allowing those who register under Level 7 to keep their wands is a pointless indulgence. However, all fairies and genies, no matter what level of magic they possess, cherish their wands and feel the need to keep them near from the day they are issued until the day death arrives. There is no known equivalent for this among humans.

Fairies and genies learn very young to ration their radia so that they will not run out. For this reason, spell-making is a small part of daily life in Feyland. Only the most reckless are willing to squander their radia on unnecessary enchantments. Few enchantments are truly necessary.

Inborn magic, once used, cannot be regenerated.

—*Orville Gold, genie historian of Feyland*

As Beryl continued frowning at Leona and me, another figure stepped out from behind a pillar. Bloodstone. His gray skin stretched tightly across his cheekbones, and his thin mouth was like a slash carved in stone.

For once, I paid no attention to him. "Beryl, are you saying you know *how* my parents . . . died?" My voice failed on the last word.

"I am saying they took careless risks, just as you have done."

"They weren't careless!" But looking at her face, I began to wonder.

Bloodstone cut in. "Your nonsense today has made both Miss Danburite and myself a full degree poorer than we were this morning." He shook his crystal watch in my face but didn't open the watch-face cover, so I couldn't see his radia reserves. He and Beryl were both Yellow. Had they really used a thousand radia each? That was a lot to lose. Too much. Quaking, I didn't dare glance at Leona.

"To correct your mistakes, Mr. Bloodstone and I had to reshuffle the entire schedule of the viewing station," Beryl fumed, "so that we could access the sending ports."

What was she talking about?

"We had to use scopes to place emergency forgetting spells on every person on Earth who saw you," Bloodstone said, scowling.

"Down to the last child," Beryl explained. "As your teachers, we are responsible for you."

"To make matters worse," Bloodstone continued, "it was no ordinary fairy who reported you today. It was a member of the High Council, Lily Morganite."

The name meant nothing to me, but then I had never learned much about the Council. When I heard Leona gasp, I realized this was serious.

"I'm sorry," I said desperately. "So sorry."

"Sorry? Zaria, have I taught you nothing?" Beryl's voice rose. "You are clearly not ready to receive your crystal watch and your wand. Nor are you, Leona. You must both wait another year."

Leona flinched. "I turned fourteen six months ago. I've already been waiting—"

"Miss Danburite," Bloodstone said. "Surely that would be an overly harsh punishment for Leona?"

Beryl whirled on him. "These two fairies have displayed contempt for the rules we have taught them. Can you imagine what they might have done if they had carried *wands*?"

Bloodstone glowered. "I agree that Zaria showed bad judgment instigating a journey to Earth," he said. "By all means, postpone her watch and wand for another year. But I have no doubt that Leona was merely trying to help a silly friend."

Leona shook her head. "*I* urged Zaria to go."

"Taking the blame for both of you is noble," Bloodstone

replied. "But I know the signs of an Earth-struck fairy. Zaria showed those signs—not you, Leona." He gave me a look of disgust as I painfully rose from the sand. My torso felt bruised.

"What happened, Zaria?" Beryl asked.

I looked down, not answering, not wanting to meet her eyes.

"The girls are equally guilty," she announced. "They must be equally punished."

"A mistake," Bloodstone told her. "However, if you insist on the same punishment, let these foolish fairies receive their watches and wands tomorrow—but with iron bands around their wings."

Chapter Nine

IT IS AGONIZING TO FEY FOLK TO TOUCH ANYTHING
MADE OF SOLID IRON, FOR IT INTERFERES WITH MAGIC,
AND FEY FOLK ARE MAGICAL BEINGS.
> —*Orville Gold, genie historian of Feyland*

I could hardly believe it. Why would Bloodstone agree to any punishment for Leona, the niece he doted on? Not only punishment, but *severe* punishment. It must have something to do with me. He had never approved of our friendship. Did he hope to ruin it?

Up to that moment, my only experience of iron was from the staff Beryl still held. I could still feel the stinging ache where it had hit my chest. I had no trouble believing that iron bands around my wings would inflict horrible pain.

I watched Beryl anxiously, waiting for her answer. I dreaded the iron, but I would rather endure a day of pain than wait another year for my watch and wand.

Beryl stood silent; it was Leona who spoke. "You want *me* to be ironbound in front of the magistria of the Council?" Twilight turned her silver wings the color of lead.

"Let it be a lesson to you," Bloodstone answered, "not to follow Earth-struck fairies. Miss Danburite? Do you approve?"

I was sure she wouldn't, but Beryl surprised me. "Very well."

My guardian made no move to intervene as Bloodstone drew on thick gloves and then brought out a band of iron set with a titanium clasp. Fiend! He must have planned this before he arrived.

"Turn around, Zaria," he ordered. "And fold your wings."

I heard a snap as the band closed around the base of my wings. It felt very cold, but not the sort of cold that numbs; it was a cold that clung and spread like cracks through broken glass, filled with slivers of piercing pain.

"In one week, if you do not break the law again, I will remove the bands," said Bloodstone.

A week! I had thought it would be only a day.

I didn't watch as Bloodstone bound Leona.

"Neither of you will speak of your crime," he said. "If you do, your punishment will be extended. And tell us: which portal did you use?"

Leona must have been in agony, but she answered quietly. "A small portal in the Golden Station."

"Did no one stop you?" he demanded. "It should have been obvious that you are much too young to journey to Earth."

"No one seemed to notice us," she said.

Our teachers exchanged glances and then drifted a little ways off. Bloodstone began waving his arms furiously, while Beryl frowned and clutched her wand.

"I'll never forgive them," Leona said. "Never." Her eyes in the fading light looked as leaden as her fettered wings.

"I'm sorry."

"It wasn't your fault."

It was taking all my strength just to withstand the pain from the iron. With each small tremor in my wings, I thought I would shatter.

"It's lucky we found the portal through the Golden Station," Leona whispered. "Otherwise the one who caught us on Earth might have watched us go back through Galena. And if the Council ever found out that my mother had made a portal in Galena, who knows what they would do?"

Just then Bloodstone raised his voice slightly. I strained to hear.

"I do not understand why the most talented fairy in our class would befriend that dim little orphan. . . ."

"Boris!" Beryl's angry whisper was perfectly clear.

"You cannot have failed to observe that Leona is exceptional."

Beryl surprised me by sticking up for me. "So is Zaria."

"Acting as Zaria's guardian has truly blinded you," Bloodstone retorted. "She is as foolish as the rest of her family."

"Lower your voice. . . ."

They drifted a little farther away, and I could no longer hear their words.

Leona looked at me. "He's a trog," she said.

"A rotten trog," I answered, wishing the Troll King could reach into Galena and pluck Bloodstone out of our lives. Maybe he could be adopted by a tribe who needed a servant.

Chapter Ten

EACH COLOR IN A CRYSTAL WATCH CONTAINS TEN DEGREES AND REPRESENTS MORE RADIA THAN THE PRECEDING COLOR BY A FACTOR OF TEN.

THE FIRST DEGREE OF RED INDICATES TEN RADIA IN RESERVE; THE TENTH DEGREE OF RED INDICATES ONE HUNDRED RADIA. (NOWADAYS, 89 PERCENT OF FAIRIES OR GENIES REGISTER AS RED.)

THE ORANGE ZONE RANGES FROM ONE HUNDRED RADIA TO ONE THOUSAND RADIA.

YELLOW RANGES FROM ONE THOUSAND TO TEN THOUSAND.

GREEN RANGES FROM TEN THOUSAND TO ONE HUNDRED THOUSAND.

BLUE RANGES FROM ONE HUNDRED THOUSAND TO ONE MILLION.

VIOLET RANGES FROM ONE MILLION TO TEN MILLION RADIA. (ANCIENT LORE INSISTS THAT ONCE UPON A TIME THERE WERE MORE THAN A FEW VIOLET FAIRIES AND GENIES, BUT NO ONE HAS SEEN THE LIKES OF THEM IN CENTURIES.)

—*Orville Gold, genie historian of Feyland*

*B*loodstone decided to escort Leona home. I didn't envy her his company on the long walk.

My walk was a little shorter, in another direction. Beryl glided ahead of me as I made my way on foot toward the house we shared, the house that stood oddly alone in Galena. My parents, Gilead and Cinna Tourmaline, had been fond of seclusion. When my brother Jett was expected, my mother and father, like all parents, were required to move to Galena. But they built our home on a lonely bar of land beside a large sonnia field, away from the larger community. No one had ever told me why.

It seemed that no one told me much of anything I wanted to know.

As I shuffled painfully along the sandy track leading home, I suddenly had a vivid memory of when I was seven. Jett had turned fourteen and received his watch and wand. My father had followed tradition, calling out my brother's color from the rooftop even though there were no families nearby to hear. *"Green!"* my father had shouted. *"Our son is a Green genie."*

Another memory moved to the surface of my mind and popped open like a bubble. I heard Jett saying, *"When a prism splits light, Zaree, we see the beauty of the spectrum. But crystal watches divide fey folk in an ugly way."*

And the last time I had seen him, Jett told me Feyland

was about to change. *"For good,"* he had said with a wide smile. *"For* good.*"*

"Beryl," I called. "Beryl, wait for me."

She stopped and turned. By starlight, the lines in her face seemed deeper, etching her long chin and short nose. "What a dreadful day," she said, sighing.

"Tell me about my family."

"Not now, Zaria."

"I deserve to know!"

"Not now."

"Do you think my mother would have let Bloodstone bind my wings with *iron*?" I burst out. "You think my father would have let this happen?"

She flashed me a look of anger. "Why did you go to Earth?"

"Why won't you tell me!" I shrieked.

She turned away and hurried ahead, leaving me to stumble on alone.

Chapter Eleven

IT IS A FATEFUL DAY WHEN YOUNG FAIRIES AND GENIES
RECEIVE THEIR CRYSTAL WATCHES AND THEIR WANDS.
ON THAT DAY, THEY LEARN EXACTLY WHAT THEIR
INBORN LEVEL OF MAGIC IS, AND THEY LEARN THEIR
COLOR OF RADIA RESERVES. THIS KNOWLEDGE WILL
AFFECT THEM FOR THE REST OF THEIR LIVES.

—*Orville Gold, genie historian of Feyland*

My wings throbbed all night, spreading pain
throughout my body. By morning I could barely lift my arms.

I staggered out of my nest. If it had been any other day, I
could not have found the strength. But I had to go to Oberon
City with my class to get our watches and wands. I had looked
forward to it ever since I understood the meaning of radia.

Beryl handed me a glass of fresh sonnia juice. "It will ease
the pain," she said.

She must have gathered the flowers very early. She gazed
at me through dull eyes as I downed it. It helped a little, but
I didn't thank her.

She said nothing else, not even a good-bye as I left.

Outside, Leona waited for me beside the field of sonnia,

her face drawn with pain. I snatched a handful of red flowers and thrust them at her. "Eat these. It helps."

Leona stuffed scarlet petals into her mouth. "Thanks," she murmured.

Meteor and Andalonus touched down nearby.

Andalonus twisted his nose. "Bound wings?" he said. "Do I smell trouble?"

Meteor didn't see anything amusing. He frowned. "What did you *do*?" he asked.

"Nothing!" Leona yelled.

"Nothing?" I imagined how Jenna, the little human girl I'd met the day before, would see Meteor. He'd look frightening. His white eyebrows stood out against his dark skin; when he frowned, they met across his nose.

"We can't tell you," I said.

"Today of all days." A lock of his black-and-white-striped hair fell into his eyes. "What did you *do*?"

"Can't tell." I gave him a meaningful glare.

Andalonus stepped behind me. "Oberon's Crown! Is that *iron*?"

Meteor's eyes went wide, then locked on my face. "Iron?"

"Bloodstone," I told him.

Andalonus slid behind Leona. He had lost his smile completely. "Bloodstone did this?" He pointed at her wings.

For once, Meteor was speechless, but at least he took some action. He turned his back to me and crouched.

"Hold on to my shoulders," he said. "I'll carry you."

I made an awkward leap onto his back. I wrenched my wings and had to choke down a scream but I hung on, and he floated gently forward, keeping close to the ground.

Andalonus offered his back to Leona. For a minute I thought she'd refuse, but she let him help her.

Silently, we headed toward our fate.

Chapter Twelve

Durable spells were put into place by the Ancients for the benefit of everyone in Feyland. Such spells allow the operation of viewing scopes, fortify appropriate barriers between territories, and protect fey children.

Durable spells are embedded in the Gateway of Galena. Only parents, children, mentors, and teachers are allowed into Galena. (Members of the High Council may pay the occasional visit for urgent matters involving the welfare of children and their parents.) If anyone else tries to enter, or if any children attempt to leave, the gateway alarm will sound and call forth the ever-waiting guards.

—Orville Gold, genie historian of Feyland

The dome that housed the Fey Order of Magic (better known as FOOM) gleamed gold and silver and platinum, edged with copper, and studded with gemstones. A giant ruby in the shape of a pyramid slowly revolved at the very top.

Going inside was like entering a prism, for the walls

were hewn from crystal. Sunlight shining through filled the entryway with every color of the spectrum. Lush carpets of red, orange, and yellow covered the floor.

More disgrace awaited Leona and me. While our classmates floated up the central space, Leona and I were directed to a spiral ramp. I believe Leona felt the shame of our bound wings more deeply than I, but she kept her eyes ahead as we toiled upward on foot and at last were ushered into a circular room.

Of course the entire class was already assembled and waiting when we entered. I hoped to avoid attention, but that was impossible.

Across the room, seated at a marble table, were three members of the High Council of Feyland, and although Beryl had prepared me for this moment, I was still awed to be in their presence—and very embarrassed about my ironbound wings.

In the central place of honor was a hefty fairy with black wings and extremely white skin. Suspended from a gold chain around her neck was a large square ruby carved with the crest of Oberon. I figured this must be the Magistria Hedda Lodestone, leader of the Council and the most important fairy in the land, after Queen Velleron.

To her left, I recognized Councilor Zircon, Meteor's father. Like his son, he had green eyes, but his lips and nose were rather thin and his white hair had no stripes. His skin was not the rich ebony of Meteor's; it was pale and shiny like onyx. Another of the rubies of Oberon adorned his wrist.

And on the magistria's right was Councilor Wolframite, the genie who five years earlier had delivered the news that my family had been declared *indeterminum detu*. He looked much as he had when I had last seen him. The ruby on his wrist contrasted with his orange skin. He was scratching his bulbous nose.

In front of the councilors knelt our teachers.

My eyes were drawn to nine fairies and genies who hovered just behind the councilors. Their faces might have been quarried from rock for all the expression they showed. They wore gold robes, and each held a wand poised and ready. The tallest of them stood directly behind Magistria Lodestone, his eyes roving vigilantly over the room.

This must be the Radia Guard, here to ensure that no one misused magic.

The fairies and genies in front of Leona and me moved aside, leaving us exposed to the gaze of the councilors. I bowed as best I could, which caused new splinters of pain to dig deep into my spine. I tried not to grimace. Leona bowed, too.

Magistria Lodestone spoke in a piercing voice. "Leona Bloodstone and Zaria Tourmaline?"

"Yes, Magistria," Leona answered.

The black-winged fairy's stare hardened. "You presume to attend this ceremony, and yet you are under punishment for breaking Fey laws."

VICTORIA HANLEY

"We apologize," Leona said.

"By rights," the magistria answered, "you should wait another year for your watches and wands, but because your teachers have vouched for you, we have agreed that you may receive them today."

My eyes flew to Bloodstone. He was still kneeling, and he looked even more rigid than ever. I wondered how much he had hated vouching for me.

"See that you do not transgress again," the magistria said.

Leona and I bowed humbly. Our teachers rose and stood on either side of the marble table.

I was grateful when the magistria shifted her attention to the whole class.

"We are gathered here today," she intoned, "because all of you have attained the age of fourteen, and your teachers have vouched for your progress. This is a solemn moment that marks the beginning of your magical development. In the years to come, you will learn to make the most of your powers, so that you may become responsible members of Feyland. Remember that magic is an important treasure, never to be wasted or treated lightly."

As a group, the class bowed low.

Councilor Zircon rose then and began to speak. "You will each receive a watch and a wand," he rumbled. "Your watches will follow Fey tradition. They will be crystal with gold backing, a silver cover, and a silver band." He paused. "Your wands, however, will break from tradition. They will all look the same. Each will be in the form of a black stylus from Earth."

Whispers and gasps! Our wands were from Earth? They would all look *the same*? We could not have been more astonished if Councilor Zircon had announced that Feyland would allow human visitors.

The councilors glowered, and the whispers stopped. "The High Council came to the decision to use these modern wands," Zircon continued. "We believe it is wasteful to keep creating elaborate wands for everyone."

He held up a slender sticklike object. It was shorter and more narrow than the pens we used for writing. Although pointed at one end, it looked nothing like any of the wands I had seen in my life.

"Humans manufacture these styluses by the thousands," he went on. "They are easy to acquire and easy to imprint with magic. The moment one of them touches your hand, it will become your wand, and respond to your magic alone."

Stunned silence.

"You may modify its appearance once you have learned how," he said dryly. "*If* you wish to spend radia doing so."

At Bloodstone's signal, we remembered our part in the ritual, and we bowed again as a group. I feared I would not be able to hide my pain much longer.

Councilor Wolframite rose. "Step forward when Mr. Bloodstone calls your name," he said.

The first student called was Cora Alabaster, a fairy with

rose-colored hair, jade skin, and bright yellow wings. She floated forward. Wolframite handed her one of the slim black plastic wands. She held out her arm, and the magistria fastened a covered watch around her wrist. Beaming, Cora took her place on the far side of the room.

One by one, my classmates received their watches and wands, while I concentrated on staying upright. Leona managed to walk with dignity when it was her turn, but by the time Bloodstone called my name, I could barely move.

I wobbled forward to Wolframite, who extended my black stylus. I offered my arm, and the magistria snugly fastened my watch onto my wrist.

Chapter Thirteen

MAGICAL LEVELS AND RADIA RESERVES TEND TO BE RELATED. FOR EXAMPLE, A LEVEL 10 GENIE IS MORE LIKELY TO HAVE RADIA RESERVES IN YELLOW THAN IN ORANGE, WHILE A LEVEL 80 FAIRY IS MORE LIKELY TO REGISTER GREEN, OR EVEN BLUE.

—*Orville Gold, genie historian of Feyland*

Our class emerged from the dome into a marble courtyard bordered by an ornamental garden, the finest in Feyland. Few of us noticed the yellow asters or rare purple lilies displayed among rough-cut gemstones. Ignoring the flowers, we clustered together.

"I warn you one final time," Bloodstone reminded us. "Do not attempt any magic with your wands until you have received instructions from your mentor."

"*One* final time?" Andalonus murmured next to me. "I believe that makes twenty thousand five hundred sixty-two final times."

"May we open our watches now?" Portia asked.

"You may," Beryl answered.

I expected Leona to be first, but it was Meteor. He flicked

open the silver cover of his watch with his thumb. Everyone stared at him avidly.

"Well?" Portia squawked.

Meteor let the moment build.

"Tell us," Cora pleaded. "What color?"

A grin spread over Meteor's face. "Blue," he burst out. "Full Blue! And I'm Level Fifty."

Classmates flocked around him, chanting congratulations and begging for a glimpse of his watch face. I didn't want to push my way past Portia and the others, so I stayed where I was. I would look at his watch later.

Bloodstone droned about what an honor it was to have been Meteor's teacher, and how few Blue genies there were in Feyland. Beryl nodded proudly.

When everyone calmed down, Cora called out, "I'm next!" Eyes screwed shut, she opened her watch and held it toward Portia. "What color?"

Portia inspected Cora's wrist. "Orange," she announced. "Almost full Orange. Level seven."

Cora's face fell. She opened her eyes. "That's all?"

All around us students began snapping open their watches. Some called out their colors, but many sighed and grumbled. Tuck Lodestone whooped when he discovered he was Level 15 Yellow. Portia astounded everyone by revealing herself to be Green.

"Full," she gushed, flirting her wings at Meteor. "But only Level Ten."

Meteor moved to my side. "See what color you are, Zaria."

I shook my head. Suddenly I didn't want to know. Whatever my color might be, I was afraid it could divide me from my friends. If I weren't equal to Meteor, would he hold his Blue over me? If I had more radia than Andalonus, what then? And if Leona's color turned out to be Orange, and mine was Yellow, would she forgive me?

Meteor nudged Leona next. "Go on," he urged.

She gripped her watch and opened the cover. Her silver eyes went wide, and then she smiled. It was a gloating smile.

Gradually the noise in the courtyard died away. When she finally spoke she had everyone's attention.

"Level Two Hundred," she announced. "And my color is *Violet*. Half full."

Meteor looked stunned. "Did you say Violet?"

"Violet." She held up her watch.

Cora shrieked. Portia cried. Tuck whirled in circles shouting, "Violet!" I heard Bloodstone roar triumphantly at Beryl, who shouted that there must be some mistake, Level 200 was unheard of, let alone Violet, Leona was playing them all for fools.

She wasn't. Of course she wasn't. I could have told Beryl so. Andalonus might have tried joking about his color. Not Leona.

"Show me your watch," Beryl ordered Leona.

"With pleasure," she answered, holding out her wrist.

Beryl brought her yellow eyes up to the crystal face of Leona's watch. Silence spread.

"You can stare forever, but it won't change," Leona pulled her wrist away. "I'm Violet."

Startled, I looked hard at Leona. She must be very angry to treat Beryl with such contempt. She had said she would never forgive our teachers for binding us with iron. I began to believe her.

Beryl's eyes watered, and everyone knew that Leona was telling the truth.

Leona strained to reach over her shoulder with her wand. She tapped the titanium clasp that held the iron band around her wings, and said something I couldn't catch. With a dull crack, the bands fell away. Her silver wings unfurled; she lifted her wand. She murmured something else, and her black stylus transformed into a slender platinum rod, set with sapphire stars.

The class oohed and aahed. Leona floated to me, her wand extended. She muttered again, and the agonizing iron let go. Sweet relief! I could move my wings. I felt a surge of power flooding through me, warm and comforting.

"Leona!" Beryl called in a croaking voice.

Leona spun lightly. "Yes, Miss Danburite?"

"You have obviously been studying spells you have not earned the right to learn," Beryl said. "And no matter what your color, you may not end a punishment assigned by your teachers."

Leona stopped twirling. "Or what?" she said.

Beryl's fingers jerked as she waved at Bloodstone. "Your uncle will explain."

Bloodstone stepped forward. "My congratulations on your exalted achievement, Leona, my dear. You are the only living Violet to grace Feyland."

"Excuse me, Mr. Bloodstone," Beryl began.

His gray cheeks flushed, as if someone had dipped him in rose granite. He cleared his throat. "Leona, it is dangerous to practice magic before you are trained and unwise to squander radia, even when your reserves are high."

"You can't stop me," Leona said. Her silver eyes burned.

He coughed. "Leona, remember that there are policies in place to prevent fairies or genies from using radia wrongly. The Council can command that your wand be taken away."

Leona looked at him as if he were a greasy beetle she wanted to step on. "Whom would they command?" she asked.

"I beg your pardon?"

"No other fairies or genies can equal my power," Leona said. "So whom would the Council command to take my wand?"

"It would not be *one* fairy or genie. It would be the Radia Guard." Bloodstone sounded as if someone had forced him to eat gravel. "The combined powers of high-level Blues and Greens and Yellows working together would be equal to a Level Two Hundred Violet."

Leona gazed at him stonily.

"As for the, er, iron bands . . . ," Bloodstone said. "Because of your elevated status as a Violet, there is no need to continue your punishment."

Beryl shook her head at this, but she seemed to have lost her voice.

"Zaria, too?" Leona challenged Bloodstone.

"Zaria?" He glanced at me. "No. Zaria must complete a week of iron."

"Then so must I," Leona answered. Gritting her teeth, she picked up the band lying at my feet. She fastened it around my wings, and the cold clamped down on me again. "Sorry," she whispered.

"I apologize for my insolence," she told Beryl and Bloodstone, her voice like wind through a mine shaft.

I knew that tone. Leona had apologized, but she didn't mean it.

Chapter Fourteen

FAIRY WINGS AND GENIE FEET ARE AUGMENTED BY
MAGIC: WITHOUT MAGIC, A FAIRY'S WINGS WOULD
NOT BE ENOUGH TO CARRY HER, AND A GENIE'S FEET
WOULD NOT BE ENOUGH TO CARRY HIM. BUT ALL
FAIRIES AND GENIES FLY, NO MATTER WHAT THEIR
LEVEL OR COLOR. THIS IS THE ONE GREAT EQUALIZER:
ALTHOUGH FLYING IS A MAGICAL ACTIVITY, IT DOES
NOT USE UP RADIA.

—*Orville Gold, genie historian of Feyland*

*A*fter Bloodstone refastened the bands around Leona's
wings, he ordered the class to return to school. "There Miss
Danburite and I will record your levels and colors."

In moments, I was standing in the courtyard with only
Andalonus and Leona. Everyone else, including Meteor, had
gone.

"Thank you for trying to help me," I told Leona.

She nodded. "I wish my uncle wasn't such a trog."

"I've never heard of Level Two Hundred magic,"
Andalonus said. "I didn't know it could happen. And Violet!
You'll be a legend, Leona."

"What about you?" she said. "Open your watch!"

He bobbed lightly. "I don't expect a high level or powerful color. I haven't felt any different since I turned fourteen." He flicked up the cover on his watch.

"Wait." I put a hand on his arm. "Whatever you find, it won't make a difference to me."

"Good," he said. "But it will probably make a difference to *me*." He looked down at his watch. Sighing, he covered it again, letting his arm drop to his side. "Even worse than I expected," he said. "My family was hoping for at least Level Seven Orange, but I'm Level Four, full Red."

Andalonus, a Red genie? He had only one hundred units of inborn radia, while Leona had five million?

He hunched his shoulders. "I'll never travel to Earth."

Leona held up her wand, turning it as if she wanted to admire every part. "If all genies could travel to Earth, it wouldn't be special to go there, would it?"

Why would she be snide with Andalonus about his color? What was wrong with her today? I shook my head at her, while Andalonus pulled his ears and said nothing.

"Now you, Zaree," Leona said. "What's your color?"

"I don't care," I answered.

"You're not going to open your watch?"

"Later."

Leona glared. "It will be the same no matter when you do it!"

I wrapped both hands around my slender plastic wand

and tried to draw the warmth of my magic into my cold and aching wings.

Andalonus did his best to help both me and Leona to school. By the time we arrived, a haze of pain covered every part of me. I didn't even try to hide it.

Bloodstone and Danburite stood at the head of the room with pens in hand, and they motioned us forward. A copper easel stood in front of them and clipped to it was a scroll listing the names of each student with a record of level and color. As expected, most names were designated as Red, and most were Level 4 or 5. It didn't seem fair.

"Andalonus?" Bloodstone asked, tapping the scroll. "Level and color?"

"Level Four, full Red," Andalonus answered.

Bloodstone scrawled his rank and then turned to Leona. A sheen of satisfaction covered his face, as if he'd stretched silk over his craggy features. "Leona Bloodstone. Level *Two Hundred*, half, full *Violet*," he wrote with a flourish. "Our class will be remembered for centuries upon centuries, Miss Danburite. We have a Blue *and* a Violet."

Beryl looked at him sourly.

"Zaria hasn't opened her watch," Leona announced to everyone.

"Come here, Zaria," Bloodstone ordered, beckoning with a knobby gray finger.

I lurched forward and held out my wrist to Beryl. She

shook her head at me but then opened my watch.

She stared for what seemed a long time, her expression blank. "Trolls and pixies," she murmured. She squinted, blinked, squinted again.

"What is it?" Bloodstone snapped. "Another Red? Oberon's Crown, Miss Danburite, get hold of yourself. I told you not to expect more."

Snatching my hand back, I looked into a dazzling crystal, polished until it was perfectly transparent. It showed six colors in equal segments on the face of my watch: red, orange, yellow, green, blue, and violet. In the center, a tiny rectangle showed a luminous number 100.

"What level?" Bloodstone asked sharply.

"Um, One Hundred," I said.

His craggy face tensed. "Are you certain?"

"Yes," Beryl told him. "I saw it."

He wrote, pressing so hard I thought his pen would snap. "And your color?" The words fell from his mouth like chips of stone.

I looked down at the watch again. Two black hands told the time: half past the second hour after noon. A third hand of gold pointed to the line between the violet and red sections.

"Your color, Zaria!"

"I don't know."

"What nonsense." He shook his pen, and ink drops spattered on his robe. "Show me."

Reluctantly, I extended my wrist. He leaned in close and did a double-take. "Not possible."

"Is it pointing to no color?" I said.

"It does not say *no* color, Zaria," Beryl answered with great calm. "It says full Violet."

I was suddenly in a separate world, a world of elation mixed with hopeless grief. Elation because Bloodstone would have to respect me now, and because Leona and I could go on being friends without worrying about rank. Grief because my mother would never know I was a Violet fairy, and my father would not call forth my color from the rooftop.

Then I became aware of my teachers, one looking as if an ordinary flower had turned into a butterfly before her eyes, the other looking as if his gray face would break into pieces.

"I will not record this," Bloodstone said. "Give me your watch, Zaria. It is defective."

"Defective?" I asked.

Then Leona stood beside me. "Stop, Uncle," she said, her voice crackling with passion. "Think of the shame if you're wrong."

Bloodstone's lips disappeared into a hard gray line. Leona stared him down. I thought he would yell out a terrible spell, but all he did was shoot me a look of pure hatred before writing *full Violet* next to my name.

I bowed. It seemed the only thing to do. He ignored me.

Leona didn't allow the awkward silence to continue. "Do

I have more power than Zaria, or does she have more power than me?" she asked Bloodstone.

He pulled himself together, and put on his lecture voice for the class. "Remember our lessons! Leona is twice as powerful because she has Level Two Hundred magic. Zaria will never be able to do magic beyond Level One Hundred."

"But Zaria has double the *reserves of radia*," Beryl put in.

The classroom was completely unsettled. Fairy wings were fluttering madly and genies were bobbing up and down.

"Mr. Bloodstone," Cora cried, "how can Leona have Level *Two* Hundred magic?"

"My mother told me that even the most advanced spells use only Level *One* Hundred!" Portia yelled.

Bloodstone took charge. "You're quite right to be astounded. I, too, have no information on spells that require more magic than Level One Hundred." He bowed in Leona's direction. "We are in the presence of greatness."

"But what will she *do* with such high-level magic?" Cora squeaked.

"That is a matter for her to discuss with her mentor," Bloodstone answered. He made a sweeping gesture. "We are finished for today. Remember, do not use your wands until you have had instruction from your mentors, who will be assigned tomorrow, our final day of class. You are dismissed."

Chapter Fifteen

FAIRIES AND GENIES HAVE ALWAYS BEEN FASCINATED BY TIME: WHAT IT IS, HOW IT OPERATES, AND THE LINKS IT PROVIDES BETWEEN TIRFEYNE AND EARTH. WHEN FEY FOLK DISCOVERED THAT THE HOURS WITHIN THEIR DAYS UPON TIRFEYNE MATCHED THE HOURS WITHIN THE DAYS UPON EARTH, THEY SHARED THE SECRETS OF CLOCK-MAKING WITH HUMANS.

PUNCTUALITY IS CONSIDERED A VIRTUE AMONG FAIRIES AND GENIES. TO BE PROMPT IS TO BE COURTEOUS. TO BE LATE IS TO SHOW DISRESPECT.

THIS IS NOT TRUE AMONG LEPRECHAUNS. THEY HAVE NO REGARD FOR PUNCTUALITY. THEY DO NOT WEAR WATCHES. THEY COULD NOT CARE LESS ABOUT KEEPING TRACK OF TIME.

IT HAS BEEN SAID THAT SOME AMONG THE ANCIENTS MASTERED TIME TO SUCH AN EXTENT THAT THEY COULD STEP OUTSIDE OF IT. THIS MAY BE TRUE, FOR THERE IS A GROUP OF ISLANDS IN THE MIDDLE OF GLENDONITE LAKE, WHERE TIME DOES NOT BEHAVE AS IT NORMALLY DOES. THE ISLANDS ARE SAID TO BE UNDER AN ENCHANTMENT THAT CHANGES THE PARAMETERS OF TIME.

—Orville Gold, genie historian of Feyland

lowed by ironbound wings, Leona and I were the last students through the doorway of our classroom. I wasn't sure if either Meteor or Andalonus would be waiting for us the way they usually did. Now that we knew our colors, maybe nothing would be the same, ever again.

But both our genie friends were hovering outside, although the rest of our classmates had gone.

"Behold the Violet fairies." Andalonus spoke lightly, but he wouldn't meet my eyes.

Meteor was smiling. "Congratulations."

"You, too," I said, wondering if it bothered him that my reserves and level were higher than his.

"I wonder," Andalonus said, "if Violet fairies or a Blue genie will agree to be friends with a common Red?"

"Don't be a fool," Meteor threw in. "Leona and Zaria will be famous and envied and talked about behind their wings. They'll need friends—real friends. And so will I."

Andalonus broke into a grin. "I'll be famous now, too— as the one who knew you well, when you were nothing more than two moody fairies and a pompous genie." He pulled an ear and laughed.

Meteor closed one eye. He began to float upward.

Andalonus took to the air. "Tomorrow, Zaree, Leona!" he shouted, catching up with Meteor.

I looked after them as they raced away. "I wish we'd

never had to learn our colors. Everything has changed," I said mournfully.

Leona tossed her head. "Nothing has changed. We've only learned what was true all along. We're important! You and I will go down in history."

"I don't want to go down in history." I wasn't even trying to hold up my wings anymore; they trailed in the sand, gathering grit. I wanted to plunge into the pool beneath Galena Falls and wash away the last two days, but the iron band would take me under.

Leona blew out a big breath. "You have ten million radia! More than anyone else in Feyland!" Her eyes glittered, and I knew she wanted me to say something about her Level Two Hundred, and how it made her the most powerful fairy ever born.

Instead, I grimaced. "My feet are sore, Leona. And my wings hurt."

She nodded, letting herself limp a little now that there was no one around but me. "The minute I get home," she said, "I'll free myself again."

"How?"

"A breaking spell," she said. "You could do it. Say, 'Resvera den.' That's the spell. Touch the titanium clasp with your wand. If you touch the iron, it won't break."

"Oh." I wondered how many spells Leona had already memorized. I didn't know a single enchantment except the simple little spell for opening locks, the spell everyone over the age of seven had heard how to do.

Leona brought out her wand, swishing it back and forth. "Meteor was right about friendship. Think how different it would be if you and I weren't friends." She gave me a sidelong look. "If there had to be another Violet, I'm glad that it's you."

Before I could ask what she meant, a crowd of fairies and genies came flying toward us at top speed, Leona's parents at their head. At the sight of them, the iron bands seemed tighter against my wings, and I stepped behind Leona as if she could shield me.

"Is it true?" Leona's mother called as soon as she was near enough to be heard. "Are you Violet?"

"Why are you wearing iron bands—is it to control your extraordinary powers?" called a genie with ears so big they flapped.

"Did you have any idea of your color before today?" yelled a pink-winged young fairy with fuzzy blue skin.

Leona waved her platinum wand, its blue stars shining. As the crowd crammed in closer, I slipped away. No one would miss me—especially not when they had Leona to admire.

I went into the nearest sonnia field and hunched low among the flowers. Grabbing a few red petals, I stuffed them in my mouth, desperate for relief from the pain. But this time, the sonnia didn't help.

Slowly, I made my way home. If anyone had seen me, they would have mistaken me for a wounded troll; I moved without any grace, thinking only of one step and then another.

I could hear parents announcing their children's colors from the rooftops. "Red!" was called without enthusiasm. "Orange!" and "Yellow!" were repeated with pride, and "Green!" was shouted with glee.

Finally I tottered through our door and closed it behind me.

Beryl had gone with Bloodstone to submit the class list; she would not return for at least a few more hours, and I was glad. I didn't want her near me. Not her, not anyone.

That wasn't exactly true. I did want someone, but that someone had left long ago and would never be back.

I settled into my favorite soft perch, thinking sorrowfully of my mother. Strange that in the past two days she'd come to mind so often, when I had put her out of my mind for years. What would she have said about my being a Violet fairy? Well, she wouldn't have led a mob of gossips to barrage me with questions, that much I knew.

The pain in my wings seemed worse than ever. I stood up, clenching my fists. *Six more days of iron?* I would go mad.

My punishment seemed an unforgivable cruelty. I could not keep my wings from shaking. The more they shook, the more the iron hurt, until I felt as if a million fragments of sharp ice were being driven through my bones.

Why hadn't Beryl fought for me? She was supposed to look after me! Instead, she had stood by while Bloodstone fastened iron around my tender wings.

I had to do something. If I didn't, my bones would come apart and my wings would never lift me again.

Drawing my slender stylus, I tried to feel the power of my magic. It had to be there. I had Level 100! Reaching deep in myself, I finally found it: a fiercely comforting fire. It leaped into my wand like flame along a fuse.

Stretching over my shoulder, I tapped the band. *"Resvera den,"* I said. *Break.*

The band snapped, falling away. My bruised wings unfurled. I sank onto a nest of pillows. Waves of warmth washed through me, filling the aching void the iron had made.

"My magic is waking," I said to the empty room.

A while later, I stood up and tripped on the iron band. Glaring at it with hatred, I pointed my wand. A second later I was looking at a pile of reddish dust settling into a hole in the floor.

The iron band had disintegrated.

What would Beryl say? What would she and Bloodstone do? I stared at what was left of their punishment. I couldn't say I was sorry. Far from it. For an instant, I imagined how it would feel to throw the red dust in Bloodstone's face and ask him how he liked it.

I opened my watch-face cover and looked for a long moment at the tiny golden hand pointing to full Violet, and the little rectangle showing the luminous 100. Leona's words came back to me: *"You have ten million radia!"*

And no idea of how to use it.

"A mentor," I said aloud. "I need a mentor. Now."

I flew up the wide stairs that my father had built for his children before we could fly. My wings buffeted the walls because I went too fast. I bumped down the hallway and fell against the door to my mother's room.

I tried the handle. It turned easily. Of course. Beryl would never have shut me out of this place. Only *I* would do that.

I had stayed away for five years.

I drifted in softly, as if I might disturb someone. My mother's room was clean all the way to the top of the lofty ceiling. Beryl must have tended it.

A mosaic of colored tiles covered the floor in a spiral pattern. Silky yellow pillows lay in a nest near the window. On the wall hung a painting of Earth trees: aspen, spruce, and pine.

I put my hand on the painting. My tired wings fluttered. Was it a family flaw to become Earth-struck? If so, I was carrying that flaw forward. Despite having my wings twisted by a human child, despite my uneasiness about the boy that Leona had met, and despite the punishment Leona and I had endured, I still felt drawn to Earth. The painting seemed to say that my mother had loved Earth, too.

She had loved Earth, and she had gone to her death there.

I turned away, looking at the side wall where copper

cupboards of all sizes hung in neat rows, cupboards tall and thin, short and wide. Could one of them be holding my mother's spellbook?

Most of the cupboards opened easily. They held nothing but hats and slippers. Then I came to one that was locked.

Meteor had been the one to teach me how to open locks. *"You say 'Upandos' before speaking the name of your favorite seed, then touch the lock,"* he had said.

What was my favorite seed? Sonnia? It ought to be: I was a fairy, and fairies lived on sonnia.

"*Upandos* sonnia," I said, placing my hand on the lock.

It didn't budge.

What was really my favorite growing thing? A vivid memory of the maple tree I had seen during my afternoon on Earth rose in my mind. Would a seed from Earth open a lock here on Tirfeyne?

Would a seed from Earth help me get the spellbook of a fairy who had been killed by humans?

Chapter Sixteen

A TROG IS A MYTHICAL CREATURE. IF TROGS EVER EXISTED, THEY DIED OUT LONG AGO. AND YET, IGNORANT FEY FOLK PERSIST IN BELIEVING THAT TROGS CAN BE FOUND LIVING DEEP WITHIN TROLL COUNTRY.

A TROG'S HEAD IS SAID TO RESEMBLE THAT OF AN EARTH TOAD, EXCEPT THAT A TROG'S EARS ARE VERY LARGE, ALLOWING THEM TO HEAR WHISPERS FROM A LONG DISTANCE. TROGS REPORTEDLY WALK UPRIGHT, CANNOT FLY, AND EXUDE A PUTRID ODOR THAT EVEN REPEATED BATHING CAN NEVER ERADICATE.

SUPPOSEDLY, TROGS HAVE SUCH VILE DISPOSITIONS THAT THEY ARE UNABLE TO FORM COMMUNITIES BUT LIVE TO ANNOY EACH OTHER AND ANY OTHER SPECIES CROSSING THEIR PATHS.

—*Orville Gold, genie historian of Feyland*

*M*aple," I said. "*Upandos* maple."

The latch clicked. The cupboard sprang open. Sure enough, inside was a book. When I drew it out, it felt strangely light in my hand, almost weightless.

Cinna Tourmaline, it said on the cover. *Spellbook.*

No young fairy was supposed to read her mother's spellbook until permission had been granted. I knew that quite well. But my mother was not *able* to grant me permission. And I badly needed her help and guidance. Now.

Scarcely breathing, I opened the cover. On the first leaf, under the seal of King Oberon—an imprint of a crown in golden wax—was my mother's record of magic: *Cinna Tourmaline, Registered Level 100, full Blue.*

My mother had been endowed with powerful magic. Yet she had lived humbly. As would I.

I began turning the pages. I skimmed past directions on how to make big soap bubbles and other trivial spells. As I skipped ahead, the page fell open to something that caught my eye.

Gag Spell

Requires Level 10 magic

This spell is not to be used lightly or for personal gain. It will render the subject unable to speak. Requires 15 radia, which will last for three hours. Each additional three hours uses another 10 radia.

A long-lasting gag spell uses 10,000 radia.

The wand must be pointed at the subject within a distance of 21 wingspans or from a viewing booth with the scope focused on the subject. Infuse to Level 10 and say, "Reducto et eloquen."

"Gag spell," I muttered, and wondered what it meant to "infuse."

At random I slid my thumb into a page farther on.

Spell of Disclosure

Requires Level 22 magic

This spell will reveal all the spells that have been cast by a given wand, back through a period of one week. Requires 50 radia.

A spell to disclose all magic worked by a particular wand, going back centuries, uses 50,000 radia.

"Fifty thousand!" I thought of the Gateway of Galena. How much radia had it taken to create spells that kept children in, and kept most adults out?

Touch your wand to the wand whose spells you will be disclosing. Infuse to Level 22 and say, "Disclosan nos enchanterel."

When I heard Beryl come back, I shoved the spellbook into its cupboard. Dreading what she would say, I crept downstairs to find her sitting on a perch, staring at the pile of iron dust. She was tucked so far forward, I couldn't see the expression on her face.

"I know you won't believe me," I said, "but I didn't mean to do it."

Beryl lifted her head. She looked even older than she had the night before. Her eyes seemed out of focus. "I do believe you, Zaria," she said. "Why do you think I was so concerned about your visit to Earth? Why do you suppose I worried about what you might have done if you had carried a wand?"

I didn't know what to say. I had expected a tirade, not weariness and worry.

"Mr. Bloodstone and I discussed you and Leona," she went on. "We agreed that in view of what we have learned today, it would be appropriate to lift your punishment."

I knew I should say thank you, but I couldn't.

Beryl's chin sagged. "I ought to report you for turning a set of iron bands to dust, but I will not."

"You're not going to tell Bloodstone?"

"Only if you tell your friends that you took it upon yourself to undo your punishment."

"I won't say anything."

"Then I will also keep this a secret." She flapped a hand at the iron dust. "You must reconstruct the bands. I know the spell." She sighed. "Visualize the object the way it was and say, '*Recre redontum.*'"

Self-consciously, I drew out my wand as she watched.

"Wait!" Beryl said sharply. "You are calling forth *all* of your magic. Do not use more than is called for; that is wasteful."

"But—"

"Imagine a furnace. How much heat is required to melt platinum? Then imagine a stove. How much heat is required to boil water? You see the difference?"

I nodded.

"Magic is like heat. Use only enough for the spell you are working. It is called *infusion.*"

"How's it done?"

"Your wand, child. Look at it. Find the line along the side that shows the amount of infusion."

I examined the stylus, which was no longer plain black. A narrow seam running down its length shone with light from base to tip.

"When your wand is full," Beryl said, "it means you have infused to Level One Hundred, which is the highest level you can produce. The reconstruction spell needs only Level Twenty. Pull back on your magic."

I imagined the magic in the wand returning to me. The light in the seam flitted down the wand and vanished.

"It takes a bit of practice to control infusion levels," Beryl said.

Thinking of all the spells I had read upstairs, I felt faint. What if I had tried working any of them? I didn't know the first thing about using my wand. I didn't know the first thing about anything!

My knees gave out, and my fluttering wings didn't catch me. I sank to the floor.

"Zaria?"

I curled my wings around myself. How I wanted to hear my mother's clear, soft voice directing me, helping me, showing me what to do.

"What is it?" Beryl asked.

"My mother." I began to wail.

"At last," Beryl muttered.

"She'll never know I'm Violet," I wept. "And she can't help me learn to use my magic. And my father . . . Jett . . . It isn't fair."

Beryl crouched beside me. "I thought you would never get around to crying for them. When they disappeared, you were so silent! Never talked of them, never went near their rooms . . ."

That was all she said. She stayed with me, though, and helped me crawl into my nest of pillows.

Chapter Seventeen

FEY MAGIC HAS BEEN DIMINISHING FOR CENTURIES. IN
ITS PRESENT DISMAL STATE, THE MAJORITY OF FAIRIES
AND GENIES HAVE ONLY LEVEL 4 MAGIC OR LESS.

NO ONE KNOWS HOW THESE LEVELS OF INBORN
MAGIC COME ABOUT. SOMETIMES A CERTAIN FAMILY
WILL SEEM TO CARRY A TENDENCY TOWARD HIGH-
LEVEL MAGIC, ONLY TO BE DISAPPOINTED BY AN OFF-
SPRING BORN WITH LOW-LEVEL MAGIC.

—*Orville Gold, genie historian of Feyland*

When Beryl woke me early, it took a little while to remember the seemingly impossible events of the day before. I was a Violet fairy with Level 100 magic. I had turned a set of iron bands to dust. And I had cried for my family.

Beryl lost no time reminding me that she expected me to reconstruct the iron bands.

Her words were short and sharp as she guided me through the spell, and I won't say it went smoothly. At first the magic in my wand kept spiking to the top and then dying down. I had to grip my concentration tightly to get it right. When the iron band had been reconstructed and lay on the newly smooth floor, Beryl sat very still. She wore a pained expression, as if someone had twisted her wings.

"Beryl?" I said. "Why did you always tell me that iron interferes with magic?"

"Because it does."

"Then how can an iron band be destroyed by magic? Or reconstructed?"

She sighed. "The truth is, Zaria, I did not know it was possible to do what you have done. Turning iron to dust!" She shook her head. "And then, to reconstruct it . . ." She folded her hands nervously. "It would be best if you tell no one about this."

"No one?"

"No one. Promise me, Zaria."

I mumbled a promise. My wings had begun to ache. Beryl wasn't acting normally. She wasn't treating me like a nuisance the way she usually did, but I wasn't sure what it meant.

She surprised me by offering to teach me a transport spell.

"Beryl," I said hesitantly, "if I'm Violet, why would I need to be careful of using radia?"

"Your stores may be rich," she said briskly, "but if you are careless, you will burn through them. Now, listen closely. The transport spell requires Level Eight. To put those iron bands into my basket, you will probably need about three radia, but if you were to move your*self* somewhere—to school, for instance—you would use at least twenty radia. That would be very wasteful."

I nodded, and waited for her to teach me the spell.

"Infuse your wand to Level Eight. That's right. Get close to the iron without touching it. Hold its destination clearly in your mind as you point your wand and say, *'Transera nos.'* The basket in front of you is the destination this time. Always be careful to focus on the exact destination or the spell may misfire and the item end up somewhere else."

I pointed my wand at the iron band and concentrated on Beryl's basket. *"Transera nos."*

The iron band clattered into the basket so fast it was as if time had not existed.

"I didn't see it travel," I said, peering at it.

"Yes." Beryl seemed even more nervous, but she congratulated me. "A perfect transport. Now listen to me, Zaria. Do not ever try to transport anything—including yourself—through the Gateway of Galena. You would set off all of its alarms."

"All right." I watched her curiously. Why was she so nervous?

"And never try to transport from Tirfeyne to Earth or from Earth to Tirfeyne. You cannot cross worlds with a transport spell," she said grimly. "If it could be done, there would be no need for portals."

"Thank you." I was glad she had told me. Otherwise, I might have tried to transport myself to Earth. I fumbled my wand back into my pocket. "Does fey magic work the same on Earth as it does here?" I asked.

Beryl's wings went rigid. "Why do you ask?" she demanded. "Is Mr. Bloodstone right about you? Are you Earth-struck? Because if you are, you had better tell me."

"Why?" I flared, rising up. "So you can sneer at me along with Bloodstone?"

"Zaria!"

I needed to get away. I banged open the door and rushed outside.

"I want to help you!" Beryl yelled after me as I took to the air.

Soaring high, I pretended I hadn't heard.

I could see almost all of Galena: the dwellings with metal roofs shining brightly enough to hurt my eyes; those covered with gemstones polished to a sparkling sheen; the school with its tiered roof; parents with infants and toddlers in colorful suits; children on their way to school, bobbing and bouncing in small groups; the great gateway with its massive pillars; the splashing water of Galena Falls . . . and I could see the boulder marking the portal to Earth, a little smudge of sandstone in a cloud of orange and yellow flowers.

The Zinnia Portal. That's what I would call it.

I spotted Leona's silver wings floating below me, and near her Andalonus's blue hair and Meteor's striped head. Diving, I caught up with them.

Leona grinned at me. "I see you're free. Did you do it, or did Danburite release you?"

I smiled blankly, remembering my promise to Beryl.

"Uncle Boris hurried over last evening to liberate me," she said. "He couldn't get through the crowds until he made them understand he was the uncle of the famous Violet fairy. He was so puffed with pride he didn't care that I'd already freed myself."

"Crowd?" I asked, looking over my shoulder, afraid we'd be mobbed again. "They followed you home?"

She nodded. "It turned into a long celebration." Leona snickered and pulled out her wand. "Look, I've added filigree." She held it up so I could see the delicate whorls of gold and silver tracing the handle.

"Beautiful."

"Show us yours."

"Nothing to see."

Leona spun neatly in the air. "Show us!"

"You'll go blind if you lay eyes on it," I said.

Andalonus sniggered, but Leona and Meteor closed in on me. "Show us!"

I drew out my plain, unchanged black stylus. Andalonus snorted.

"Everyone will think you have no radia to spare," Leona scolded. "You won't get the respect you should have as a Violet fairy."

"Why should I get respect for being lucky?" I cried. "And if I keep my wand plain, no one has to know I'm Violet."

"Everyone already knows," Meteor called after me.

"Everyone can forget!" And I flew as fast as I could, away from my friends.

Chapter Eighteen

AT FOURTEEN, FAIRIES AND GENIES LEAVE ORDINARY
SCHOOL. THOSE WHO HAVE REGISTERED WITH LEVELS
ABOVE 7 AND RESERVES OF RADIA PAST ORANGE ARE
THEN ASSIGNED A MENTOR TO GUIDE THEM. MENTORS
ARE SUPPOSED TO TEACH THE CORRECT WAY TO USE
MAGIC RESPONSIBLY AND GIVE INSTRUCTION ABOUT
SPELLS, WHICH STUDENTS RECORD IN A SPELLBOOK.
HOWEVER, NOT ALL MENTORS ARE CONSCIENTIOUS;
SOME HAVE BEEN KNOWN TO MISLEAD THEIR
STUDENTS WITH INEFFECTIVE SPELLS AND WRONG
UNDERSTANDING ABOUT MAGIC. FOR THIS REASON,
TRIED AND TRUE SPELLBOOKS ARE OFTEN HANDED
DOWN WITHIN FAMILIES, PRESERVING KNOWLEDGE
THAT WOULD OTHERWISE BE LOST.

—*Orville Gold, genie historian of Feyland*

t school that day, Beryl issued our magic records and
ordered us to guard them carefully so we could show them
to our mentors. When I received mine, I stared at the seal of
Oberon over the inscription: *Zaria Tourmaline, Registered Level
100, full Violet.*

Then Bloodstone made a big display of handing out mentor assignments to those of us who had registered Yellow or more. There weren't many: Rumpel Garnet, Tuck Lodestone, Portia Peridot, Leona, Meteor, and me. Bloodstone reminded us to keep the identities of our mentors a secret. He scowled at me as he said it. I didn't know why he would single me out. I could keep a secret.

When he gave me my mentor scroll, he actually smiled. What could make Bloodstone smile?

I waited until he went on to Portia before reading it. *Magic Mentor for Zaria Tourmaline: Lily Morganite. Report to 3750 Morganite Towers in Oberon City.*

Lily Morganite? Wasn't she the one who had reported our visit to Earth? No wonder Bloodstone had smiled. Had he and Beryl discussed it and decided on someone who would disapprove of me? Did they hope to cure me of being Earth-struck?

Bloodstone started his good-bye speech to the class. "Now that you have your crystal watches, you may all explore Oberon City," he droned. "Those of you with levels above seven and reserves of radia past Orange will train with your mentors, who will expect to meet with you tomorrow morning. The rest of you may consider your education complete."

Complete. How I envied Andalonus!

"The term for this class is at an end," Bloodstone continued. "What we began together seven years ago . . ."

He kept going on and on. I didn't listen. I couldn't pretend to be sorry about the end of school. If not for my mentor assignment, I would have been completely happy. No more days spent with Bloodstone!

But I would have to train for another three years with my mentor. Why? Why couldn't I study my mother's spellbook on my own?

I tried to console myself. Maybe my mentor wouldn't be too terrible. Maybe she wouldn't hold my visit to Earth against me. She was a Council member, so she would know more than most fairies. Maybe she could help me.

"Dismissed," Bloodstone said at last.

A few fairies and genies stayed to say farewell to Beryl and Bloodstone, but most of us packed the doorway eagerly.

Outside, Portia teetered on tiptoe in front of Meteor, her green wings unfurled. She blinked so fast I thought she had a bug in her eye. "Would you like to go into Oberon City with me?" she asked him.

Meteor turned to Andalonus, who waved him on. He cast a look at me. I shrugged. Leona spread her hands. "If you go with me, you'll be mobbed," she said.

Meteor nodded abruptly at Portia. They floated off together.

"You're expecting another horde?" Andalonus asked Leona.

"I'm Violet!" she said. "The news will have spread by now, and all the fey folk who aren't allowed in Galena will be on the other side of the gateway, waiting for a glimpse of me. And Zaria."

"Not me," I told her.

"You can't hide forever, Zaree."

"I can hide today." I wanted to talk to her, about Lily Morganite. "Leona—"

She rose, beckoning me to join her.

When I stayed on the ground, she flared her silver wings, turned, and flew away, leaving me with Andalonus.

"I hate this," I mumbled.

Andalonus pulled his ears. "Zaria, is it so bad to be Violet? You'll never run out of radia. I have to guard mine carefully or I'll use it all in the next hour." A breeze sprang up, stirring his hair into a blue nimbus. "Imagine all the good you'll be able to do."

"Andalonus Copper, it's *you* who should have been Violet." I tried to smile, but felt I would choke.

He squinted at me. Andalonus, the genie who made everyone laugh, looked serious and sad. I didn't like to see him that way.

"I'm going home," I said. "Maybe I can learn a spell that will turn me into a better fairy."

"I'll see you soon, Zaree."

I nodded. Lifting off, I soared into the sky. I left a gaggle of children in my draft as I flew homeward.

I landed with a bump and hurried inside. At least Beryl was still away, no doubt lingering at school, discussing the new group of seven-year-olds who would soon begin. Or maybe she was talking with Bloodstone about her troublesome Earth-struck charge.

In Oberon City, the gawkers would be gathering, expecting to see the Violet fairies swoop through the Gateway of Galena. For now, I had a little time alone, but what about tomorrow—and every day after? Would I ever have peace again?

I'm not sure how long I lay in the perch of our front room, counting the stones in the wall. I don't remember how or when I made one of the biggest decisions of my life. I remember only that by the time I went upstairs to my mother's room, I was intent on finding a spell that would make me invisible.

How I wished I could talk to my mother. Then again, maybe it was just as well she wasn't there. She would try to stop me from doing what I had planned.

I took out her spellbook and skipped to the advanced spells near the end.

There it was.

Spell of Invisibility

Requires Level 50 magic

The invisibility spell will render the subject invisible to any onlooker by causing the subject and anything the subject may be touching to appear to be part of the surroundings. (The subject may also be the one performing the spell.) Ten minutes of invisibility uses

50 radia. Each additional ten minutes uses another 50 radia.

It is inadvisable to attempt a long-lasting spell of invisibility.

The wand must touch the subject. Infuse the wand and say, "Verita sil nos mertos elemen."

When I had memorized the spell, I stood beside my mother's window and steadied my wings.

I was going back to Earth.

Chapter Nineteen

ONCE UPON A TIME, FEY GODMOTHERS OR GODFATHERS WOULD INTERVENE IF THEY PERCEIVED THAT THEIR GODCHILDREN WERE IN TROUBLE, BUT THIS HAS BECOME RATHER RARE. THE MAJORITY OF GODMOTHERS AND GODFATHERS BEING RED, THE CAPACITY TO GIVE ASSISTANCE TO HUMANS HAS DECLINED.

HOWEVER, MOST FAIRIES AND GENIES STILL LOOK IN UPON THEIR GODCHILDREN BY USING THE FEY SCOPES. THE SCHEDULE OF VIEWING BOOTHS REMAINS BUSY, DAY AND NIGHT.

FEY SCOPES THAT VIEW EARTH ARE A GLORIOUS CREATION OF THE ANCIENTS. A SCOPE CAN TRACE THE MOVEMENTS OF ANY PERSONAGE——INCLUDING NOT ONLY HUMANS BUT ALSO INHABITANTS OF TIRFEYNE WHO ARE VISITING EARTH: FAIRIES, GENIES, LEPRECHAUNS, PIXIES, GREMLINS, TROLLS, GNOMES, ET CETERA. THE ONLY THING NEEDED TO FIND AN INDIVIDUAL IN A SCOPE IS TO KNOW THAT INDIVIDUAL'S NAME.

THERE IS ONE BLIND SPOT IN THE SCOPES. THEY CANNOT PENETRATE EARTH'S SURFACE TO SEE UNDER-GROUND.

—*Orville Gold, genie historian of Feyland*

As I soared lightly over the pool below Galena Falls, not one of the children playing there glanced in my direction. The invisibility spell seemed to be working. I was looking through my own special one-way window to the world. I could see them, but they couldn't see me. I liked it that way.

When I got to the sandstone boulder of the Zinnia Portal, I didn't pause before stepping straight through it.

Earth's sky greeted me, beautifully blue. Soft breezes showered me with scents. As I flew gently above the ground, Earth seemed to have a heartbeat the same as my own. The golden light falling across the grasses told me I had been right to come here. I needed a refuge, a place where no one would ask what I was doing or why.

And as long as I was here, what harm could it do to look for Sam and Jenna? I could just peek at them from inside my invisibility. I wouldn't talk with them or do anything that they might remember.

I renewed the invisibility spell before it lapsed. Lily Morganite or Boris Bloodstone could look through a viewing booth as much as they liked; I wasn't going to be found.

There were only a few people in the park where I'd met Sam and Jenna: a white-haired man and his brown dog, twin girls in pink sunhats, a mother trundling a baby.

I floated down a street leading away from the park, past silent houses, reaching out with my magic but not knowing how to use it to find the particular people I wanted.

I flew slowly, one hand resting on my wand. Feeling slightly silly, I tried talking to my magic. *Show me. Show me Sam and Jenna.*

I drifted three streets east, then felt drawn to stand in front of a house with a maple growing in the yard. The tree's branches reached upward, and again I marveled at the pattern of each leaf. Green paint covered the house. The shades were up, and I saw movement flickering on the other side of the windows.

Just to be safe, I renewed invisibility again before going up the flight of steps that led onto a porch. I peered through the windows, but the sun's glare reflecting off the glass made it hard to see inside. But the front door opened easily, and I slipped through.

I knew I had found the right house when I saw Jenna standing near Sam in a big room with beige walls. She was smiling at the open door. Sam turned, and his eyes seemed to find me. I wondered if the spell could have faltered, but then his gaze slid past me to the doorway.

"You didn't close the door all the way," a woman's voice said. "The flies will get in." She stood beside a table, her hands restlessly sorting piles of envelopes. Her profile showed a freckled nose and thin cheek, and a long fall of red hair. She wore a black dress belted around her waist.

Sam strode to the door. He pushed it shut with the heel of his hand. "No flies, Mom."

"I'm going to Denver to give your dad's boss a piece of

my mind," she said, flinging the envelopes down on the table. "That man had better tell me what he knows about why we haven't heard from your father." She faced Sam, her blue eyes blazing. "If he won't take my calls or answer e-mail, I'll see how he likes it when I barge into his office." For a small woman, she looked fierce.

Their father? Was he *missing*?

"Do you want me to go with you?" Sam asked.

The woman seized a ring of keys from the table. "No. You need to take care of Jenna." She grabbed a handbag, black and shiny like her shoes. The little girl ran to her, hugging her legs. "Be good, sweetie," her mother said, planting a quick kiss on the top of Jenna's head. "I'll be back. Sam, order a pizza."

Her heels clicked past me on the flooring, and she left by the door that Sam had just closed.

"Will Daddy come back?" Jenna asked her brother.

"Of course he will." Sam smiled at her, but his eyes were worried. He picked up his little sister. "Let's watch my cell-phone videos."

"Okay." She brightened.

I trailed after them down a stairway so narrow I had to clutch my wings tightly against my back to keep from batting against the walls. I watched from the doorway, looking into a room painted a very light yellow. Sam plunked a red object onto a desk. He picked up a black stylus that looked like my wand and used it to tap against colored symbols and numbers on the front of the red thing.

A screen on the desk lit up. I thought at first it was television, which I had learned about in Human Culture class. When Bloodstone had first told us about it, Meteor had objected.

"I thought you said humans have no magic."

"Correct," Bloodstone had assured him.

"But how can they show something that happened in the past, without powerful magic?"

"It is called technology," Bloodstone answered. *"And it is changing Earth faster than magic ever could."*

Looking at the screen in front of Sam and Jenna, I had to agree with Meteor. Scenes went by on the screen, scenes of places and people who were not in the room. How could that be?

Sam held Jenna in his lap. She laughed and pointed at the screen, but he didn't seem to be paying attention. With his father missing, I figured I knew what was on his mind.

Jenna squealed. "Fairy!" She joggled Sam's arm. "Look, she's flying."

Sam leaned his face around her, staring at the screen. "Whoa. What the—?"

There I was, flying away. My image looked back once, hovering an instant before rising higher.

"Who's been messing with my phone?" Sam asked. His hand jerked out to cover something on the desk. He moved his fingers, and my flight reversed to the moment when my face was visible. My image stood still; all my movement had ceased; I seemed to be frozen in that one moment from the past.

Technology *was* magic.

"She has purple eyes," said Jenna.

"Someone has seriously hacked my phone!" Sam cried.

I wished I could see his face. What did he mean when he said *hacked*?

"And purple wings," Jenna babbled.

"Yeah. She's beautiful," her brother said. "Got to be Jason who put her there."

Put her there?

"Purple, purple, purple," Jenna said, singsong. She twisted around to look up at him. "How can she fly?"

Sam drew a deep breath. "I wish I knew."

Jenna gasped. Her eyes fastened on me. "Look!" she cried, pointing.

I had lost track of time. The spell had lapsed and Jenna could see me.

I heard the squeak of Sam's chair as it revolved and he faced me. Little bursts of gold lit his eyes—rays of amber, hazel, and brown. He looked astounded.

I should do something, renew the spell instantly, but I felt frozen, like my image on his screen.

"Hi, fairy!" Jenna said. "What's your name?"

This time I could speak. "I'm Zaria."

Jenna jumped out of Sam's lap. She touched my gown. "You're real," she gurgled.

"I should leave." If Sam and Jenna could see me, so could any snoop in Feyland.

"How did you get in my phone?" Sam asked.

"Stay!" Jenna said.

"I can't," I told her gently. I drew out my wand, infused it, and touched my head, murmuring, *"Verita sil nos mertos elemen."*

Jenna tumbled back to Sam. He gazed at the spot where I was and put out a hand as if to call me back. I hurried from the room and up the stairs, out the front door.

Never had my world seemed so far away.

Chapter Twenty

FIFTY YEARS AGO, THE LEPRECHAUN EDICT WAS PROCLAIMED BY THE HIGH COUNCIL OF FEYLAND. IT PROHIBITS LEPRECHAUNS FROM TRAVELING TO EARTH. THE EDICT WAS ENACTED TO ADDRESS TWO PROBLEMS. FIRSTLY, LEPRECHAUNS COULD NOT BE PERSUADED TO STOP TEASING HUMANS. THEY WOULD PUT POTS OF FEY GOLD IN PLAIN SIGHT, THEN CAUSE THEM TO VANISH. HUMANS HAVE NO SENSE OF HUMOR WHEN IT COMES TO GOLD: WHEN THEY REALIZE THEY HAVE BEEN TRICKED, SOME OF THEM DEVELOP DANGEROUS GRUDGES. SECONDLY, LEPRECHAUNS BEGAN SMUGGLING HUMAN BEVERAGES INTO FEYLAND, WITH DISASTROUS RESULTS.

TO FACILITATE THE EDICT, ALL LEPRECHAUNS WERE SENT TO THE IRON LANDS, WHERE THEY LIVE IN WHAT IS KNOWN AS THE LEPRECHAUN COLONY. THE GROUND THERE IS MADE OF IRON ORE. NO MAGIC IS POSSIBLE, INCLUDING PORTALS TO EARTH. ANY ENCHANTMENTS BECOME NULL AND VOID FOR THE DURATION OF A STAY IN THE IRON LANDS.

—*Orville Gold, genie historian of Feyland*

$\mathcal{I}$ decided to return to Tirfeyne by way of the one lawful portal I knew about. From Sam's house I searched until I found the Cornfield Portal again. I stepped through it into the Golden Station. This time, I didn't worry about being seen.

There were big advantages to being invisible.

I flew out, high over Oberon City. In my mind, I went over what had happened on Earth, what had been said and done, how the humans had looked and sounded.

The boy had called me beautiful. Me. Beautiful.

I floated, looking down, wondering where my friends might be. The great FOOM dome stood out, bigger and brighter than all the rest.

Then I saw the crowd.

A buzzing frenzy of fairies and genies hovered one on top of the other, showing every color of wing, every shade of hair. Something was happening on the ground.

Cautiously, I flew lower, trying to get close enough to see. My view was blocked. Just as I was about to give up, a group of genies moved enough to give me a glimpse.

It was Leona. She stood next to the ornamental gardens in the courtyard and seemed to be basking in the attention of the great crowd. She certainly wasn't trying to get away.

Instantly, I flew high again. I couldn't understand why Leona would enjoy putting herself on display for such a mob, when I would rather live with trolls than have a crowd staring at me that way. It made me uneasy. Leona had been my closest friend ever since we could fly. Now, she was acting as if she cared about crowds of strangers more than she cared about me. I couldn't even get near enough to talk to her.

Below me, Feyland looked like a great flower expanding in all directions. I saw Galena as a petal with the gateway at the nectary point. On the other side of the city another petal caught my eye, but no one seemed to be flying there.

No flights. Of course. The Iron Lands, where the leprechauns lived.

I don't know why I decided to head toward the Leprechaun Colony. After seeing Leona holding court, I was feeling gloomy, and maybe I just wanted to go somewhere that matched my mood. Or maybe I was only curious to see what it was like closer to the wall that bordered the Iron Lands. But somehow, I felt drawn in that direction.

The farther I went from the center of Oberon City, the more thinly spread the domes and towers became. Some of them were clearly in disrepair, marred by crumbling stones and tarnished metal. The few fey folk I passed frightened me a little. Their red-rimmed eyes seemed overly wide, and they flew with strange, sputtering movements. Ragged threads trailed from their clothes. What was wrong with them? Were these the "lawless hooligans" Beryl was always warning me about? Just looking at them made my wings feel tired.

I decided to turn around. Just as I did, a fairy came

flying straight at me. I darted sideways, and she barely missed hitting me.

It took a full second to realize who she was, and then I was very relieved to be under the invisibility spell. The fairy had orange wings, tawny hair, and a horribly drab gown. It was Beryl Danburite.

What was she doing here?

I took off after her, surprised by how hard I had to work to keep up. I hadn't even known she could fly so fast.

I managed to renew the invisibility in mid-flight. The last thing I wanted was to be discovered following my guardian through a seedy area of Oberon City.

The scenery changed. No more domes, just collections of slag. The air smelled oddly fragrant, but I didn't recognize the scent. Beryl flew lower and lower, and then she touched down.

I wasn't expecting her to stop where she did; I landed with a bit of a jolt. My feet skidded against gravel. Beryl looked toward the sound, frowning. She listened while I stood perfectly still.

We were in front of a one-story building patched together from uncut stones. Mortar had been carelessly spread— it bulged from the wall in sloppy drips. The copper door was completely unpolished; its sheet of mottled green hung raggedly on dented hinges.

Behind the building, about ten wingspans back, a huge granite wall twisted along bare ground. I must be looking at the border of the Iron Lands. I shuddered and wondered why I had wanted to get anywhere near it.

The only other building to be seen was about fifty wingspans away, and it was nothing but a fallen-down wreck.

Beryl gazed at the sign in front of us: THE UGLY MUG. Her lip curled. "Reeks of Earth," she muttered disgustedly.

And then she went in.

I sprang into motion, flinging myself after her before the door could close.

The moment I crossed the threshold, the aroma I had noticed earlier intensified. It was unlike anything I had ever smelled: a rich, smoky scent, silken and powerful. It filled the air, and as I breathed in, I felt as if I had been knocked into a forbidden land, a land that would like to capture me and hold me forever.

I stood behind Beryl in a long, low room, dim and noisy and filled with brass tables teeming with patrons. Beryl advanced, but I hung back, glad to be invisible.

Murmurs and shouts and raucous laughter swelled around me. The room was packed with fairies and genies of every hue. I also saw a few short, stocky folk; cautiously, I edged after Beryl so I could get a closer look at them. The one nearest me had a long beard, long nose, and long feet decked in boots with turned-up toes. Heavy eyebrows, wide mouth. His stubby fingers held a steaming mug topped with something foamy and white.

A leprechaun? What was a leprechaun doing *outside* the

Iron Lands? The Ugly Mug was close to the border wall, but it was not inside it—not at all. And what was he drinking? Peering around, I saw that most everyone was sipping something similar.

What was Beryl doing here?

She stepped briskly past several wobbly bronze tables. "Banburus Lazuli?" she called, using her teaching voice to cut through the noise. "Banburus?"

A tall genie stood up from a table near the back and moved toward her. In the dusky light, his skin looked somewhere between dark blue and black. A tangle of dirty grayish-blue hair framed his face and fell to his bony shoulders.

"I don't usually bother with all the syllables," he said when he got close enough to be heard. "Call me Laz. What do you want?"

Just then a leprechaun jumped up beside Beryl and plucked her sleeve with his free hand. "When's the Council going to reverse the Lep Edict?" he cried.

Beryl stiffened. "Hands off, if you please."

He hung on. "I used to travel to Earth—me and all m'friends. Now look at me—banned!"

"A fine example you are," Beryl said.

"Not fair!" he groused. "A few leprechauns get into trouble teasing humans, and the Council outlaws traveling to Earth for every one of us!"

Beryl leaned toward him. "You are mucking my gown. What *is* that on your hands?"

"Nothing!" Abruptly, the leprechaun let go. He wiped his fingers on his shirt, leaving dark streaks of something soft and sticky on the faded green cloth.

He had left his handprints on Beryl's gown. *"Chocolate!"* she exclaimed, and drew back. "I might have known."

Chocolate? I had heard whispers of this delicious contraband, a bittersweet substance made on Earth by humans and then smuggled onto Tirfeyne by desperate outlaws. It was said that once fey folk tasted chocolate, they could never get enough of it; that they would give up everything they had for the chance of a steady supply.

"Not so!" the leprechaun protested, but his denial seemed ridiculous. Not only his hands but also the edges of his mouth were coated with gooey smears; even as I watched, he licked his lips as if he couldn't help himself.

"And if the stench in my nose tells the truth, you have been drinking coffee, as well." Beryl smoothed her stained skirts with narrowed eyes.

I had heard of coffee, too. One of the many beverages favored by humans, it was brewed from special beans into a drink that could keep fey folk up for days and nights at a time. Its effects were supposedly worse than spending hours dancing with pixies.

Was the aroma that circulated through THE UGLY MUG coming from coffee or chocolate or both? Beryl had called it a stench, but I didn't believe that even she could really find it anything but exciting.

Beryl glared at the little man. "Lucky for you I am not here to investigate." Her back straight, she turned from the leprechaun to the tall genie who called himself Laz. "May we speak privately?"

He shrugged, calmly grabbed a bowl-sized cup from the nearest tabletop, and headed toward the door. I slipped aside or they would have bumped into me on their way out.

Chapter Twenty-one

THERE IS ONE METHOD FOR FEY FOLK TO GAIN MORE RADIA. THIS IS DONE BY TAKING A TRANSFER FROM SOMEONE ELSE'S WAND. DEPENDING UPON AVAILABILITY, IT IS POSSIBLE TO TRANSFER ANY AMOUNT OF RADIA FROM ONE WAND TIP TO ANOTHER.

TRANSFER OF RADIA REQUIRES CONSENT. THERE IS NO SUCH THING AS AN INVOLUNTARY TRANSFER, FOR EVEN THE MOST POWERFUL COMPULSION SPELL WILL NOT BE EFFECTIVE IN FORCING ANY OF THE FEY TO GIVE UP RADIA UNWILLINGLY.

—*Orville Gold, genie historian of Feyland*

Outside The Ugly Mug, I tagged after Beryl and Laz as he led the way around the corner of the building. They faced each other on a patch of gravel. I stood behind Beryl so I could see the genie's face.

"You're a smuggler, aren't you?" she asked in her sharpest tone.

The color of his eyes matched his hair—a murky blue-gray. "You know my name, but I can't return the pleasure," he said, ignoring her question.

"Beryl Danburite. I am a teacher in Galena, though I never had the honor of seeing *you* as a student. You must have belonged to a different group."

He took a swig from his cup, which left a whitish film on his upper lip. "And?"

"*Must* you drink coffee while I am speaking to you?"

"Cocoa." Laz glared sourly at Beryl. "And what I drink is my own business. Since you don't care to partake, I have to assume that something else brings you here."

Beryl huffed. "You should be ashamed of yourself!"

Staring straight into her face, the genie deliberately took another drink. "Perhaps you'd care to tell me why I should listen to anything more?"

Beryl fidgeted a moment before saying, "You are Samuel Seabolt's genie godfather."

Samuel? Was she talking about the human boy I had met? Had she seen me appear in front of him today?

Laz gave Beryl a considering look. "What of it?"

"You have not been keeping an eye on him!"

Laz flicked his cup with the fingers of one hand, making a pinging sound. "Something wrong? Last I checked, all was well with Sam."

"No thanks to you."

"Spare me the lecture. Humans get along just fine without us." The genie swiped his filthy sleeve across his mouth.

"*Other* godfathers help and protect—"

"These days? Not many," he scoffed. "And if they take

credit for their godchildren surviving to adulthood, they're liars." He leaned close to Beryl and breathed out slowly. "Tell me why you're here."

Beryl wrinkled her nose but didn't move back from him. "Two fairies in my class broke the rules and made a visit to Earth," she said brusquely. "I cast forgetting spells on the humans who saw them, of course, but I found one memory I could not eradicate. It was in a gadget belonging to your godchild."

I began to feel a little better. Evidently this was not about my latest journey to Earth.

Laz's chuckle sounded like gravel poured into a culvert. "Gadget?"

"A machine that *remembers.*"

A change came over Laz's face: his bleary eyes widened and his jaw went slack. He looked purely astonished. "Mighty magic," he said, as if awestruck.

Then I realized his gaze was locked on *me.* Once again, I'd allowed the spell to lapse. Oberon's Crown! Beryl would take me to the Council and insist they take back my wand.

I looked into Laz's face, shaking my head pleadingly.

"Not magic!" Beryl said irritably. "Human technology."

He shifted his gaze, rolling his eyes to the sky. "Technology," he said. "Of course. And how long since you traveled to Earth yourself, Miss . . . Danburite?"

I got my wand tangled in my gown as I frantically drew

it. Before Laz finished speaking, I had whispered, *"Verita sil nos mertos elemen."*

"Not long," Beryl answered. She turned her head. "Did you hear something?"

"Not long? How long is 'not'?" Laz asked, sneering.

"No more than thirty years," Beryl said.

He laughed, a snort that ended in a cough. "And those fools at the Council have *you* teaching youngsters!" He raised his cup to her mockingly. "The gadget was probably a video camera—or might've been a cell phone. Either one could have recorded your fairies."

Beryl shook her finger at him. "Because of genies like you, all of Feyland is infected with human customs, human mannerisms, and human speech!"

"Genies like me, eh?"

"I can spot an Earth-traveling genie when I see one. You pick up those vile human habits and spread them everywhere. Not to mention those loathsome confections and concoctions that corrupt anyone who tastes them."

"And what do *you* want? Maybe you'd like to do away with the last few hundred years of history?" Laz shook his cup lazily, and creamy brown liquid sloshed over the sides. "Free advice for you: modernize!"

Beryl bristled. "We *are* modernizing."

The genie rolled his eyes again. "You're obsolete." He tipped his head back, draining the cup, then turned toward the building.

"Wait," Beryl cried. "How do I get rid of the memory in the gadget?"

Laz turned back. "You go to Earth. You find where it's stored. You delete it." He lowered his brows. "Not too much for you, is it?"

I couldn't believe it when Beryl asked, "Will *you* do it?"

What was the matter with her? Why would she trust a genie like him? It was as if she were afraid of going to Earth herself.

A slow grin showed all of Laz's teeth. "For a small price."

"What price? You should do it out of duty to your godchild."

He seemed unimpressed. "It's not as if Sam could be harmed by the sight of a fairy on a screen," he said. "For all I know, it would do him some good. Broaden his horizons." He flung the empty cup; it crashed against a corner of the building and broke into little pieces. "I don't ask much. Fifty radia."

"Fifty! But going to Earth and back uses less than one!"

He blew out a slow breath. "Fifty or nothing."

For a moment Beryl's wings actually quivered. "Very well," she said, croaking her words. "I expect it to be done tonight."

What?! Hadn't she taught me that only fools and criminals traded in radia? That it would lead to nothing but trouble and loss? Why would Beryl Danburite strike a bargain with a genie who drank coffee and associated with leprechauns?

"Sure," Laz said. "I'll pay a visit while he's asleep."

I watched Beryl take out her wand. The carnelian rod glowed, and Laz produced a wand with a lapis tip. He touched it to the danburite tip of Beryl's wand, and the glow transferred from her wand to his.

And that was all. She said nothing about checking to be sure he did what he said he would do. Had she sniffed Banburus Lazuli and decided his word was good?

I watched as they turned from each other. Beryl streaked away, and Laz headed for the door to The Ugly Mug.

Chapter Twenty-two

ONCE THEY HAVE FINISHED ORDINARY SCHOOL, FAIRIES
AND GENIES WHO ARE GIFTED WITH HIGH-LEVEL MAGIC
AND ADEQUATE RADIA RESERVES ARE ALLOWED ACCESS
TO THE CROWN LIBRARY, WHERE THEY MAY READ THE
ANCIENT TEXTS ABOUT ADVANCED MAGIC. HOWEVER,
YOUNG FEY FOLK SUIT THEMSELVES ABOUT WHAT
THEY STUDY AND WHEN. THIS IS A DEPLORABLE STATE
OF AFFAIRS, FOR ONLY TRUE SCHOLARS, MOTIVATED
BY THEIR OWN DEEP CURIOSITY, ACQUIRE ENOUGH
KNOWLEDGE TO PROTECT THEMSELVES FROM THOSE
WHO ARE EXPERIENCED BUT UNSCRUPULOUS.

—Orville Gold, genie historian of Feyland

I arrived home well before Beryl. She didn't come back until late, and by then I was pretending to be asleep, though my restless thoughts ran from Leona to Earth to The Ugly Mug.

The next morning, Beryl shook me awake very early. Her visit with Laz seemed to have put her into a mood. She was scowling as if she wanted to deepen every wrinkle, and her yellow eyes snapped. She waved a hand in a shooing motion. "Get up."

"Why so early?" I yawned.

"You are due to meet your mentor this morning, and you do not want to be late!"

The mention of my mentor threw me into a mood of my own. Sitting up, I frowned at Beryl. "Why are you still punishing me? Wasn't the iron enough?"

"What in Oberon's name are you talking about?"

"My mentor assignment."

Beryl folded her arms. "I do not even know who your mentor *is*."

"Then how did Bloodstone know?"

"Bloodstone did not know! Mentor assignments are secret, as we have taught you again and again. What does it take for you to learn something, Zaria? Apparently it is not enough to repeat a lesson over and over. Now get up."

I flopped out of my nest to stand in front of her. "Yesterday, when Bloodstone handed me my scroll, he gloated so much he almost broke his face."

Her orange wings began to unfurl. "That is extraordinarily disrespectful, Zaria. Being named Violet seems to have gone to your head. You and Leona had better—"

"Tell me why Bloodstone would be so happy about Lily Morganite!" I interrupted.

"What?"

Beryl's knees folded, and her wings failed to catch her. She *fell* into my nest!

Confused, I watched her fight for control. On the fourth try, she managed to heave herself out of the nest, but she didn't stay upright. She sat on the edge.

"Beryl?"

"Lily Morganite," she said tremulously. "Your mentor? I do not believe it."

I scooped up the scroll from the nook beside my nest and held it out to her.

Magic Mentor for Zaria Tourmaline: Lily Morganite
Report to 3750 Morganite Towers in Oberon City.

"It cannot be." Beryl's wings flapped convulsively. "What am I to do?" She seemed to be talking to herself. "Oh, Cinna, what can I do?"

Cinna. My mother's name.

Beryl sighed so deeply it sounded like a sob. "Zaria, this is not something I can help you with. Mentor assignments are decided by the Council, and they do not consult your teachers. Mr. Bloodstone could not bring this about. He is not part of the Council, much as he would like to be." She straightened a little and seized my wrist. "Listen to me. You must not *ever* discuss personal matters with Lily Morganite. Nothing, do you understand? If she asks about your parents, tell her you do not remember them. Same with Jett. Are you listening?"

I had never listened more closely to anyone.

"Do not let her get the best of you," she went on. "Do not let her lull you into revealing a single thing about yourself." Her grip on my wrist was painfully tight.

"Why? Who is she?" I tried to pulled away, and Beryl finally let go.

"She is diabolical." Beryl covered her face with both hands. I'd never heard her label anyone that way.

Her hands dropped into her lap like two dead birds. "Lily Morganite is all the more dangerous," she went on, "because she has the other Council members fooled."

"Fooled?" I heard myself asking.

"Fooled into thinking she has the best interests of Feyland at heart. Ha! She pretends to care so much." She looked me in the eye. "This assignment as your mentor must be *her* doing, Zaria."

"But *why* would she want to be my mentor?" I asked after an awkward silence.

Beryl swallowed hard. "You are Violet, and now she wants you in her clutches." How pitiful she looked, collapsed on the edge of my nest, her orange wings quaking against the pillows, her face haggard and drawn. "Promise you will not tell her anything at all about you, your parents, your brother, your friends, your life."

I promised.

Chapter Twenty-three

THE ANCIENT DURABLE SPELLS MUST BE REFRESHED
WITH LARGE AMOUNTS OF RADIA FROM TIME TO TIME,
OR THEY BEGIN TO LOSE THEIR POWER.

ALL FAIRIES AND GENIES WHO REGISTER ABOVE RED
ARE REQUIRED TO PAY A RADIA TAX TO HELP SUPPORT
THE DURABLE SPELLS. THE TAX IS COLLECTED AND
DISPENSED BY THE FORCIER OF FEYLAND.

ONLY THE MOST HONORABLE AMONG FAIRIES AND
GENIES MAY BECOME A FORCIER.

—*Orville Gold, genie historian of Feyland*

Beryl gave me directions to Morganite Towers. "And
do not be put off your guard by its beauty."

"I'm not a baby."

But looking at the graceful spires of Morganite Towers,
I had to admit it was hard to believe a diabolical fairy could
be living there. I flew up to the thirty-seventh floor at the
top, alighting on the balcony marked *3750*, and tapped on
the door. When it opened, I found myself unable to breathe.

Standing in a shimmering white gown was the fairy I
had seen on my visit to the viewing station—the godmother

who had given such a bad gift to her human godchild.

Up close, her pink skin was flawless, and every one of her saffron hairs was smooth. Her white wings hung soft and still. "Zaria Tourmaline?" She enunciated my name clearly. Her voice was unusual—sweet and light, yet it grated on my ears.

The scent of lilies washed over me as I nodded. I exhaled, sounding like a whistling teakettle.

"I am Lily Morganite." Pearly eyes ran over me. "Come in, child." She extended an arm, and I saw the imposing ruby carved with the crest of Oberon sparkling on her wrist as she led the way into a lofty dwelling.

Perches filled with embroidered pillows lined the walls. Books and ornaments rested on shelves high above exotic carpets. I could imagine sitting on the wide window ledges to look out over the city.

"May I offer you sonnia juice?" my mentor asked.

"No, thank you."

"As you wish. I am glad to see you are ready to begin." She flitted up to a perch and patted the pillows next to her. "The first thing we will do is put your registry into your new spellbook."

I sat beside her, but as far away as good manners would allow. I decided I didn't like the scent of lilies, a scent that seemed to be intensifying.

My mentor brought out a large heavy-looking book with a pink cover. She laid it in her lap. "Your spellbook."

I hated that book on sight. My spellbook should be light

as air and blue, like my mother's. I opened my mouth to ask if we could study Cinna Tourmaline's spellbook instead, but then closed it again. Beryl had warned me not to mention my family!

Lily asked for my record of registry. Fumbling in my gown, I brought it out and I handed it to her. *Zaria Tourmaline, Registered Level 100, full Violet.*

She examined it. "You are very fortunate to be Violet. You will have the chance to practice many spells."

I looked at her warily as she spread glue on the back of the document. "I could do an adhesion spell," she said, "but I want to set a good example, so I will not waste radia." She opened the book and pressed my registry onto the first page.

I laced my fingers together to keep from fidgeting. "How are mentors chosen?"

"By the wisdom of the High Council," Lily said too quickly. "We discuss each new assignment together. And because you are Violet, we needed someone especially well qualified to train you."

"Qualified?"

She measured me with her eyes. "I have served on the High Council for ninety years, working for the good of the land." I thought of Beryl's words. *She pretends to care so much.* "And," she continued, "I am Blue. Level One Hundred. So you see, I have much to teach you."

Level 100 meant Lily Morganite could do any spell I

could do. And she probably knew a thousand spells I'd never heard of.

She handed me the book as if it were made of delicate spun glass. When I took it, it felt like a load of lead.

"This is one of the most important days in your life—the day you begin the study of magic. Remember, spellbooks and their contents are secret. Guard your book closely and never discuss it with anyone but me. It will belong to you, but you will keep it here, until you are ready to practice magic without my supervision."

"Supervision? But—"

"Zaria, I know you have already broken laws."

Of course she knew. She'd reported it.

"The Council cannot risk a high-level Violet running amok," Lily continued. "As your mentor, I am responsible for you. Therefore, you are not to practice magic of any kind without my permission." She gave me a metal stylus with a sharpened tip. "This pen is designed to engrave the pages of your spellbook. Begin by signing your name."

Rolling the strange pen between my fingers, I felt suddenly tired. I put down the pen and hefted the book without opening it. "Why is it so heavy?"

"It is made of an unusual alloy," she said. "I will explain later. Sign your book, child. We have a great deal to do."

I opened the book. "What will I learn first?"

"How to control the level of magic you put in your wand."

I wasn't going to let her know that Beryl had already taught me to control the level of magic in my wand. I picked up the pen again and rubbed my hand across my eyes, then sat a little straighter, trying to shake off a desire to sleep.

"No one informed me you were a slow student," Lily said. "Please sign your book, Zaria."

I put the pen to the page, but I was seized with an overwhelming feeling that if I set my name there, I would become forever less than I was now.

Beryl's quiet words boomed inside my head. *She wants you in her clutches.*

I let the pen drop and shoved the spellbook from my lap. It fell, landing with a thud on the carpeted floor, its pages splayed like a broken fan.

Lily's pearly eyes went wide. "What is wrong with you?"

"Too heavy." My tongue felt thick and fuzzy. I reached for my strength, but it seemed faded and far away.

I had to get out.

Chapter Twenty-four

ONLY THE ANCIENT LANGUAGE IS CAPABLE OF CON-
DUCTING THE MAGIC NEEDED FOR ADVANCED SPELLS.
TO CAST EFFECTIVE ENCHANTMENTS, PARTICULAR
SPELLS MUST BE CAREFULLY MEMORIZED, WORD BY
ANCIENT WORD.

—*Orville Gold, genie historian of Feyland*

In clumsy haste, I threw myself onto Lily's balcony. I felt as if I had to break through a sticky web fastened to my wings, but I lifted off and spun dizzily away from Morganite Towers.

Weak and slow, caught in a gummy haze, I flew, expecting to be overtaken at any moment by my horrible mentor. Then my wings began to fail. I drifted downward, unable to stop myself.

Spotting the azure fronds of some bannerite bushes in a garden far below, I aimed for them, hoping they would break my fall. Tumbling and rolling, I crashed through the bushes and hit the ground. I lay half-stunned, staring through a tangle of twiglike branches at the sky. Fronds of bannerite tickled my face.

Bannerite is famous for its soft, pretty leaves, but they are terribly bitter. If a bannerite twig so much as touches the tongue, it fills the mouth with an acrid taste. I closed my lips tightly.

What was happening?

Lily Morganite must have put a spell on me. Nothing else could explain the way I felt.

I drew out my wand and infused it with as much magic as it would hold. I gazed dully at the glowing seam along the black stylus, trying to think.

Oh, how I wanted to sleep.

"Don't sleep," I murmured. I had to reverse the enchantment. But how?

If only I had my mother's book. There must be a spell to take away the foul magic that seemed to be coating my thoughts as well as my wings. There must be!

I felt even more tired, my mind more thickly clouded. I lay still, and hopelessness crept into my heart. My arms felt stiff as stone.

I laid the tip of my wand against my aching forehead. "Undo it," I muttered. "Undo any spells on me."

My hand flopped to the ground, and I lay unmoving.

I took a full breath. The bannerite close to my nose smelled pungent. My wings had relaxed, and my head was clearing. I could feel my power thrumming again.

Either my makeshift spell had worked or Lily's spell had expired.

It was probably Lily's spell that had expired. Everyone knew it was impossible to work magic using ordinary words. If common words could conduct magic, fey folk would cast spells by accident.

What should I do now? I was in deep trouble. I had offended a powerful fairy.

A *diabolical* fairy.

I didn't want to go out and face Feyland, but I didn't want to stay in the bannerite bushes, either. I wanted to disregard the advice in my mother's book and cast a long-lasting invisibility spell on myself. That way, I wouldn't have to worry about Lily Morganite ever again. Tempting as it was, I knew it would be very foolish, so I put my wand away and crept out of the bannerite. Carefully, I dusted myself off and checked my wings. They were bruised but otherwise unharmed.

After several big sighs, I decided to look for Leona. She understood the world of grown fairies better than I. Maybe she'd know of a way to change mentors.

The first fairy I asked told me that Leona's mentoring sessions were held inside the FOOM dome. "As befits a Violet . . ."

When I got to the dome, a crowd hovered in the courtyard. I dove to the front, heedless of any wings I might ruffle. The fairies and genies I jostled got huffy; a blue-faced fairy scolded me: "No manners, no elegance . . . backward parents . . . uppity . . ." Her voice sounded like hammers striking granite.

I held my position, but it didn't matter. When Leona emerged, the crowd rushed forward, and I lost my place.

"Any truth to the rumor that, Magistria Lodestone is your mentor, Leona?" the blue-faced fairy screeched.

"Has the Council let you know what they have in mind for you?" yelled a red-haired genie.

Questions spattered from all sides.

Leona just smiled. "Naturally, I can't reveal who my mentor is," she said when she could be heard. "And I'm much too young for the Council to consult me about anything."

I'd never needed her friendship more, and I couldn't even talk to her without an audience. If I showed myself, she would probably introduce me to the crowd as her sister in Violetness.

I edged sideways through the tangle of fairies and genies until the curve of the dome could hide me. Then I spread my wings and headed for Galena.

Maybe I could find Andalonus or Meteor. But if I did, how could they help me? Andalonus would make light of my troubles unless I told him the entire story, but telling him the entire story would be risky because he wasn't good at keeping secrets. And Meteor would disapprove of everything I'd done since my first visit to Earth, especially performing an advanced spell before I'd had any sessions with my mentor.

Disconsolate, I drifted home. But instead of going through the front door, I lifted the latch on my mother's window. I wanted to read more of her spellbook.

The instant I stepped into her room, I knew something was different. Outwardly, nothing appeared to be disturbed. The pillows were arranged just as I'd left them, all the cupboards neatly shut. But a scent hung faintly in the air.

Lilies.

The first thing I did was rush to open the cupboard that held my mother's book. It was empty.

My wings trembled like petals in a strong wind. "Beryl must have put it away for safekeeping," I told myself, not believing my own words. "She must have."

I opened the door. Murmuring voices drifted up from downstairs. I recognized Beryl's tones, and I was afraid I recognized Lily's, too. I closed the door softly and went back out the window.

Entering by the front way, I saw Beryl with Lily Morganite.

Beryl sat scrunched on her perch. "Zaria," she said flatly when she saw me. "We have a guest."

Lily sat upright on the threadbare pillows of our highest perch, which was only a wingspan off the floor.

She gave me an aloof stare. "I have told your guardian about your rudeness earlier."

"What are you doing in Galena?" I burst out.

"Our guest is not only a councilor but also your mentor," Beryl said. "She can pass through the gateway if she sees fit."

"Not a very courteous greeting, Zaria." Lily had the air of someone who knew she could expect nothing better from me, but her voice was sweet. "Miss Danburite tells me she cannot understand why you would forget your manners. Prove her right. Apologize."

I wanted to scream the question that ran through my mind like a furious gremlin: *Did you steal my mother's spellbook?*

"Come now," Lily went on. "No shame in apologies when you have done something wrong."

"I'm sorry, Councilor Morganite . . . ," I began.

A smile spread over her face.

"I'm sorry, but I don't want you as my mentor."

The smile vanished. Lily's eyes narrowed. "I have not consented to mentor anyone for over fifty years. You should be honored." She rounded on Beryl. "Although you could not be expected to know you were raising a Violet, Miss Danburite, you ought to have instilled better manners in Zaria."

"But—" Beryl said.

"Under your guidance, she seems to believe she is a law unto herself," Lily said, waving a finger at Beryl. "I see it will be up to *me* to educate her. And I am sorry, but I must inform the other Council members about this wayward child."

Beryl began to sputter. "Why you . . . inform the Council . . . you cannot . . ."

"Certainly I can," Lily answered, smiling coldly. She rose. She swept up to me and put her face close to mine.

"Remember, there are penalties for discussing your spellbook with anyone but me."

I was close to calling out that she was a liar, and that she'd enchanted me for no reason, and that I'd never let her come near me again. But I didn't speak.

I watched her as she left. She was carrying a pink bag. It had a bulge the size and shape of my mother's spellbook.

Chapter Twenty-five

BAD-TEMPERED FAIRIES AND GENIES HAVE PLAYED AN ESTABLISHED ROLE IN FEY HISTORY. WHEN ANGERED, THEIR VENGEANCE OFTEN TAKES THE FORM OF MALICIOUS ENCHANTMENTS, CAST NOT ONLY UPON HUMANS BUT ALSO UPON FEY FOLK UNFORTUNATE ENOUGH TO OFFEND THEM. ALAS, ONE DESPICABLE DEED BY A WICKED FAIRY OR GENIE RECEIVES MORE ATTENTION THAN COUNTLESS ACTS OF GENEROSITY BY GOOD-TEMPERED FEY FOLK.

IT IS UNWISE TO ANGER A POWERFUL FAIRY OR GENIE.

—*Orville Gold, genie historian of Feyland*

Five years ago, I had lost my mother. I couldn't bear to lose her legacy now. Before Beryl could say a word, I flew out the door. Skimming into the sonnia field, I ducked down among the lush red flowers.

"Verita sil nos mertos elemen." Invisible, I hurtled after Lily.

I had to find out for sure what was in the pink bag. Once she got it safely back to Morganite Towers, I'd have no chance.

But how could I take it from her? I was gaining on Lily, but what could I do when I reached her? If I so much as touched the bag she carried, she would cast a spell. And for all I knew, there were spells to turn me visible again.

Unless I took her wand. If I did that, she wouldn't be able to cast any spell beyond a Level 7.

The thought of stealing a wand shocked me. A few days ago I'd been a good fairy who never did anything more disobedient than sneak out for a starlit flight alone over Galena Falls. Now I found myself breaking the law more often than I kept it.

"She seems to believe she's a law unto herself," Lily had said. Could she be right about me?

Directly below us grew a patch of sonnia flowers. A few children played Leaping Leprechaun in a sand field off to the right. They weren't paying attention to Lily flying above them, and they couldn't have seen me even if they had looked.

I had almost caught up to her. But the Gateway of Galena wasn't far ahead. All too soon, Lily would pass through it.

If only I knew a spell to make her stop flying and give me her bag. But the only spells I knew could not help me now. I was going to have to give up.

Rage and frustration made me infuse my wand even though I knew it wouldn't do any good. I pointed it at the back of her head. "I wish you would fall asleep here and now," I whispered.

And then Lily was tumbling over and over, on her way to the ground.

Horrified, I plummeted after her, managing to catch hold

of the hem of her lustrous skirt. I yanked upward. There was a long, drawn-out ripping sound as her skirt began to tear, but I was able to break her fall.

She landed in a sonnia field. Deep in sleep, she lay with one arm flung out, holding the pink bag. Juice from crushed sonnia plants stained her torn gown.

Shaking all over, I touched Lily's head with my wand. No one must see her here. *"Verita sil nos mertos elemen,"* I cried.

She—and the bag she carried—winked out like a star in daylight.

Breathing hard, I felt along the ground, seeking the bag. Finding it, I slid my hand inside as gently as I could and pulled out a nearly weightless book. As soon as I touched it, it popped into my vision.

I remembered what the spellbook had said about the way invisibility operated. *The invisibility spell will render the subject invisible to any onlooker by causing the subject and anything the subject may be touching to appear to be part of the surroundings.*

I could see the book now, but no one else could.

Cinna Tourmaline, Spellbook. I hugged it close.

Lily murmured in her sleep. How much longer before she woke?

"You're a sneaking gremlin," I said. "Why would you steal from me?"

Why, why, why? I doubted she needed my mother's book for the spells. My mother had never been a councilor. She wouldn't know spells Lily had never learned.

Then it occurred to me that Lily Morganite might not want the book for herself. Maybe she only wanted to keep it away from me.

Lily and I were equal in our level of magic, but her skill with spells would give her the advantage. She might be afraid that if I learned everything in my mother's book, I would become troublesome.

So she had tried to steal my heritage.

Rotten, sneaking gremlin.

I wanted to take her wand, to keep her from enchanting me again. But if I did, I would be a true thief. My mother's book did not belong to Lily, so getting it back wasn't stealing. But taking her wand? Theft, plain and simple.

Still, Beryl had called Lily diabolical. If I took a diabolical fairy's wand, I might be doing a favor for Feyland.

I pocketed my stylus and quieted my shivering wings. I groped for Lily's wand.

The instant I touched it, a siren began to screech. I leaped back. Drawing my own wand, I infused it with magic. "Be silent!" I wailed, pointing.

The siren shrieked on. Children were running toward the sonnia patch, calling excitedly. What a fool I'd been, triggering such an obvious spell, a spell with no remedy. Lily's wand would never respond to magic from another!

I rose unsteadily into the air. For a moment I watched the bewildered children as they sought the source of the howling siren. More children, some of them with grown-up fairies and genies, were hastening to the scene.

In fewer than ten minutes, Lily would become visible. There was no way to guess how long she would sleep. Maybe her racketing wand would wake her up immediately.

In midair, I renewed the invisibility spell on myself. Then, holding tight to my mother's spellbook, I turned and fled.

Chapter Twenty-six

THERE HAVE BEEN SEVERAL ACCOUNTS OF ENDURING
FRIENDSHIPS BETWEEN FEY FOLK AND HUMAN BEINGS,
AND THESE ACCOUNTS ARE TRUTHFUL. HOWEVER,
ALL SUCH FRIENDSHIPS BELONG TO THE PAST, BEFORE
THE EDICT OF THE UNSEEN—AND WELL BEFORE THE
INVENTION OF GUNS.

—*Orville Gold, genie historian of Feyland*

I flew toward home, but how could home protect me?
And where could I possibly hide the book so it wouldn't be
found?

In that time of need, I thought of the Zinnia Portal. It
wasn't far. I could use it to go to Earth and calm myself. If
only I could think clearly, I could decide what to do.

I raced to Galena Falls. I skidded to a landing by the
boulder hung with zinnias, then dashed through it.

The boulder on the Earth side of the portal lay quiet in
the waving grass. Farther up the slope, trees reached to the sky.

Sun poured golden warmth across my wings as I floated
up the ridge into the trees. I sat beneath a tall evergreen with
great sloping branches full of blue-green needles. I knew

what sort of tree it was: blue spruce. I leaned against its trunk.

What had I done?

They would be looking for me. If they didn't find me, they would search. What if they found the portal in Galena? My only hope was to return before being missed.

And how could I hide the book?

I thought of burying it. We had been told that fey scopes could not see godchildren who happened to be in basements or deep caves. If a scope couldn't see a child underground, maybe it wouldn't be able to find a buried book, either.

Going to my knees, I poked at the moist ground under the spruce tree. The dirt yielded easily to my frantic hands. It seemed to be made mostly of old, crumbling spruce needles. Soon, I had a hole big enough.

I laid the spellbook in the ground and covered it. Then I drew out my wand. The black stylus looked so bland and unimpressive. It was a good thing I hadn't changed it. Who would suspect such a wand of doing advanced magic?

Lily Morganite would. What if she persuaded the rest of the Council that I must surrender my wand?

A wild idea formed in my mind. My wand was a stylus that had been made on Earth. I had seen one like it in Sam and Jenna's house. What if I borrowed Sam's stylus and took it back to Feyland? Then if the Council ordered me to surrender my wand, I could give them Sam's stylus.

Beryl had taught me the transport spell, so I could be at Sam's house in an instant. I focused on my destination: a pale yellow room where a black stylus waited. Infusing to Level 8, I touched my head. *"Transera nos."*

I didn't have time to blink before I stood in the room where Sam and Jenna had gazed at me in surprise. A stylus lay on the desk. I grabbed it and compared it to my wand. They looked identical.

I was about to transport back to the grove when I heard someone crying. Poised to leave, I listened and knew right away that it wasn't a child making those despairing sobs.

I hurried upstairs toward the sound. Sam's mother was sitting in the main room, alone in a cushioned chair, her face in her hands, disheveled red hair falling around her shoulders. She lifted her head for a moment, showing dark-circled eyes. She looked as if she hadn't slept since I'd last seen her.

Their father must still be missing.

I wanted to help, but urgency pounded me, telling me to go back to the grove and then into Galena, where Lily Morganite would surely be awake by now.

Infusing my wand, I pointed it experimentally at Sam's mother. "Rest," I said.

She leaned back in her chair, her eyes closing. In seconds, she was asleep, breathing evenly.

My thoughts whirled. Again, I had cast a spell with ordinary words. How could that be?

There was no time to stop and wonder about it. I focused on the spot where I'd buried the spellbook. *"Transera nos."*

Instantly, I was beside the blue spruce again. I knelt and

put the two styluses next to each other. The one from Sam's house *looked* just like my wand but *felt* completely unmagical. No fairy or genie above a Level 6 could possibly believe it was really my wand.

I sighed. Surely, I should make at least one attempt to transform Sam's stylus into something more believable.

Infusing, I watched the thin plastic seam light up. How many times had I gone to Level 100 today? I couldn't remember and wondered fleetingly how much of my radia was gone forever.

I set Sam's stylus on the ground and visualized it becoming a thing of magic. Then I pointed my true wand. "Transform," I commanded.

When I picked up Sam's stylus, it felt slightly magical.

I had done it again, cast a spell using everyday words. I couldn't wait to tell my friends. What would Leona say? Meteor would probably wag his head, warning me about wasting radia. Andalonus would ask me to try a special spell to make myself look ridiculous.

I caught myself smiling and pushed the thought of my friends out of my mind. I had a dire decision to make. Should I leave my true wand behind?

If Lily *did* persuade the full Council that I should turn over my wand, keeping the true wand along with the fake could be horribly risky. They might find it somehow, exposing my deception.

But if I left it on Earth, I would be without any power

to cast spells beyond Level 6. I would be cut off from the fullness of my magic.

Kneeling beside the blue spruce, I vacillated, even though I didn't have a second to spare. At last I decided it would be best to leave my true wand with my mother's spellbook.

I renewed invisibility and then flipped open my watch-face cover to glance at the time. A few minutes past three in the afternoon. I had ten minutes to get home before the invisibility spell expired.

Scrabbling in the hole beneath the spruce, I uncovered the spellbook and laid my true wand inside the front page. I patted dirt over them, brushing needles and leaves across the top to look natural.

Leaving them there felt like losing a wing.

I stowed the false wand in my gown and then raced for the portal. As I burst out of the grove, I couldn't believe my eyes. Below me, down the ridge in the grass, close to the portal, stood a human boy and a fairy. The fairy's silver wings rose like sparkling mist and her hair streamed dark in the wind.

Leona had returned to Earth.

Chapter Twenty-seven

GNOMES ARE OF A SIMILAR STATURE TO LEPRECHAUNS, SHORTER AND STOUTER THAN FAIRIES AND GENIES. LIVING ON POWDERED GRANITE, THEY DWELL ON ALL PARTS OF TIRFEYNE BUT HAVE VERY LIMITED MAGIC. THEY CANNOT FLY OR CAST SPELLS.

GNOMES MAKE EXCELLENT GUARDS, BECAUSE A SPELL CAST DIRECTLY UPON A GNOME HAS NO EFFECT. HOWEVER, THEY ARE NOT IMPERVIOUS TO MAGIC THAT HAS BEEN CAST UPON SOMETHING OTHER THAN THEMSELVES. FOR EXAMPLE, AN OBJECT WHOSE NATURE HAS BEEN ALTERED BY ENCHANTMENT— SUCH AS A FLYING CARPET—WILL RETAIN ITS MAGIC AROUND GNOMES; A PERSON WHO IS UNDER A SPELL OF INVISIBILITY WILL REMAIN UNSEEN.

GNOMES ARE EXCELLENT WORKERS. IN FEYLAND THEY CLEAN, MAKE REPAIRS, SEW CLOTHING, DIG IN THE MINES, AND HELP TO KEEP ORDER. IN OTHER PARTS OF TIRFEYNE, SUCH AS TROLL COUNTRY, THEY PERFORM DIFFERENT DUTIES.

—Orville Gold, genie historian of Feyland

I'd been wanting so badly to talk with Leona. Now she was in front of me without a mob of fawning fairies and genies around her, but she was standing next to a human, and I had no time to stop. Also, I was invisible, so she couldn't see me.

When I got close enough, I recognized Jason Court, and I wanted to grab Leona and shove her through the portal along with me.

But Leona would be offended. She would argue. I would have to explain everything to her, and I didn't have time. I had to get home: my invisibility spell was ticking away and without my true wand, I couldn't cast another.

I dodged past Leona and Jason and slipped through the sandstone boulder into Galena. I took to the air, shaking out my gown as I went. After all that had happened, it would be senseless to be caught with spruce needles clinging to me. I scrubbed my hands against the insides of my pockets, trying to get rid of the dirt.

Approaching home, I saw a small crowd of children and parents around our door. There were more than a dozen pairs of hovering wings. I couldn't see past them.

I pushed on. The view of my front doorway might be blocked, but the crowd did not extend to the back of the house.

No gawkers there, but something that frightened me much more: two gnomes were watching the windows. Gnomes inside Galena, standing guard over my home! It could mean only one thing. Someone who lived in my house had been accused of a crime.

I drifted downward, landing just behind the gnomes without making a sound. I checked my watch. One more minute before my invisibility expired.

I picked up some pebbles and then flew to my mother's window. I tried the latch. It turned easily. With one hand on the latch, I threw the pebbles between the gnomes. When they looked at the ground, I slipped inside the window, fastening it behind me. One of the gnomes, a fellow with a cleft chin and tufts of hair growing out of his forehead, was quick to look up. Knowing I'd reappear any instant, I ducked away from the window.

I crossed to the door. Opening it, I listened on the landing and heard Beryl's angry tones. "Come in, then, if you must," she was saying.

I heard our front door clang shut just as my invisibility spell expired.

Beryl flashed me a look of relief and worry as I came downstairs. I tried to look unruffled, but it wasn't easy. Our front room held three members of the High Council: Wolframite, Zircon, and Morganite.

Lily must have drawn a spell to mend her gown, but she had left the sonnia stains, and they stood out in red streaks. Her saffron hair was tangled, her white wings folded. The genies flanked her, their expressions earnest and grave.

Would Beryl betray me? She knew, of course, that I'd been gone. The day before, I would have been sure that she would turn me over to the Council at once, denouncing my behavior. But since our conversation about Lily Morganite, I no longer knew what she might say or do.

I bowed politely in the direction of the councilors.

A deep spark flared in Beryl's yellow eyes. "A misunderstanding has occurred, Zaria," she said. "Councilor Morganite accuses you of attacking her and trying to steal her wand."

I looked at Lily. "Why would I do such a thing?"

"Miss Tourmaline," said Councilor Zircon. "We must ask you to tell us where you have been for the past half hour."

I told them I had been resting.

Councilor Wolframite's gaze bored into Beryl. "Can you verify this?"

I held my wings tightly against my body as Beryl drew herself up. "Zaria was very tired after meeting with Councilor Morganite," she said.

I didn't dare show any expression. Beryl had neither answered Wolframite's question nor revealed that I'd been gone.

"Utter nonsense," Lily said. She pointed at me. "That young fairy performed an invisibility spell so she could attack me."

I wanted to cast a different spell right then, one that would make her tongue curl and her wings drop off.

Zircon held up a stately hand. He tilted his head at Lily. "Shall we find out whether Zaria performed the spell?"

"You are quite correct, Councilor." Lily bowed her head. "And let the burden be on me. *I* will incur the loss of radia for a spell of disclosure." She extended a graceful hand, palm up. "Your wand, please, Zaria."

"Why?" I asked.

Wolframite explained: "Councilor Morganite will disclose any spells you may have done."

"But we were told our wands would not respond to anyone besides the owner," I said.

"True," Wolframite growled. "Except for the disclosure spell, which is very effective." He paused, probably wanting me to scream a confession.

"I haven't done any spells with this wand," I said, glad that it was the truth.

"Then you have nothing to fear," Wolframite answered. He stuck out *his* hand. "Your wand, please."

Hoping no one would notice the grime on my knuckles, I drew out Sam's stylus. Wolframite's knobby fingers closed over it, and he handed it to Lily.

She placed it on a small shelf then held up her wand, which was smoky quartz with a morganite tip. She infused it to the halfway mark, while the councilors and Beryl watched avidly. I tried to hold on to my wings, but they fluttered like those of a dying butterfly.

"*Disclosan nos enchanterel,*" Lily said.

Sam's stylus lit briefly from base to tip and then went black again.

Lily infused her wand a second time. *"Disclosan nos enchanterel."*

The same thing happened.

Zircon cleared his throat noisily. "Councilor Morganite, clearly there are no spells to be revealed."

I almost danced like a pixie.

Lily turned, her wand still upraised. "Forgive me, Councilors, but I am not yet satisfied. I find it difficult to believe that a Violet fairy would not test her powers with at least one or two spells, and yet this *wand*"—she pointed disdainfully at Sam's stylus—"revealed not a single one." She raked me with a glance. "It is possible that Zaria has somehow acquired a false wand and is hiding the true one somewhere. We must search her—and her home."

"What?" Beryl cried.

I forced my wings to keep still. Lily had guessed almost exactly! How? How could she know what I would do?

I was so thankful that I'd left my wand behind on Earth. Thankful for the invisibility spell, too—without it, someone could have watched me digging beside the blue spruce.

Lily was paying no attention to Beryl; she focused on Zircon and Wolframite. Her voice sweetened. "I hope you will allow me to perform one more spell? I can easily determine whether another wand exists upon these premises." She gave a charming smile.

Wolframite scratched his nose. Zircon frowned.

"The expenditure of radia will be mine, of course," Lily

continued, "and if Zaria turns out to be innocent, I will be more than glad."

Both genies nodded gravely at that.

"For my part, I believe it is important to determine the truth," said Zircon.

"Agreed," Wolframite rasped.

"Wait!" Beryl stepped forward, her orange wings quivering. "I will not allow—"

"It's all right, Beryl," I said quickly. "Let them."

Beryl looked at me, dread in her face. I nodded at her, trying to tell her with my eyes that she had nothing to fear. She sank onto the nearest perch. "Very well," she said.

Lily infused to the halfway mark. Level 50. *"Cerch nos es vonden,"* she said, waving her wand in a circle.

Four chimes began to sound. One came from Zircon's direction, another from Wolframite, a third from Beryl, and a fourth—not as loud as the others—from the shelf where Sam's stylus lay. The chimes were not in harmony at all; the sound of them together hurt my ears.

"Four chimes," Zircon said. "My wand, Wolframite's wand, Miss Danburite's wand, and Zaria's wand."

Lily swished her own wand forcefully. The chimes stopped.

Her face showed nothing. "Congratulations, Zaria," she said, faint sarcasm in her voice. "Evidently you are simply what you appear to be—an innocent fourteen-year-old fairy, more dutiful than most." Her eyes found mine. "It appears I must hunt down the one who attacked me."

"Apologies, Miss Tourmaline," Zircon said. "I hope you understand that this was entirely necessary."

"Perhaps," said Beryl. She rose slowly from her perch. Her eyes looked sunken and sad. "But given the accusations made against Zaria, she ought to be assigned to a different mentor." There was a wheeze in her voice I had never heard before.

Thank you, Beryl! I looked at her gratefully.

"Oh no, I would not dream of abandoning Zaria," Lily replied.

"But—" I said.

Wolframite put a blotchy hand on my shoulder. "It is quite an honor to be mentored by Councilor Morganite." The expression in his beady garnet eyes was completely sincere. "She made an error tonight, accusing you—but the error was understandable. She *was* attacked."

"But—"

He pressed more heavily on my shoulder. "Youth is impetuous," he said. "You are young, with rich stores of radia. Everything pointed to you."

How could I get them to understand what Lily had done, without revealing that I had tricked them?

Beryl helped me again by saying, "Leona Bloodstone meets with her mentor in FOOM chambers. Zaria is due the same treatment."

Wolframite finally took his hand from my shoulder. He raised an eyebrow at Zircon, who nodded. "There would be no harm in changing the location of mentoring sessions."

Lily smiled earnestly, her pearly eyes glistening. "Then I shall expect you, Zaria, at the FOOM dome at nine tomorrow morning."

After giving their formal apologies, the councilors left.

As soon as they did, Beryl drew her wand. She waved it, saying, *"Lygos nos vindage el dur."* She dropped onto the nearest perch. "That will keep sound from escaping. If someone is listening outside, they will not be able to hear a thing, but if anyone knocks, we will know it."

The councilors' visit must have upset her even more than I had guessed. Beryl was not in the habit of spending radia.

I sank onto another perch. "Thank you," I said, "for not telling them I left."

Beryl heaved a deep sigh. "I need to know. What happened today?"

I looked at Sam's stylus still lying on the shelf where Lily had left it. I didn't reply.

"Zaria. Your wand did not reveal either the reconstruction or transport spells *I* taught you."

I stared at her through a fog of distrust. She had helped me tonight. But I didn't believe she would forgive me if she knew all the laws I had broken.

"I beg you to tell me the truth," she said.

"Then tell *me* the truth. Tell me why you never go to Earth and why you despise humans. And what Lily did to *you*."

Beryl looked down at her hands. "Earth is dangerous," she answered. "Humans are treacherous. Fey folk have done so much for them. As you know, it was fairies and genies who taught humans to tell time and build dwellings . . . not to mention the untold numbers of magical gifts we have given to human children. But are they grateful? Not in the least."

"You don't know if they're grateful or not," I said. "How could they show us gratitude if we don't let them see us?"

"When they see us, they want only to catch us. They are not to be trusted."

Not all of them are the same, I thought. "Why do you say Lily is diabolical?"

Beryl's wings sagged. There was a long pause. "I suppose I always knew this day would come," she said. "And always hoped it would never arrive."

"What day?"

"The day I tell you about Lily, and about your parents."

A thrill of hope traveled from my heart to the tips of my wings. Would Beryl really unveil the secrets hanging over my life? I was afraid of breaking the fragile moment, so I tried not to look too eager as she gathered herself.

"I have waited until now to talk to you because Lily Morganite has been holding something over me," she began.

"Something?"

"Yes, but I believe you are old enough to understand."

And then, unbelievably, a knock sounded. A tap on our

door that turned into loud battering when we didn't answer.

Beryl cast up her eyes. "What now?" She infused her wand and pointed it. *"Lygos nuy."*

"Zaria!" someone called. "Zaria, are you there? Open up. Please!"

It was Leona's voice.

Chapter Twenty-eight

FAIRIES OR GENIES WHO HAVE LEVEL 7 MAGIC OR ABOVE HAVE THE ABILITY TO READ THE NATURE OF A HUMAN. ONCE HIGHLY VALUED, THIS SKILL IS SELDOM PRACTICED ANYMORE, BECAUSE IT USES RADIA, AND FEY FOLK HAVE GROWN CAUTIOUS ABOUT SAVING THEIR DWINDLING RESERVES. SPENDING RADIA ON HUMAN CHILDREN IS NOW CONSIDERED EXTRAVAGANT—UNLESS USED TO FULFILL THE BASIC OBLIGATIONS OF A FAIRY GODMOTHER OR GENIE GODFATHER.

NOWADAYS, MANY LEVEL 7 FEY FOLK ARE WITHOUT INSTRUCTION ON HOW TO ACCOMPLISH READING A HUMAN'S NATURE.

—*Orville Gold, genie historian of Feyland*

The instant I opened the door, Leona grabbed my arm. "You have to come with me," she said.

I pulled back. "Not now. I can't."

Her eyes, puffy and frantic, fixed on my face. She lowered her voice to a whisper. "Zaree, I wouldn't ask, but I can't trust anyone but you." Her silver wings rippled.

Leona wasn't easily shaken. Something terrible must have

happened. But this was the very worst moment for her to ask me to leave.

"But, Leona, I—"

Beryl rose from her perch. "Leona? Is something amiss?"

Leona controlled her wings. "It's nothing, Miss Danburite. But I wondered if Zaria could visit me?"

Beryl hardly hesitated before giving her permission. She looked relieved. It didn't surprise me—now, she would be able to put off talking with me.

"Beryl," I said. "Promise me that when I come back—"

"I promise, Zaria. I will still be here when you return."

Beryl had never broken her word to me, but what if she changed her mind this time?

"Wait." She hurried over with Sam's stylus. "Your wand."

I jammed it into a pocket of my gown and flew out with Leona.

The sun was low on the horizon, and beams of light struck the tourmalines embedded in our roof. Thankfully, the curious fey folk who had hovered outside were gone.

"Where are we going?" I asked as Leona and I soared into the air.

"Earth," she declared, flying faster.

"Earth! We can't." I pushed to keep up with her.

What might Lily Morganite be doing this very minute? She might still be discussing things with Zircon and Wolframite. But what if she had gone to a viewing booth? She seemed to have a strange understanding of me. It was almost as if she knew what I would do before I did it. What if she guessed I'd end up on Earth again tonight? How much worse could things become?

Leona turned a grim face. "You can do an invisibility spell. I'll teach you how."

"I don't have my wand."

"Yes, you do. Beryl gave it to you. I saw her."

"Leona, I've been wanting to find you, but you're always surrounded. I—"

"Thank Oberon, that disgusting mob from the city can't follow me into Galena or to Earth," Leona said bitterly. "You were right about avoiding them, Zaree. I wish I could turn to shadow like you."

"Leona, listen to me."

But she streaked on, forcing me to use all my strength to keep up. Soon she touched down beside the Zinnia Portal. The orange and yellow flowers glowed like a cluster of jewels.

"The invisibility spell," she said, panting. "Infuse your wand and say—"

"Verita sil nos mertos elemen."

She squinted at me. "You know the spell?"

"Yes, I found my mother's spellbook."

"Good! Hurry."

"Leona, I'm trying to tell you," I whispered. "*I don't have my wand.* The one Beryl handed me is a fake."

She looked as if someone had bound her wings and taken all her radia. "No," she said. "That can't be true."

"It's true."

"A fake? Why? Was your wand stolen, too?"

"Stolen? No, I . . ." Stopping, I stared at her. Suddenly her frenzy made sense. "Your wand was *stolen*?"

She shook back her hair. "You can never tell anyone."

"Of course not."

Her eyes watered. "You're a true friend."

I made a quick decision: much as I feared getting caught on Earth again by Lily, Leona was more important. "We'll get your wand back," I said. "Follow me." I glanced left and right to be sure no one was near before I stepped through the portal.

On the other side, golden fire trimmed a bank of purple clouds in Earth's sky, while streamers of light lit the outlines of trees on the ridge. I flew up the slope to the grove that held the blue spruce, Leona right behind me. I knelt to dig.

"What are you doing?" Leona said as she dropped to her knees beside me.

"Shh." I scrabbled in the dirt. When I pulled my little stylus free, warmth and strength flowed through me, reviving me, restoring my sense of hope. I felt half-giddy with the joy of being reunited with the fullness of my magic.

"What is your wand doing *here*?" Leona cried.

"Shh!" Infusing, I tapped her head. *"Verita sil nos mertos elemen."*

She disappeared. Her disembodied voice thanked me.

I repeated the spell on myself. "Where are we going?"

"Wait. Zaree, why was your wand on Earth?"

"I'll tell you later. Where's *your* wand?"

"Jason Court," said Leona in a brittle, angry voice.

"*He* stole your wand?" I gasped. "How?"

"It doesn't matter."

"But how will we find it?"

"The moment I realized it was missing, I went into Oberon City to find a viewing booth. I had to go to an old broken-down station beside the Malachite Towers, and I had to flatter the attendant before he would let me in. Total humiliation. The scope was blurry, too. But now I know where Jason is."

Hurriedly, I smoothed dirt over my mother's spellbook, wishing I could bring it along. My fear of Lily rose up again. What if she had seen us here?

I infused my wand and touched it to the ground. "You are protected," I said softly, wishing I knew a better spell.

I felt magic moving out of me into the earth and hoped it would be enough.

"What did you say?" Leona asked.

"Let's go get your wand," I answered.

I held on to Leona's sash as we flew over the human town.

"The brick house below," she said, after we'd gone several miles.

We touched down. "I'm going to renew the spell for both of us," I whispered.

She waited while I said the words. I looked at my watch. Two minutes past seven o'clock.

The house we approached wasn't far from Sam's, but it was much larger, shaped like a great heavy box. An iron balustrade marked a stone stairway leading to wide wooden doors. I followed the soft rustling of Leona's wings to the entrance.

"*Upandos* zinnia," I heard her say. It surprised me, somehow, that the humble zinnia would be Leona's favorite seed.

The doors swung open, giving plenty of space for our wings. An expanse of polished flagstones in the entryway led into the house.

"Go left," Leona hissed.

I turned, gliding carefully down a hallway. I could hear Leona ahead of me counting doors under her breath. We passed three, and then she stopped.

"Here," she whispered, turning the doorknob.

I darted through after her. But when I saw who was in the room, I almost lost my balance.

Surely that was Sam standing with his back to an enormous window? No other human could have that same shock of fiery hair and those same gold-toned eyes. What was he doing with the thief who had stolen a fey wand?

Jason stood across from Sam, a big smirk on his handsome face. A massive bed stood in one corner, big enough to sleep five. Clothes were strewn across the carpets. Shelves on one wall held books, trophies, and dozens of other items I didn't recognize.

Jason almost collided with me as he kicked the door shut. He turned back to Sam. "I keep telling you, I'm not the one who hacked your phone," he said.

Sam frowned. He shoved his hands in his pockets.

Jason folded his arms across his chest. "But now *I've* seen something strange—and it wasn't on my phone. It was for real."

"What are you talking about?" Sam's frown deepened.

"I was out by Coyote Ridge and saw this girl all dressed up like a fairy. Wings and everything. Great costume. And dude, she's a female magician, better than David Blaine. I don't know how, but she did a disappearing act. All for me."

"For you."

"And before she vanished, she kissed me." Jason raised his eyebrows.

Involuntarily I floated backward, almost bumping into the wall. Leona Bloodstone had *kissed* a human?

"Kissed you," Sam said. "Right."

I knew as surely as if he'd spoken the thought aloud that Sam believed Jason was talking about me. I wanted to scream.

"It's true." Jason grinned. "And I can prove it."

"Right," Sam said again.

Jason opened a wooden drawer and lifted out Leona's wand. "Look at this," he said, holding it up.

In that room made by humans, the fey wand glistened

with otherworldly light. It looked wrong to see Jason's hand gripping its winding tracery of gold and silver.

Sam stared. "She *gave* that to you?"

"Nah. I took it." Jason brushed the filigree.

The wand jerked out of his hand and disappeared. Jason jumped back, banging into the wall. "What the——?"

"*Pyt verucca,*" I heard Leona say.

An ugly wart appeared on Jason's nose. It was slightly off center, large and red with black hairs growing out of it.

Leona's wing bumped mine. The door opened and I heard the swish of her skirts as she left.

Sam stared at Jason. He put up a hand as if to protect himself. "Zaria?" he whispered.

He thought *I* had put a wart on his friend's nose!

I glanced at my watch. Less than a minute before the invisibility spell expired. I rushed from the room, down the hall, and out the front door to Leona.

"*Verita sil nos mertos elemen,*" she said, tapping my head. "Let's go."

"How long?" I asked her.

"It's a ten-minute spell, remember?"

"I mean, how long will the boy have that wart?"

"It's not long-lasting." She sounded impatient. "I'm only teaching him a lesson."

I took a look behind us. Sam appeared in the doorway alone, lamplight striking his red hair and shadowing his face.

On the way back to the portal, Leona was silent. She didn't ask why my wand had been on Earth; she didn't ask anything at all. Only the quiet rhythm of her wings told me she was still there.

I guessed that she was embarrassed because Jason had said she kissed him. I wanted to ask her if it was true—and if it was, what it was like. But I couldn't quite get the words out.

When we passed the grove on the hillside, I didn't stop to bury my wand again. I would take my chances bringing it back. I didn't want to leave the spellbook, either, but I also didn't want to try to hide it in Feyland.

Our invisibility wore off just after we crossed back through the portal. Leona's wings shimmered eerily in the twilight as we flew over Galena Falls.

"Thank you for coming with me, Zaree," she said. "I never want to be without my wand again."

I shivered. "Neither do I."

Chapter Twenty-nine

DILIGENT STUDENTS OF THE ANNALS OF MAGIC MAY GLEAN IMPORTANT BITS OF KNOWLEDGE IF THEY ARE PATIENT ENOUGH TO SIFT THROUGH THE MANY PASSAGES THAT ARE EITHER WOEFULLY UNCLEAR OR DOWNRIGHT IRRELEVANT. THE VOLUME SUFFERS FROM A STYLE OF WRITING THAT SEEMS DESIGNED TO MISLEAD THE READER.

—*Orville Gold, genie historian of Feyland*

The thought of the wart on Jason's nose and Sam whispering my name was disturbing, but Beryl's promise to tell me about my parents and Lily helped put what had happened on Earth out of my mind. I was so eager to hear what Beryl had to say, I almost bruised my wings dashing into the house.

It was not a happy homecoming.

Beryl was crumpled in the shabby old perch beside the far wall. Patched cushions supported her wings. She didn't even try to rise when she saw me.

"Beryl?" I approached hesitantly and hovered beside her.

Sorrow spilled from her dry eyes. She pointed to her throat with a closed fist.

"What's wrong?" I asked.

She touched her throat and shook her head.

"You can't speak?"

She nodded.

I ran for a scroll and pen and ink. When I returned with them, Beryl held a fist in front of my eyes. I examined her hand: the fingers seemed fused. I tried to pry them apart but it was like handling stone.

Anger turned in my heart like a wheel of fire. "Did Lily do this?"

No answer.

What should I do? Would it be safe to let Beryl know I had discovered how to make up my own spells using common words? She'd disapprove, no doubt, but I had already lived with her disapproval for five years.

I drew out my wand. Light streaked from the base to the tip as I infused it, but she shrank from me, shaking her head as if I had threatened to injure her.

"Beryl? What's wrong? I can reverse the spell."

She crossed her fists in front of herself protectively, terror in her eyes.

I lowered my wand. "All right. I won't help until you agree."

She let out a sobbing sigh.

With great care, I pulled the infusion out of my wand, fearing the force of my rage would explode into unintended magic, turning our home to dust.

Lily Morganite would pay for this if it took every last bit of radia I possessed. For it must have been Lily—who else would silence Beryl?

What is Lily holding over her?

"I'm going out," I told my guardian.

She reached toward me, a pleading gesture, but I turned away.

At the door I looked back. Beryl tottered to her feet. Her wings quivered as she took a step. She motioned at me with her enchanted fists. I shook my head, and she sank back onto the tattered perch.

I whisked out the door and flew hard toward the Gateway of Galena. I was getting close to it when a voice spoke beside me. "Where are you going?"

I whirled. "Meteor?"

Starlight outlined his shoulders and gleamed on the stripes in his hair. "Where are you going?" he repeated.

"Are you following me?"

"My father told me what happened tonight."

I slowed, peering at him. "Councilor Zircon *told* you?"

"He said you'd been falsely accused and exonerated."

"That's comforting." I couldn't keep the sarcasm out of my voice.

The pillars of the gateway were just ahead. I didn't want

Meteor following me into Oberon City, so I turned in midair, fuming, and flew slowly along the inside border of Galena. Meteor stayed right beside me.

Fey lights outlining the boundary revealed his face, dark and serious. It suddenly occurred to me that it had been years since he and I had been alone together. He never sought me out unless Andalonus was there, too.

"You can't fight her, Zaree," he said. "Not now."

"What?" I hovered uneasily. "Fight who?"

"Lily Morganite. She's too powerful."

I nearly choked. Meteor had guessed what I meant to do! "She has no right to put spells on me and Beryl!" My wings beat erratically, forcing me downward.

Meteor floated smoothly to the ground after me. He held up a hand and then checked the surrounding area. "There's no one near," he said. "Why do you believe she put spells on you?"

I thought of Beryl, alone and suffering. "Beryl was going to tell me something—something important about my family! But when I got back, she was under a gag spell. And her hands were locked into fists."

"Zaria, have you thought about how dangerous this could be?"

"I have to do something!"

He stepped back. "Tell me what happened."

And I did. I talked fast, not really looking at him as my story poured out. I told him the truth—or most of it. I left out my visits to Earth. It seemed like the wrong time to confess all the laws I had broken. And I didn't mention my discovery that ordinary words could be used for casting magic. I wasn't ready to tell anyone about that yet.

But I did tell him that Lily was my mentor and that she'd stolen my mother's spellbook. And I told him how I had deceived the councilors with a false wand—though I didn't say where I'd gotten it.

When I stopped, Meteor was so quiet he seemed to have quit breathing.

"Say something," I cried.

"This is bad," he muttered.

Aghast, I realized I'd confided in a councilor's son. "I shouldn't have told you."

"Why not? You had to tell someone, and I'm your friend." He looked worried. "But we should ask for help."

"Who could help? We can't tell the Council."

"What about Mr. Bloodstone?"

"What?" My wings unfurled with a snap.

"Bloodstone. He would know what to do for Miss Danburite."

"*Bloodstone?*"

"He would know what to do," Meteor said stubbornly.

"No," I said. "Bloodstone would find a way to use this against me."

"Zaria, he—"

"*No!*"

Meteor folded his arms. "All right," he said. "We'll go back to your house together. I'll help you if I can. I know a little about spells."

I hesitated. "Do you know *enough*?"

"More than you. I know that wherever you hid your mother's spellbook, it's still in danger of being found."

"Found?" My wings fluttered.

"The only way to conceal something from magical tracking is to bury it on Earth. Lily Morganite touched the book, which means she can track it."

I stared at him. "Bury it on Earth?"

"According to the Annals of Magic, it's the only thing that could keep her from tracking it."

"Annals of Magic?" I sounded like an echo.

"The Crown Library, Zaree—remember? With your level and color, you can study there anytime. I've been going there every day."

Elation filled me. I had somehow guessed right about burying the book on Earth. Lily could perform spells until she used up all her radia but she'd never find my mother's legacy. "Thank you, Meteor. If you can tell me what to do for Beryl, I'll do it. However much radia it takes."

He gave me a look. "What did I say to make you happy?"

"Nothing." I rose into the air.

Chapter Thirty

SONNIA IS THE ONLY FOOD THAT FEY FOLK ABSOLUTELY
REQUIRE FOR HEALTH AND STRENGTH.

CHILDREN LIVE UPON SONNIA EXCLUSIVELY. THE
LARGE CRIMSON FLOWERS OF THE SONNIA PLANT ARE
CHEWED FRESH OR MADE INTO A VARIETY OF NECTARS
AND TEAS.

ONCE THEY ARE GROWN UP, MANY AMONG THE FEY
ACQUIRE A TASTE FOR OTHER BEVERAGES.

—*Orville Gold, genie historian of Feyland*

Beryl lay in the same position I'd left her, flopped in a perch beneath the light of a fey globe. I hurried to her side. She gave me a look I'll always remember, as if she were trying to say something with her eyes. But whatever it was, I couldn't understand. And then Meteor came in.

The instant she saw him, Beryl sat up and smiled cheerily. "Meteor! Welcome."

Confused, I drifted backward. Meteor's eyebrows lifted to his hairline.

"Beryl?" I squeaked. "You can talk?"

"Of course, child. Age has not yet taken my powers of

speech." She sprang up. "Would you like some spiced son-nia tea, children?" She glided toward the potbellied copper stove. "I suppose I should not refer to you as children any-more, now that you have received your watches and wands." She poured water into a kettle and added dried sonnia leaves.

No gag spell. No frozen fists. Just a complete personality change.

I sidled up to Beryl and peered at her face. All her features were the same: long chin, short nose, yellow eyes, wrinkled skin. But how could this pleasantly smiling old fairy be the guardian that I knew? Beryl Danburite would not behave this way. She would frown and demand to know what Meteor was doing here so late. She would grill me about where I'd been. And she would not forget a gag spell.

Watching her stir the tea, I rubbed my aching eyes, then turned to Meteor. He stood motionless against the wall.

"Don't drink it," he said softly.

"What?"

He crossed the room and took my arm. He tugged me through the front door.

Outside, he didn't let go. "Zaree, you can't stay here tonight."

I looked up at him. "Why?"

He shook my arm. "You have to go somewhere else until you find out what spells are at work here."

"Then you believe me?"

"Miss Danburite isn't acting like herself. Not one bit."

"Meteor, when I told Beryl I would try reversing the gag spell, she was terrified. Do you know why that would be?"

Meteor's eyebrows met in a long line. "You offered to reverse the spell?"

"I—" No wonder he seemed shocked. He knew I never studied.

But apparently Meteor wasn't thinking about whether I could have learned a spell of reversal. "Layered magic," he said in a stricken voice.

"What?" I had never heard of layered magic.

He finally dropped my arm. "Of course. I should have seen it." His whole face tensed. "I was reading about layered spells only yesterday. They're wickedly dangerous. Reversing them requires advanced magic I know nothing about." He glanced anxiously at the door. "Whatever she serves us, don't drink it!"

Strings of panic knotted inside me.

He drew his wand. He had changed it: it was striped black and white with a zircon tip. "We need protection," he said. "I once saw the spell against layered magic. . . ." He frowned in concentration. "Level Thirty," he said, nodding. *"Fendus altus—"*

The door opened. Beryl, still smiling, stepped out. Before I could blink, a warm mug was in my hand, and Meteor held one, too. "Try it," she urged. "I added inga flowers."

Meteor straightened his arm and dropped the mug. It smashed on the stones of our little courtyard, and the brew splattered his feet.

He staggered back. His eyes found mine. "Zaria?" He sounded bewildered, as if he didn't expect to see me.

I looked at his feet. Most young genies go barefoot, and Meteor was no exception. Drops of tea had fallen on his skin. Very carefully, I glided backward. I hurled my mug sideways and heard it shatter.

"Zaria!" Beryl sounded hurt.

Meteor looked dazed. "I don't remember coming here."

Beryl wagged her finger at me. "You know better than to put spells on your friends."

My mouth fell open. Meteor's expression went from dazed to furious. "Wait," I cried. "You know I'd never do such a thing."

"*Someone* enchanted me," Meteor said. "I doubt it was Miss Danburite."

I wanted to throw aside caution and do experimental spells on both of them. But Meteor had talked of layered magic. And already in the course of the evening, Beryl had behaved as if she were under a gag spell, a spell to freeze her fingers, and some other insidious enchantment that had made her a stranger.

A stranger who would try to turn one of my dearest friends against me.

What if the brew that splashed on Meteor contained

layers, too? How could I risk having my magic misfire?

"Meteor," I said, "I did not do this."

Beryl sniffed. Meteor looked hard at me and then rose into the air.

He didn't look back.

Beryl and I faced each other. Although I knew she was in the grip of an enchantment, I couldn't forgive her. She had let this happen. She must have known about protection spells, but she'd never seen fit to tell me about them. If she had, I would gladly have donated radia to keep her safe.

She had kept silent about the most important things in my life, things I had every right to know—about my family, and about Lily, and about Earth.

"Your criminal nature is showing, Zaria," she said. "As I always knew it would."

I wondered if Lily might be watching through Beryl's eyes. How bitterly glad I was that I hadn't told Beryl about the fake wand or about my visits to Earth.

"Criminal nature?" I asked.

Her mouth puckered sourly. "Look at what you have become! A thieving liar."

I pointed my wand at her head. "Don't come near me. You know how dangerous untrained Violet fairies are, when our magic gets away from us." I kept my wand raised as I slowly circled behind her and then burst into the house.

I flew up the stairs into my mother's room and shut the door behind me. Oh, how I needed a haven.

I heard Beryl on the stairway. Pointing my wand at the door, I spoke softly. "Open to none but me tonight." I did the same with the window.

The door rattled. "You will regret this, Zaria Tourmaline. After all I have done for you, you vile, ungrateful fairy!"

"Go away."

I waited until she stopped calling insults. Then I sank into my mother's nest, folding my wings.

Alone, I mourned for all I had lost.

Chapter Thirty-one

LEPRECHAUN MAGIC DIFFERS FROM THAT OF FAIRIES AND GENIES IN MANY IMPORTANT REGARDS.

LEPRECHAUNS CANNOT FLY; THEY TAKE ENORMOUS FLYING LEAPS INSTEAD.

ALL LEPRECHAUNS HAVE THE SAME LEVEL OF MAGIC: THE EQUIVALENT OF LEVEL 10. BEFORE THE LEPRECHAUN EDICT, THEY COULD TRAVEL FREELY BETWEEN TIRFEYNE AND EARTH.

LEPRECHAUNS HAVE NEITHER THE MEANS NOR THE NEED TO MONITOR EXPENDITURES OF MAGIC, FOR THEIR MAGIC IS SELF-RENEWING. THEY CAN DO SPELL AFTER SPELL WITHOUT RUNNING LOW, AND THEIR MAGIC OPERATES WITHOUT THE NEED FOR A WAND.

HOWEVER, THEY ARE INCAPABLE OF TRANSFERRING MAGIC.

—*Orville Gold, genie historian of Feyland*

I opened my eyes to find myself slumped in my mother's nest. My crystal watch told me that Lily Morganite expected me at the FOOM dome in two minutes.

She was the very last fairy I wanted to go anywhere near.

Slowly, I rose. I infused my wand to Level 30, the level Meteor had said was needed to cast a protection spell.

I spoke an improvised spell. "I, Zaria Tourmaline, am protected from any and all enchantments today."

I checked to be sure I had both wands—the real and the fake.

"I won't give up the real one," I promised myself. "Not to anyone."

I wanted to do something to reinforce my decision, something powerful to help me keep that promise no matter what happened. But what? Beryl had never taught me any special rituals, and I had been too young when my parents disappeared to have learned any from them.

I looked around the room and saw the spiral pattern on the floor, the painting of trees on the wall, the row of copper cupboards. How many dreams had my mother left behind when she took her last journey? For that matter, what had Jett been hoping to do when he told me Feyland would change "for good"? And how had my father felt when he went away to search for his missing son?

Had any of them ever suspected that I, Zaria, would be the only one remaining to carry their legacy forward?

I stood in the center of the floor, the spot where the spiral began. "Here, today, I take my vow on my family's honor," I said. "I will never give up my true wand."

The room answered with silence, but I felt different

inside, as if the strength of my whole family had gathered in my heart.

"Thank you," I whispered.

Glancing at my watch, I realized it was past nine o'clock. However fast I pumped my tired wings, I would be late meeting Lily.

Unless I transported myself.

Beryl had warned me not to transport *through* the gateway. To get to the FOOM dome, I would have to do two transports—one to the Gateway of Galena, and once I had passed through the gateway, another to the dome.

At seven minutes past nine, I stood beside a trellis of inga flowers in the ornamental gardens behind the FOOM dome. And there, two wingspans away, hovered Lily in a white satin gown.

When she saw me, her face tightened. "Good morning," she said. "I see you have been practicing transport spells."

I said nothing. Why hadn't she waited for me at the front of the dome? Why did she seem to have some uncanny power to guess everything I would do?

Lily smiled frostily. "Did you sleep in that gown?" She looked at me as if I were a diamond so rough I could never be polished. "Come with me," she ordered.

Inside the dome, she led me through wide corridors, her wings unfurled just enough so she could skim gracefully, the scent of lilies drifting behind her. I should have been dazzled by the opulence of the dome—the same opulence that had awed me only days earlier—but I wasn't. The shining walls and colored floors seemed nothing more than a magnificent bottle holding a venomous brew.

I followed Lily through a zirconium door into a room carpeted in pale yellow. A suspended crystal, cleverly cut, split rays of sun from a skylight into hundreds of butterfly-shaped rainbows.

I felt sickened. I hated the prettiness of the room. I would rather be in The Ugly Mug surrounded by boisterous leprechauns sitting at battered brass tables.

The door clanged shut and Lily turned to face me. "You have been squandering radia," she said. "Transporting yourself is abominably wasteful. Consider: if you transported yourself four times a day for a year, you would use over thirty-six thousand radia. In a hundred years, you would part with close to four million for no purpose." With a pink finger, she tapped my temple. "And if I am not mistaken, transportation is not the only spell you have been playing with."

Because of you, I thought.

"Nothing to say? Perhaps you believe you have plenty, a wealth you could not spend if you tried?"

"No," I answered. "My guardian told me to be careful."

"So you *can* speak."

I flinched and thought of Beryl, lost in layers of enchantment. How I'd love to see Lily stripped of her wand. *Ad eternum.* Forever and always.

She switched to another subject. "One of your teachers noticed you show signs of being Earth-struck."

I looked down at the soft yellow carpet.

"Tell me, Zaria, has anyone explained to you why there are durable spells on the portals to Earth?"

I lifted my chin. "Portals?" How much did she know about the portals I had taken?

"That interests you?" Her eyes looked like frozen pearls.

"What spells protect portals?" It annoyed me that Lily was so tall I had to look up at her.

"Spells to keep humans out."

"But I thought . . ."

"Yes?"

"It takes magic to pass through the portals, so if humans don't have magic, why would we need enchantments to keep them out?" I asked sullenly.

"Very good, Zaria. Perhaps teaching you will not be a hopeless endeavor. The answer is: not all humans are without magic. A surprising number possess the equivalent of Level Five."

"No one told me."

She smiled knowingly. "You have much to learn."

I slid my hands into the pockets of my gown and gripped my true wand. If I had to, I would put another sleep spell on Lily, though I doubted she would have left herself unprotected again.

"Zaria. Listen to me, child." She spoke softly and sounded

kind. "A mentor is the most important person in a young fairy's life. I was carefully chosen just for you." I stared at her white wings while she kept talking. "No one will interfere with my teaching methods, for it is understood that I, and I alone, know what is best when it comes to your training."

I thought of Beryl again. She had tried to interfere. Was that why she was now under layered magic?

"You should not presume to question what I do," Lily went on, "but because we are only beginning to work with one another, I will attempt to explain what happened yesterday." Her eyes shimmered, full of goodwill. "I gave you your first test."

"What *test*?" I blurted out.

"To find out if you could detect the presence of magic. There was a spell on your pen. Unfortunately, you left before I could finish the lesson."

"Lesson? But I—"

"No harm would have come to you," she said. "The spell was cued to be sure you reached the ground before you fell asleep. But I am surprised you were able to fly home. You must be stronger than you appear."

"I am," I mumbled, trying to remember just how sleepy I had felt, and when.

"Good. As a Violet fairy, you will need *all* your strength." Lily smiled warmly. "Now, before we continue, let me remind you that your lessons here are not to be discussed with anyone else—including your friends."

"Why not?"

"You are *Violet. Level One Hundred*. That sets you apart, Zaria. Very far apart."

"Not from Leona."

Lily set her jaw. "You should never discuss magic with another Violet. Powerful fairies must work for the good of all, not for the advancement of friends."

"But—"

"Stop and *listen*, Zaria. I am here to teach you." She held out her hand. "Your wand, if you please, so that I can give you your next lesson."

Without arguing, I gave her the false wand.

Lily dangled it between a finger and thumb. "I hope," she said, "that you do not intend to try any deception with me."

Before I knew it, I was speaking my thoughts aloud. "*You're* the expert on *deception*," I cried.

She drew her wand in a flash. She pointed the morganite tip at me. *"Reducto et eloquen!"*

For a second I saw a shield of violet light. A loud hum circled the room and then died away. "*Gag* spell?" I said, and felt a surge of triumph because my protection had worked.

Lily's eyes stabbed like pearl-handled knives. "I understand why an orphan like you would be distrustful at first, but one day you will learn that I am the best mentor you could have." She tapped the false wand I'd given her. *"Disclosan nos enchanterel."*

The stylus lit briefly, then went black.

Lily nodded. "This so-called wand shows no activity." She dropped the stylus to the floor as if it were a piece of trash. "And yet I saw you transport this morning, and you have surrounded yourself with a protection spell."

I stared at Sam's stylus, a slim black line on the carpet.

"Only three days with a wand," Lily said, "and you have deceived the High Council of Feyland."

"Because of you," I shouted. "You took my mother's spellbook!"

At the look in her eyes—satisfied, gloating—I wished I could take it back. Beryl had warned me not to reveal anything about myself or how I felt.

"Impressive, Zaria. A sleep spell on your mentor. Invisibility. A false wand. You show yourself to be as resourceful as your father."

I gulped. "My father?"

"Did you not know? Gilead Tourmaline was renowned throughout Feyland as a very resourceful genie."

My father famous throughout Feyland? Why had no one told me? I wanted to shower Lily with questions, but my throat closed up as if her gag spell had succeeded.

"Now, show me your true wand." She held out her hand again.

"T-tell me about . . ." I couldn't finish the sentence.

"First your wand, Zaria, and then I will tell you about Gilead."

She was offering me what I wanted most. How tempting

it was, to stop fighting her, let her do as she wished. She knew so much more than I, about radia, and Feyland—and about my father. How could I pass up the chance to learn the truth that everyone kept hiding?

If I gave Lily my wand, she would know what sort of spells I had done and how many. But she wouldn't know how often I'd gone to Earth or that I'd helped Leona take back her wand from a human; she wouldn't know about the portal in Galena; she wouldn't know I'd seen Beryl in The Ugly Mug at the borders of the Leprechaun Colony or that I had buried my mother's spellbook under a tree.

But she *would* tell me about my father.

Slowly, I drew out my true wand.

"Good," Lily said, as if she respected me.

But then I hesitated. Less than an hour earlier, I had vowed on my family's honor that I would never give up my wand to anyone. *Never.* To *anyone.* How could I consider breaking my vow already—and to Lily Morganite of all fairies?

Hastily, I put the wand back in my gown.

She leaned toward me. "I can force you to turn your wand over to the Council," she said calmly. "But I would much rather do the spell privately, just the two of us."

I felt the power of her determination pushing against me. She would never give up!

I reached back to the moment when I had vowed on my family's honor, the moment when I had felt the strength of my father, my mother, my brother, together with myself. "No," I said.

Lily sighed. "Zaria, you are so very lost and alone. You need a guide. And I *can* guide you through all the perils of high-level magic. I only tried to take your mother's spellbook for safekeeping. Have you any idea of how dangerous it was to leave the book in such a vulnerable place? Beryl Danburite means well, but clearly she does not know how to look after the interests of a Violet, nor does she understand the temptations you would feel to practice the spells found in your mother's book—spells that would deplete you of radia and expose you to perils you could not possibly comprehend."

I waited for her to ask me where the spellbook was now. She didn't.

"Trust me, child," was all she said.

I waited longer, and then finally spoke. "If you want me to trust you," I said, despising the quaver in my voice, "take away the spells on Beryl."

Her forehead crinkled. "Is something amiss with your guardian?" She sounded truly concerned.

"You know there is."

"I am afraid I know nothing about it. What is wrong?"

"I don't know," I mumbled.

"Which is why you *need* a mentor." Lily sighed again and looked at her watch. "You have two days to consider allowing me to do the disclosan spell. By the third day, if you have not allowed it, I shall notify the Council of your deception." She pointed her wand at the door. It opened silently. "Go."

There was no dignity in stooping to pick up Sam's stylus, but I did it anyway.

Chapter Thirty-two

GREMLINS, THOUGH SMALL, ARE LARGE NUISANCES. THEY HAVE NO MAGIC TO SPEAK OF, BUT THEY ARE ABLE TO MOVE WITH SUCH SPEED THAT THEY HAVE SOMETIMES BEEN SUSPECTED OF PERFORMING MAGIC. GREMLINS ARE DEDICATED TO MISCHIEF, WHICH THEY CREATE BY REMOVING SMALL, CRUCIAL PARTS OF WORKING MECHANISMS.

SOMETIMES, GREMLINS EMIT A HIGH-PITCHED, PIERCING SHRIEK. IT IS A DREADFUL NOISE THAT NONE BUT OTHER GREMLINS CAN BEAR TO HEAR.

—*Orville Gold, genie historian of Feyland*

As I left the FOOM dome, I barely noticed the rose marble of the courtyard. The radiant flowers in the garden only pained my eyes. My thoughts churned. Should I take Lily's offer to tell me about my family in exchange for a spell of disclosure? And if I refused her, what would I do when the Council demanded my wand?

"*She wants you in her clutches,*" Beryl had said.

If only I had been given a true mentor, someone I could trust, someone to answer all my questions about magic.

I should go to the Crown Library and study, try to find out what could be done for Beryl. I should talk to Meteor and see if he might listen to me about what had happened yesterday evening.

But I couldn't bear the thought of Meteor's anger. My wings beat sluggishly, barely keeping me aloft as I headed for Galena. I passed through the gateway, but the closer I got to home, the more I wanted to avoid Beryl. What might she say and do today?

Last week, I would have sought out my friends. But now, Meteor thought I had practiced enchantments on him, and I had no idea where Leona might be. I hadn't seen Andalonus since the day of our last class together; he probably believed I had lied when I told him his color wouldn't matter to me.

My wings ached as if bound with iron as I remembered what Andalonus had said. *"Is it so bad to be Violet? . . . Imagine all the good you'll be able to do."*

But I had not done any good.

I had used an uncounted amount of radia trying to protect myself. Lily was right about one thing—at this rate my reserves would be gone before I was fifty years old. Maybe sooner.

I opened my watch and brought it close to my face. The tiny golden hand that registered radia had moved very slightly. It was no longer pointing straight at the line between Violet and Red, the line I had thought meant "no color" but which Beryl had called full Violet. By the time the hand had moved enough to hit the first degree within Violet—one tenth of the color—I would have used up a million radia. I still had a long way to go before that happened. But the hand *had* moved, even though I had received my watch only a short time ago. Not good.

I flew up to the high spot above Galena Falls. I had some vague hope of finding Leona there, but the place was deserted.

My eyes were drawn to the drab sandstone boulder of the Zinnia Portal. If I went to Earth, I could read my mother's spellbook. Maybe Cinna Tourmaline would have made notes about layered enchantments.

I glanced around. Children played in the pool far below; I saw no one above me.

I drew my wand. *"Verita sil nos mertos elemen."*

A chilly wind greeted me on the other side of the portal. Earth's sky was so full of dark clouds that not a single strip of blue peeped through. I was glad to be invisible, for not three wingspans away, Jason Court and Sam Seabolt were approaching.

How relieved I was to see that the wart on Jason's nose was gone.

Both wore jackets against the cold. Wind tousled their

hair and blew loudly enough to conceal the sound of my beating wings as I hovered near them. What could they be doing this close to the portal?

Jason's jaw jutted forward as he went right up to the boulder covered with zinnias and rapped it with a fist. "Here," he said. "She walked straight into this rock and disappeared."

Trolls and pixies, how could Leona have been so reckless?

I thought of what Lily had said that morning: *"Not all humans are entirely without magic. A surprising number possess the equivalent of Level Five."*

What if either of these humans had the ability to go through the portal? I doubted Leona's mother had set up any barricades. She would have believed this lonely spot to be safe.

Jason kicked the boulder and then kicked it again. I drew a breath of relief. If he'd had any magic, the portal would have opened.

"Forget about it," Sam said.

"She put a wart on me," said Jason.

"But you're okay now. Call it even."

Jason shook his head. He reached into his jacket. "When I see her again, I'll give her something to remember me by." A gun with a rounded tip waved in his hand.

We had learned about guns in Human Culture class. Bloodstone had said humans used them to hurt each other, sometimes even kill each other. But this gun looked different from those we had studied. It was sleeker and completely black.

"Is that what I think it is?" Sam sounded alarmed.

Jason grinned. "Isn't it a beauty? My dad got it."

"A laser gun?" Sam took a step back.

"With this, I can put a mark on that girl's forehead." Jason aimed up the hill toward the grove. A red beam of light shot up the rise and hit the great blue spruce near where I'd buried my mother's spellbook. As Jason held the gun steady, a branch ignited.

"What the heck are you doing!" Sam yelled. He began pelting up the hill.

I gathered my strength and flew past Sam, reaching the tree before he did. The small fire was taking hold on the end of the branch, helped by the wind. I didn't understand where the spark had come from. Was this more "technology"?

I flew close to the blaze. Rising smoke made me cough as I pointed my wand. *"Resvera den,"* I said. "Break."

With a loud crack, the flaming branch broke near the trunk of the tree. It caught among the thick blue-green needles of the branches just below. I grabbed the broken branch and flung it away. Sparks bounced over the ground below, and several hit my gown. I flew higher, shaking out the cinders that clung to my skirts.

Sam pounded toward the burning branch, pulling off his jacket as he ran. When he reached it, he beat at the flames with his jacket. He moved very fast, whipping his arm up and down, breathing hard. I hovered above him, flicking sparks from my gown while he smothered the fire.

Then Jason strolled up.

"That was close," Sam said.

"Sorry," Jason answered. "I'm still learning how to use this thing."

He gazed at the tree, his eyes narrowing. He touched the spot where the branch had snapped when I cast the breaking spell. "Look at this."

"Look at *what*?" Sam glared at Jason. "The way you almost started a forest fire?"

"Branches don't break that way by themselves." Jason lifted his weapon again.

Sam faced his friend. "For God's sake, you'll set the whole ridge on fire!"

"Come out, come out, wherever you are," Jason called, ignoring Sam. Another red beam blasted the air just above my head.

"Stop!" Sam shouted.

I shot toward the portal.

I wish now that I had flown to the other side of the ridge instead. I wish I had calmed myself and then watched over the portal.

But fear makes fools of us all, and I am no exception. The bolts of red light had terrified me, and all I could think of was escape.

Chapter Thirty-three

O<small>N THE DAY THAT FAIRIES AND GENIES RECEIVE THEIR</small>
<small>CRYSTAL WATCHES, THEIR COLORS ARE ANNOUNCED</small>
<small>TO THE WORLD. A</small><small>FTER THAT, ONLY MEMBERS OF THE</small>
<small>HIGH COUNCIL HAVE THE RIGHT TO VIEW ANOTHER'S</small>
<small>RADIA RESERVES.</small>

<small>R</small><small>ESERVES ARE FORMALLY INSPECTED ONCE A YEAR</small>
<small>WHEN THE FORCIER ASSESSES RADIA TAX. SUCH</small>
<small>INSPECTIONS ARE DISAGREEABLE TO FEY FOLK; THEY</small>
<small>ARE THEREFORE DONE IN PRIVATE.</small>

<small>I</small><small>N FACT, GROWN FAIRIES AND GENIES ARE QUITE</small>
<small>SECRETIVE ABOUT THE DEGREE OF THEIR RADIA</small>
<small>RESERVES. UNLESS THEY ARE ALONE, THEY KEEP THEIR</small>
<small>WATCH-FACE COVERS CLOSED. EVEN AMONG FRIENDS,</small>
<small>IT IS CONSIDERED IMPOLITE TO ASK HOW MANY RADIA</small>
<small>SOMEONE HAS LEFT.</small>

—Orville Gold, genie historian of Feyland

I had to warn Leona about Jason's weapon, but where would she be? A few days before, I would have known. Not anymore.

Sometime during my flight, I became visible again. I zoomed through the Gateway of Galena toward the FOOM dome. Though Leona seemed to have changed her mind about crowds, it was possible she could be dazzling a mob in the courtyard.

She wasn't there. Several gnomes pushed brooms across the marble. A few fairies hovered in a group near the back gardens, and a couple of genies slouched on benches beside one of the fountains.

Reluctantly, I dipped toward the Crown Library's emerald dome. It was the most likely place to find Meteor—and maybe he would be able to tell me where Leona was. I didn't want to ask him, didn't even want to see him, but he might know where to look for her.

The doors of the library were crystal etched with gold. Inside, stacks of metal shelves rose haphazardly. Had they laid out this place as a test of flight skill? I was afraid I would bump into one of the teetering stacks. I could just see it toppling slowly, the shelves crashing and clanging, a musty load of books thudding onto the stone floor.

I tried to move quietly as I searched for Meteor. I spotted him quickly; the white stripes in his black hair stood out against the red cushion where he reclined. His dark face was half hidden by a book. Lounging next to him, her green wings fanned out to display every shimmer, was Portia Peridot. She looked as if she were posing for an illustration in a human fairy tale.

Portia saw me but pretended she hadn't. Meteor remained totally absorbed in his book.

"Meteor," I whispered.

He looked up. His eyebrows came together in a withering frown.

"Have you seen Leona?"

He turned a page, ignoring me.

"Meteor! Please. Tell me if you've seen her."

"No, I haven't."

I turned away, my eyes clouding with tears. In all the years we'd been friends, we had argued many times, but Meteor had never looked as if he hated me.

I took to the air outside, asking everyone I met if they happened to know where Leona, the famous Violet fairy, might be found. Everyone had heard of her, but no one knew where she was. Leona must have truly tired of her fame, just as she'd told me the day before when she said she wished she could turn to shadow.

Was she hiding under an invisibility spell? Had she gone to Earth to get away from the crowds making much of her in Feyland?

I had to find her, warn her to stay away from the portal in Galena. Once she was on her guard, we could work together to take away Jason's weapon and get rid of it.

I flew back to Galena. I stood behind a pillar at the gateway until twilight had turned to darkness, waiting for Leona. She never arrived. Meteor passed through with Portia and Andalonus, but no Leona.

In the darkness near my home, I infused my wand. "I, Zaria Tourmaline, am protected from any and all enchantments tonight and tomorrow."

I went in, dreading what I would find. How would Beryl greet me? What sort of blankness would fill her eyes? Would she play the concerned guardian—or someone else?

But Beryl wasn't there. I went over the whole house. When I was sure she'd gone out, I crept to my own room. My nest looked so inviting, but I found that there were more enchantments lurking. The protection spell I had cast prevented me from getting within a wingspan of my comfortable nest. It was the same in my mother's room, too.

I ended up sleeping on my floor.

I woke at dawn to tapping on my door.

"Zaria?" Beryl's voice.

I dragged myself off the hard stones and opened the door. Beryl shuffled in. She leaned against the wall, wings folded, her face more haggard than I had ever seen it. "Do not worry, child," she said. "I have shaken the spells."

Hope rose in my heart. "Who enchanted you?"

"I did not see. I believe it was done under invisibility." She shook her head. "Why would anyone spend that much radia on me?"

Hope died. Beryl would know that Lily had motive, and only a spell would keep her from saying so.

I forced my face to be expressionless. "I believe I'll go out early," I said.

"Please, Zaria. I apologize for what I said last night. I was not myself."

"I know." That much was true. I brushed past her, mumbling about gathering sonnia.

"Wait. I have something important to tell you."

I stopped, turned around, and gazed at her pitifully worn face. Her yellow eyes, filmy and dim, seemed ready to close with exhaustion. "You need to rest, Beryl," I said as gently as I could.

"But—"

"Please, Beryl. Rest now." I wished I knew how to help her. Today, I would find out more about layered magic. I'd go back to the library, this time to study. "But be careful of your nest—it may be enchanted," I told her.

She nodded again. "I know," she whispered. "I know."

I looked at her intently. How I longed to trust her. But I knew I must not confide in her. And if I listened to her, she might feed me hurtful lies.

"Good-bye, Beryl."

Outside, I gathered a handful of sonnia. I chewed the red flowers morosely as I flew toward Leona's, hoping to catch her before she left for the day.

I knocked at Leona's dwelling. The door opened a chink, and she looked out. Glad to see her, I smiled.

She didn't smile back as she motioned me inside.

Chapter Thirty-four

ON EARTH, THERE ARE SKILLED HUMAN SURGEONS WHO CAN MEND DIRE INJURIES. IN THIS REGARD, HUMANS HAVE FAR SURPASSED FEY MAGIC, FOR ON TIRFEYNE, HEALING SPELLS DO NOT EXIST.

AS CHILDREN, FAIRIES AND GENIES ARE CAREFULLY NURTURED IN GALENA SO THAT NO INJURY MAY BEFALL THEM. LAWS AGAINST HARMING ONE ANOTHER ARE STRICT, FOR THOUGH MINOR INJURIES WILL HEAL FOR US JUST AS THEY DO FOR HUMANS, WE HAVE NO ENCHANTMENTS THAT CAN MEND A BROKEN WING OR RESTORE A SIGHTLESS EYE.

THERE ARE ONLY TWO HEALERS IN FEYLAND: SONNIA FLOWERS AND TIME. SOMETIMES, NEITHER IS ENOUGH.
　　　　　　　—Orville Gold, genie historian of Feyland

looked for you yesterday," I began. "Leona—"

A whimper behind her made me stop. I looked past Leona and saw her mother, Doreen Bloodstone, on a low perch. One of her eyes was swollen shut, and just above it was the mark of a deep burn.

"She went to Earth last night," Leona said shortly.

Oberon's Crown! Doreen must have used the Zinnia Portal—and met Jason Court and his laser gun.

Shivers traveled over my wings. How could he have been so cruel?

"I've used ten thousand radia trying to take away her pain," Leona said. "Nothing helps."

Ten thousand radia was a full degree of Green. Leona must have known there were no spells of healing, but she had tried anyway. I would have tried, too, if someone I loved had been harmed so terribly. For the first time, I understood how much Leona loved her mother, loved her even though they never seemed to agree on anything.

"I don't know what happened," Leona whispered. "She hasn't told me." She spoke louder so Doreen could hear. "I want to know who attacked you, Mother."

Doreen's good eye rolled back and forth. "It was a boy, maybe your age." Her voice sounded feeble.

"Why did he do this?" Leona asked.

"He did not explain," Doreen answered. "I had never seen him before, but he seemed to be waiting for me. He was just outside the portal."

"I hope you turned him into a toad," Leona said.

"A toad?" her mother sputtered. "Fairies do not harm humans. You know that."

"We did once upon a time—if they hurt us. He was harming *you*."

"Leona." Doreen shifted on the pillows, pain in her face.

"As I told you," she said evasively, "I had never seen him before."

Leona drew her wand; it glittered dangerously. "If you won't tell me who did this, I can compel you."

Doreen held up a hand. "No. Against the law to compel."

"The law doesn't matter to me." Leona's silvery eyes darkened to slate gray.

"No," Doreen said weakly.

Leona touched her mother's head with her wand. *"Enjorum es explia."*

Doreen jerked. Her shoulders drew back and her mouth dropped open.

"Who burned you?" Leona asked.

And Doreen answered in a flat voice, giving an exact description of Jason, down to the color of his jacket.

I saw the news hit Leona. Not only her wings, but her whole body began to shake. She laid her wand against her heart.

I didn't dare move.

After a long pause, Leona resumed. "Did anyone help him?"

"No," Doreen said. "No one else saw me."

I let out the breath I'd been holding.

"Did you use the portal you made in Galena?" Leona asked.

"Yes. The boy caught me there. I ducked back through the portal to get away."

Leona waved her wand. *"Dos elemen restora,"* she said,

taking the compulsion spell off her mother.

Doreen's eyes ran with tears; it was terrible to see them leaking from the swollen crease of her injured eye. Had I ever believed that she laughed too much?

"Never do that again," she said.

"I'm sorry." But Leona sounded enraged. "We should go, Zaree," she said abruptly. "Can't be late for our mentor meetings." She hurried past me out the door.

"Good-bye," I told her mother. "I hope you get better soon."

Doreen didn't answer, and I hurried out.

Leona was flying fast toward the gateway. I felt dizzy and sick as I beat the air beside her.

"What are you going to do after we meet with our mentors?" I ventured.

She faced straight ahead. "Don't ask me to tell you."

I hesitated, my breath short. "Do you want me to go with you?"

"No."

"But what if something goes wrong?"

"I am not my mother," Leona said. "And when *I* go through that portal, I'll be invisible."

"But—"

"You would get in my way."

She believed invisibility would protect her, but I knew different. I couldn't forget the red beam from Jason's gun.

• • •

I remembered to draw a protection spell against Lily before meeting with her—but it was wasted. She didn't try any magic on me that day.

She smiled a welcome. She wore an elegant pink gown and opal necklace. "Have you decided about the spell of disclosure?" she asked right away.

"You said I had two days."

"I hoped you would make a decision."

I shook my head and imagined a bird of darkness devouring the rainbow butterflies flitting over the walls.

Lily sighed. "Still distrustful? Well, perhaps it will help if I tell you a little more about myself."

I watched her suspiciously. What could she tell me to make me trust her?

"I am a high-level, high-ranking member of the High Council," she began. "I have many responsibilities. Not only have I served the Council for ninety years, but for the last ten, I have held the position of Forcier of Feyland."

"Forcier?" I vaguely remembered several lessons about the Forcier, something about refreshing the durable spells.

"I collect radia taxes. I dispense radia to the durable spells that need to be refreshed. It is difficult work, made even more difficult than it was in centuries past, because there is less radia available now. In these times, there are far too many Reds and not enough of the other colors." A rainbow butterfly darted across her face.

"Why?" I asked. "Why are there more Reds now than there used to be?"

She spread her hands. "No one knows. But it is a dangerous situation. Lately, it has become impossible to refresh all the durable spells that need radia. Some are in danger of *failing*." She gave me a sad smile. "But you, Zaria, with your rich stores of radia, will be able to help. You will be very important to the future of our world."

A small alarm began to wail deep inside me. "I don't want to be important."

She laughed. "You *are* important, whether you want to be or not."

Hating her laugh, I tried desperately to turn the subject. "I have a question for you," I said abruptly. "As my mentor."

"Speak up." She smoothed the lace at her neck.

"What happens to humans who hurt the fey?"

Lily stood in disapproving silence for several moments before she spoke. "Is this about your family, Zaria?"

Her words felt like iron barbs. "My family?"

"Surely you have heard that your family was lost after taking a portal to Earth?"

I couldn't make myself speak.

"You want to hear about it," she said. "Naturally, you do. And I can tell you, Zaria. The whole story. But only if we have trust between us."

I wanted to shout that I would never trust her, not ever,

not for anything. But she was all too right that I wanted to know about my family. My resolve crumbled.

"Trust requires an honest foundation," she continued. "If you allow me to do the spell of disclosure, we can begin to build that foundation."

I dug my toes into the thick yellow carpet. "Not today," I choked out. "Not yet."

By the time Lily dismissed me, a crowd had gathered in the courtyard. They must be waiting in hopes of seeing Leona. Good. That meant she had not yet left for Earth.

I sped to Galena Falls. Invisible, I settled in to watch the Zinnia Portal. Whether she wanted it or not, I would go with Leona.

Chapter Thirty-five

FEY FOLK ARE DEPENDENT UPON HUMAN HAPPINESS, FOR THE LEAVES OF SONNIA PLANTS CONVERT HUMAN HAPPINESS INTO THE NOURISHING FLOWERS THAT FEY FOLK EAT. THE METHOD IS AKIN TO PHOTOSYNTHESIS, WHERE GREEN PLANTS CONVERT SUNSHINE INTO OXYGEN.

JUST AS SUNSHINE IS ENERGY, SO, TOO, IS HAPPINESS. IT ARRIVES UPON TIRFEYNE FROM EARTH IN A MANNER SIMILAR TO THE ARRIVAL OF LIGHT AND HEAT FROM SUNSHINE. THERE ARE DEGREES OF HAPPINESS, JUST AS THERE ARE DEGREES OF HEAT. WHATEVER THE DEGREE, THE WORLD OF TIRFEYNE HAS THE CAPACITY TO SOAK IN THIS ENERGY OF HAPPINESS, AND THEN SONNIA PLANTS CONVERT IT INTO NUTRIENTS.

IF HUMANS CEASE TO PRODUCE HAPPINESS, FEY FOLK WILL EVENTUALLY DIE DUE TO A LACK OF NEEDED "SUNSHINE" FROM THE HUMAN WORLD. HOWEVER, MOST OF THE FEY HAVE FORGOTTEN THAT THIS IS TRUE; ONLY SCHOLARS SEEM TO REMEMBER. THIS FORGETFULNESS IS A PUZZLING CIRCUMSTANCE THAT I HAVE ATTEMPTED TO REMEDY, BY DOING MY BEST TO PRESERVE THE HISTORICAL RECORD.

—Orville Gold, genie historian of Feyland

hen I saw the flowers of the Zinnia Portal moving even though there was no wind, I knew it was Leona, invisible like me, passing through. Leona, heading to Earth for vengeance upon Jason Court.

Slipping after her, I floated above the familiar hillside. Out of habit, I glanced up toward the grove. There I saw a lonely human figure pacing back and forth beside the towering blue spruce. Reddish-gold hair caught the sunlight.

Sam.

My wings began to pump. What if Leona recognized him as Jason's friend?

I flew fast, but not fast enough. Before I reached the grove, Leona had popped into view directly across from Sam. What a sight she was, a raging fairy with shining wings, black hair pouring over her shoulders, silvery eyes filled with sparks of brilliant darkness.

She and Sam stared at each other as I flew closer. Sam's eyes widened.

"Where is your friend?" Leona asked.

He seemed transfixed.

"Where is Jason?"

"Please," Sam said. "Don't go near him."

"Where?" She drew her exquisite wand. Its blue stars sparkled fiercely.

Why didn't he run? But then, where could he run that she would not follow?

The wand's tip touched his head. *"Enjorum es explia."* Leona's mouth turned up in a feverish smile. "Where is Jason?" she repeated.

All emotion left Sam's face. "I think he's at home," he answered in a hollow voice. "He asked me to come over, and I said I would, but I didn't. He's probably waiting for me."

She swished her wand. *"Dos elemen restora."*

Instantly Sam's expression changed to one of desperation. "Whoever you are, don't go near Jason. He has a dangerous weapon."

"I don't think you quite understand the meaning of danger." She pointed her wand. *"Reducto et eloquen."*

A gag spell! But Sam had never done her any harm. He was trying to protect her. Why couldn't she see that?

"Now you won't be able to warn your friend that he will have a surprise visitor," Leona said.

Sam clutched his throat. He opened his mouth but no words came.

"Stay here if you know what's good for you," she said menacingly.

He held out both hands to Leona, but she turned and lifted into the air. Her wings almost brushed me as she flew away.

I wanted to help Sam, but if I lost Leona now, the next time I saw her, she might be mutilated by a laser gun. Not only that, but what might *she* do to Jason in her anger?

I could try reversing the gag spell on Sam with a spell

of my own, but if I got it wrong I would waste precious moments. So with a regretful glance at Sam, I flew after my old friend.

In flight, I renewed invisibility. A second later, the silvery speck of Leona winked out. She, too, was invisible again. I poured on speed, hoping to arrive at Jason's house before she did.

Spotting the big brick house with the iron balustrade, I descended to land on its roof. From there, I viewed the grounds.

The yard in back of the house was surrounded by a tall wooden fence. Trees stood like many-armed giants, their gnarled fingers garlanded with leaves. Under the trees, grass grew in patches around several stone benches. A human stood near one of the benches: I recognized Jason's pale hair and black jacket.

If Leona was there, she had not yet made her presence known.

Jason was holding the laser gun and muttering to himself. He kicked the bench in front of him, then kicked it again, so hard it tipped over.

He aimed his gun at the fallen bench. A red beam caught the white stone. He held the beam steady until part of the bench blackened and crumbled away.

Jason scowled. "I'm not waiting all day, Sam." He pointed his gun at the sky and waved it in an arc. I heard a muffled cry.

Leona!

I drew my wand. Infusing, I swooped toward Jason. "Sleep," I ordered.

Jason dropped to the ground, but he was still clutching his weapon, and now the red beam ran through the grass to the fence. Where it touched the wood, a fire started.

Darting forward, I kicked the gun out of Jason's grip. When I did, the beam went out.

"Leona?" I called softly. "Leona, where are you?"

"Here," said her voice.

And then she appeared.

A charred line slashed the margin of one of her quivering wings. Livid burns crossed the fingers of the hand holding her wand.

"Leona!" I bounded toward her.

She glared furiously at Jason lying on the ground beside the fallen bench. "Sleep spell?" she asked.

I nodded.

"Wake him," she said. "But first, get his weapon."

"This place is on fire! Humans will be swarming here."

"All the more reason to get his weapon," she said darkly. "Please, Zaria. Pick it up. I would do it, but my hand is burned."

I stooped to the smooth black thing lying quiet in the grass. I lifted it cautiously, afraid of its deadly beam. "I have it," I said. Behind Leona, rising flames crackled, and I heard the wails of sirens heading toward us. "Let's go."

"Not yet. Wake him up."

"Leona! The fire. You don't know if you can fly." I looked doubtfully at her stricken wing.

"Wake him."

"I don't know the spell for waking," I said uneasily.

"Then reverse the sleep spell."

Flames were consuming the fence, spitting sparks and ash into the grass. Smoke billowed; some of it blew in my face. I coughed, and my eyes watered. I shut my eyes. "What do I say?"

"*Chantmentum pellex,* Level Thirty," Leona said impatiently. "But first hide the weapon."

I hesitated.

"It's harmless unless you squeeze the trigger," she said.

Vaguely, I remembered the class during which we had studied guns. Yes, there had been something about the trigger. But no one had taught us about a gun that would shoot red beams that could burn through stone.

The sirens howled louder. Very carefully, I put the laser gun into the deepest pocket in my gown.

"Now wake him. Please." Leona's face was distorted with pain.

I pointed the wand at Jason. *"Chantmentum pellex."*

Jason stirred. His eyes opened and saw the spreading fire. He leaped to his feet.

Leona was ready for him, her wand alight. *"Trans amphib bufon nos."*

It was Jason who leaped; it was a large brown toad that landed on the ground.

"Did you think you could harm a fairy and nothing would happen to you?" she cried, her voice carrying over the sirens. "How wrong you were." She jabbed her wand at the toad. "And this time, my spell won't wear off so soon." She infused all the way to the tip.

"Leona, don't!"

"*Chantment dura solaran,*" she chanted, ignoring me. "You'll be a toad for a year—if you survive that long."

Just then, four humans came running around the corner of the house—men in heavy clothing, carrying big hoses. "You girls get out of here!" one of them yelled as they ran past. "What do you think this is, a costume party?"

They began squirting jets of water at the fence.

"Leona, let's go!"

I saw the infusion travel up her wand again. I grabbed at her arm, but she twisted away. She pointed her wand at Jason's house. *"Pyro los dred."*

As if a great bonfire had imploded in its center, the house collapsed with a rending crash. Flames began coiling toward the sky in great clouds of smoke.

The men stood quite still for a moment, their lips moving soundlessly, as if they were under gag spells. Then they burst into motion, running at Leona and me.

"Move!" one shouted. "Move, move!"

"Get back!" shouted another.

Just before the nearest man got close enough to touch her, Leona cast the transport spell. *"Transera nos,"* she said, and disappeared.

The men stopped short, blinking disbelievingly, heads turning back and forth in search of what was no longer there.

And on the ground at my feet, a large toad hopped back and forth in frenzy.

Maybe I should have stayed and reversed Leona's spell upon Jason. But with smoke rolling toward me and heat searing the air, all I could think of was getting away.

I shot skyward.

Chapter Thirty-six

HUMANS ARE UNAWARE THAT THEY ARE DEPENDENT UPON FEY FOLK TO KEEP FROM BECOMING TOO DOWN-CAST AND HARDENED.

THE HUMAN WORLD IS OVERBURDENED WITH A CERTAIN TYPE OF REALITY THAT HAS STRICT LAWS OF PHYSICS, HEAVY AND SOLID. THE FEY WORLD IS MORE EFFERVESCENT AND AIRY; ON TIRFEYNE THE LAWS OF PHYSICS ARE MORE YIELDING AND RESPONSIVE.

ENCOUNTERS WITH MAGIC (SO LONG AS THAT MAGIC IS NOT OF THE WICKED, MALICIOUS VARIETY) ARE BENEFICIAL TO HUMANS, ALLOWING THEM RELIEF FROM THE MORE PONDEROUS ASPECTS OF EXISTENCE.

THUS THE WORLDS OF TIRFEYNE AND EARTH ARE MEANT TO BE RELATED TO EACH OTHER, PART OF A LARGER HARMONY WITHIN WHICH EACH PLAYS A CENTRAL PART. IN THIS ONGOING CONNECTION, HUMANS AND FEY FOLK ARE ESPECIALLY CLOSE, SUPPLYING EACH OTHER WITH IMPORTANT INGRE-DIENTS FOR LIFE AND HEALTH.

—Orville Gold, genie historian of Feyland

$\mathscr{M}$y wings trembled as I flew, and my thoughts felt scrambled. I was breathing hard, trying to comprehend what had happened.

Then it struck me: what if there had been humans inside Jason's house?

There couldn't have been. If other people had been home, they would have noticed the burning fence. They would have rushed out when the sirens arrived.

But I had to know.

Turning back, I sped through the afternoon sky. I saw a child looking up at me and belatedly remembered to renew invisibility. Then I tried frantically to recall how much time Leona and I had been visible.

Time enough.

The invisibility had worn off for both of us before I woke Jason, before Leona turned him into a toad and blew up his house. If any fairy or genie had been looking through a viewing scope at this neighborhood, we would be barred from Earth for decades, if not forever.

How could I bear that?

The memory of the leprechaun who had plucked Beryl's sleeve rose up in my mind. *"I used to travel to Earth—me and all m'friends. Now look at me—banned!"*

How terrible it must be for them.

At Jason's place, men were holding water hoses to a

blackened pit of smoking rubble. The only thing left standing was the iron balustrade.

While I hovered, cars arrived with blue and red lights flashing. Men and women dressed in dark blue poured out of them.

"What happened here?" a woman asked, staring at the smoking ruin.

"Don't know, ma'am. We were called to a small fire, but it turned out to be a big one," a man answered. "We suspect an incendiary device."

She wrote on a pad of paper. "A bomb?"

"Haven't had a chance to investigate, ma'am."

She scribbled hurriedly. "Any fatalities?"

"None that we know of."

I sighed with relief. Leona's vengeance had not taken anyone's life. Unless a big-booted man had stepped on a toad by mistake.

I scanned the ground several times but didn't see any toads, big or small. I admit it was a halfhearted effort. Jason had stolen a fey wand, and he had hurt two fairies with a human weapon. Maybe he deserved to be a toad.

But only for a little while. Not for a year. And Leona should never have blown up his house.

The human boy's wickedness seemed to have spread to my friend, changing her into someone I hardly knew, someone who fought cruelty with cruelty and rage with rage. Someone frightening.

I wished I could undo some of the worst of Leona's magic, but I didn't know how to rebuild a human house. I didn't believe anyone could, despite exaggerated tales about the famous genies of old.

I took a last look at the destruction below, then flew away again, worried now that Leona might have decided to go after Sam, too, even though he had nothing to do with injuring anyone.

But when I got back to the grove, I found Sam sitting alone with his back to the blue spruce, gazing down the hill. His curly hair stuck out in all directions.

I knew I should simply release him from Leona's spell and leave, but the longer I looked at him, the more I wanted to stay. There was something about him that drew me. Maybe it was because his father was missing, and I knew what that was like. Maybe because he was kind to his little sister and he'd put out the fire Jason started in the blue spruce. All in all, he seemed to be a good sort of human.

I lingered until my invisibility expired. When Sam saw me appear, wariness crept into his face.

I drew my wand. *"Chantmentum pellex."*

Sam looked even more wary.

"Can you speak?" I asked.

He cleared his throat. "Zaria?"

I nodded.

Sam blinked. "What was wrong with my voice?"

"An enchantment."

"Enchantment." He put a hand over his neck.

"Are you all right?"

"Guess so." He squeezed his eyes shut and then opened them again. "How do you do it?" he asked. "Appear and disappear."

"I'm a fairy."

"A fairy." He looked troubled. "I saw the other one . . . *flying.*" He rubbed his temples with his fists. "She was going to find Jason. He has a laser gun. I hope he doesn't hurt anyone."

"That's over," I said.

He gave a half smile. "Over? Is he covered with warts now?"

"No. He doesn't have the gun anymore." I couldn't bring myself to tell him about the toad, or the explosion.

"Good." Sam picked up a handful of dead spruce needles and let them trickle through his fingers. He pointed to the blackened branch lying on the ground. "It was you, wasn't it?" he said. "You helped me keep the woods from burning up."

"I was there, yes."

"I came here hoping . . ." He shook his head. "I'm not making sense."

Puzzled, I waited for him to say more.

"My dad's missing." His eyes watered.

"I'm so sorry." I wished I could say something to help him.

"Now I'm seeing fairies and hearing voices." He blew out a breath. "I'm losing it, aren't I? Losing my mind."

His face was so close I could clearly see the reddish speckles on his nose. "I'm quite real, if you're wondering."

He sat still for a moment. "So you have real magic?" he asked.

I looked out across the hillside. The lowering sun was beginning to streak the sky, the clouds like purple roads leading beyond the horizon. At that moment, I wanted to glide down those roads and see how far my magic could take me. Maybe I could find another world, one without the problems of either Earth or Tirfeyne.

Tirfeyne.

The thought of my world sent panic tearing through me. I was on Earth without the protection of invisibility! Once again I had forgotten Lily Morganite and Boris Bloodstone and every other meddling fairy or genie. What if they saw me with Sam? What might they do—to him? They would erase his memory at the very least.

Instantly, I drew my wand. *"Verita sil nos mertos elemen."*

Sam jumped up. He passed a hand across the air in front of his face. "I've been hallucinating," he muttered.

I grabbed his hand. "I'm real," I said softly. "Real as you."

He squeezed my hand and pulled me toward him. "If you have magic," he said in my ear, "can you help me find my father?"

His father!

Feyland's viewing scopes burst into my mind. If I could get into a viewing booth, I could look. But if I did, I would be breaking another law.

"We're not allowed to use magic on behalf of full-grown men and women," I said, moving back from him. "It's absolutely forbidden."

Sam tensed. "But what about me and Jenna? Don't you understand? It's killing us not knowing where he is."

I knew all too well what he meant. I drew a long breath. "I would need his name."

"Michael Seabolt," he answered, color flooding his face.

I exhaled. "I'll look for him."

"Please," Sam said, "don't say you'll do this unless you mean it."

"If I can," I whispered, "I will. Wait for me on your porch tonight." But even as I said it, I decided that if I found out his father was dead, I would not let Sam know.

His face was so hopeful. "Okay," he said.

"Now, please go."

He smiled, his gold-toned eyes alight. Then he turned and ran through the grass toward the human town. I watched him for a moment before I knelt beside the blue spruce again.

It didn't take long to bury the laser gun next to the spellbook.

Afterward, I infused my wand. "This ground and all that it holds cannot be disturbed by anyone but me," I said, and felt magic flowing out of me. "*Ad eternum.* Forever and always."

Chapter Thirty-seven

HUMANS THROUGHOUT HISTORY HAVE DISPLAYED A
DISTURBING WILLINGNESS TO HARM OTHERS OF THEIR
KIND. INDEED, THEY HAVE APPLIED CONSIDERABLE
INVENTIVENESS TO THE CREATION OF WEAPONS THAT
CAN KILL AND MAIM.

—Orville Gold, genie historian of Feyland

I emerged into Galena to see Leona in our favorite spot, looking wretched. The burn on her wing stood out in a charred line. Pain filled her eyes.

I landed next to her and waited until my invisibility expired.

"What took you so long?" She sounded weary.

"I checked to be sure no one was burned or killed." I watched carefully to see her reaction.

A tear trickled down her cheek. "I was so angry! When I realized what I'd done, I was afraid of myself." She bowed her head.

I was relieved to see her cry. "I was afraid of you, too," I said truthfully. "But no one was burned, and no one died."

"That much is good." She sighed. "What did you do with the weapon?"

"It's buried," I answered. "And I'll never tell where it lies."

She nodded. "Thank you for coming after me," she said. "Without you, I might be nothing but a heap of ashes." She used her sleeve to wipe her eyes. A tremor ran over her burned wing. "My wing will probably be scarred."

I touched her shoulder gently. "Can you still fly?"

"I can get airborne but I flap. And it hurts as if my wing and my hand were on fire."

How I wished I could help her.

"I don't ever want to go back to Earth," she said gloomily. "Our teachers were right. It's dangerous. And *I'm* dangerous when I'm there." She shifted, staring straight at the Zinnia Portal. "I wish my mother had never put a portal in Galena."

Listening to Leona, I felt suddenly faint with hunger. I couldn't remember the last time I had eaten. "I'm going to get some sonnia," I told her.

A patch grew just above our rocky refuge. As I plucked handfuls of flowers, a stray wind rustled around me. For a minute I longed to follow that wind wherever it blew, but instead I brought blossoms to Leona. We crammed the food into our mouths.

"Zaria, if anyone saw us on Earth, the Council will command us to surrender our wands—and probably keep them for the next ten years." She drew her wand and began tracing the handle with her finger. "But I can't be without my wand. Even if they send the Radia Guard after me, I will never let them have it."

I thought of all Lily's attempts to get me to hand her my wand. She said it was for a disclosure spell, but it occurred to me now that once I gave it to her, I would have no power to take it back. I shuddered to think of how close I had come, and inwardly renewed my vow that I would never give up my wand.

"I won't, either," I said solemnly.

Leona looked at me sideways. Her wings twitched. "Magistria Lodestone is my mentor," she said.

"I heard the rumor."

"It's true. She's Level Eighty, Blue." Leona arched an eyebrow. "And she says you and I should not be friends."

"My mentor says the same."

In the pause that followed, we smiled grimly at each other.

"I know why," she said. "Our friendship is dangerous. But not to us." She studied her beautiful wand. "We're Violet. As long as we stand together, they cannot oppose us."

"I'll stand with you, Leona."

"Magistria Lodestone *commanded* me to stop being your friend." She grinned. "What a trog she is."

"Rotten trog," I said.

A giggle escaped her, then we both burst into sudden wild laughter. If anyone had seen us, they would have taken us for a pair of shrieking gremlins.

When we finally stopped laughing, I glanced at the sun.

Twilight would fall soon. "Leona, I have things to tell you."

I began with Lily Morganite: how she'd stolen my mother's spellbook and how I'd taken it back. "That's why my wand was buried on Earth."

"And you fooled the Council with an Earth stylus? Brilliant!" Leona seemed delighted.

"So now you know something about *me* that you must never tell."

"Never."

I went on, pouring out the story of the layered magic on Beryl. The longer I talked about it, the more serious Leona looked. "Meteor forgot what had happened and then wouldn't speak to you?" she exclaimed. "He must be under a dire enchantment! He would never forsake your friendship."

"But he did."

"We'll go to the library tomorrow and study layered spells," she said. "We need to learn how to protect ourselves and our wands."

How glad I was to confide in her. Leona was still a friend I could trust.

Then why hadn't I told her about my journeys to Earth without her, visiting Sam and Jenna, and my promise to look for their father? Should I tell her?

"Magistria Lodestone keeps making tragic predictions," Leona was saying. She rolled her eyes. "Predictions about how weak the durable spells have become and how desperately Feyland will need my talents."

"Lily says the same."

Leona bounded up suddenly. "Did you hear something?" She pointed her wand behind my head.

I leaped and whirled around, but twilight's shadows were long gone, and full night surrounded us. "Hear what?"

She flew into the dark above our rock.

I followed, drawing my wand. "What is it?"

My ears caught a faint whooshing sound, as if a genie had breezed by me on swift magic feet.

"Spy." Leona's wand shone eerily in the faint starlight as she shook it at the sky. *"Chantmentum—"*

"Wait!" I charged into her and knocked her wand loose. It fell.

She bent, seizing her wand. The tip wavered in front of my face. "Are you a spy, too?" she yelled.

I held up my wand to oppose her. How puny my stylus appeared. "Stop. Leona, what if the spy carries a layered spell? Reversing it could backfire on you!"

"Backfire?" Her wand shook, a pale streak of platinum trembling in the dark. She lowered it and slid to the ground. Resting it against her knees, she gripped both ends.

I sank into the sonnia beside her.

"I thought you were trying to take my wand." Her head drooped. "I almost put a statue spell on you."

A statue spell? I shivered. Where had Leona learned to do a statue spell? They were forbidden.

But so were compulsion spells.

"I've got to get control of myself," she said. "I can't be throwing spells the way I've done today."

I had to agree, but I didn't say anything.

"How much of what we said was overheard?" Leona whispered next.

I tried to remember everything I'd told her. I had revealed so many secrets about Lily and Beryl. And Meteor. "Who would spy on us?"

She lifted her head. Her silver eyes had a dark lonely center, reflecting the night. "The invisibility spell takes Level Fifty, so it could be anyone with Level Fifty magic who can pass through the Gateway of Galena." She gripped her wand more tightly. "We've got to seal the portal. If the spy heard us talk about it, he'll know my mother put it there. If the Council found out, they would send her to the Iron Lands. We can't let the portal be found!"

"I'll help you seal it," I said, trying to hide my sadness. Leona was right. The Zinnia Portal had to be closed.

"Thank you. I'll ask my mother how it's done and meet you back here."

Opening my watch, I squinted at it. Eleven! Time had flown past me, and Sam would be waiting on his porch. "I have to make a quick trip into Oberon City first," I said.

"What for?"

To look for Sam and Jenna's father. "Something I promised to do. But it won't take long at all. I'll hurry."

"Guard your wand, Zaree. Spies could be anywhere."

Chapter Thirty-eight

HUMANS HAVE COME TO RELY UPON AN INCREASING NUMBER OF MACHINES FOR PURPOSES OF TRANS-PORTATION. THESE MACHINES ARE CAPABLE OF MOVING AT HIGH SPEEDS, SOMETIMES EXCEEDING THE VELOCITY OF FEY FOLK AT FULL POWER. ACCIDENTS INVOLVING THESE MACHINES HAVE BECOME MORE AND MORE FREQUENT.

—*Orville Gold, genie historian of Feyland*

The thought of spies made the air around me seem to buzz with phantoms. I tapped my head. *"Verita sil nos mertos elemen."* I didn't want to continue using up radia, but what choice did I have?

I remembered what Leona had said about locating Jason Court. *"I had to go to an old broken-down viewing station beside the Malachite Towers."*

I could get to the Malachite Towers quickly, by using two transports.

I went through the Zinnia Portal. From there I transported straight to the Cornfield Portal. There I paused before going into Feyland.

It was time to draw the best protection I could imagine. I closed my eyes and thought carefully until I was satisfied that I could create a spell that would protect my wand wherever I went or whatever I did.

I didn't believe the councilors who had told us that our wands were safe from all magic except our own—or a spell of disclosure.

"No spells but mine can affect this wand," I said. "*Ad eternum.* Forever and always."

Magic swirled through the little stylus in my hand as the spell took hold.

Once more, I infused to Level 100 and enunciated clearly. "Any harmful spell cast upon me will rebound upon the one casting it and have no effect upon me. *Ad eternum.* Forever and always."

I wanted to check my watch to see how much radia I had spent, but it was too dark to see. It didn't matter anyway. I would have protected myself whatever the cost.

Steadying my wings, I stepped through the Cornfield Portal into the Golden Station. From there, I transported to the dingy Malachite Towers in Oberon City.

I snooped around until I found an old, run-down viewing station. Inside, a genie with greenish skin and black hair stood morosely watching the booths. The glass doors were webbed with cracks, and what little I could see of the scopes showed tarnished, dented instruments.

A yawning fairy with mottled brown wings floated in

after me. She crossed the chipped tile floor to the attendant. "Evening, Seth. I hope the scopes are working better than they were during my last visit. Night is best for watching my godchild." She sniffed. "She looks better asleep than at any other time."

The genie grunted. "A fine way to talk about your god-child, Shirelle."

She shrugged. "What does it matter? I couldn't help her even if she needed me. I'm a Red, remember?" She drifted toward a viewing booth, muttering as she went.

A stout genie in ragged robes stuck his head out of one of the other booths. "Seth," he said with irritation. "My scope is so blurry I can't see my boy."

Seth sighed. "I keep asking the Council for an infusion, but they can't be bothered." He clenched a fist. "That high and mighty Morganite fairy was here last month. Paraded her wand like it was Velleron's scepter and gave us an infusion of fifty radia. The scopes didn't improve one jot."

At the mention of *that high and mighty Morganite*, the stout genie hastily left.

"Will the Council listen to me? No." Seth kept grumbling, though I was the only one left to hear and he didn't know I was there. "This station's falling down around my ears. And me paying my radia tax faithfully." He sounded more and more aggrieved. "They don't forget *that*, now do they?"

The ragged genie had left the door to the vacant booth ajar. I darted inside. The booth was clean, but the dented scope creaked when I adjusted the eyepiece.

Peering through the scope, I whispered Michael Seabolt's name. The view was a hazy blur. I gripped my wand. "Focus," I ordered the scope, but it didn't respond. I fiddled with every knob, trying to clear the image. Nothing helped.

How was I going to find Sam's father? If I went to a better station, all the booths would be filled.

I glanced around the shabby walls, an idea dawning. Seth had said this station needed radia. What if *I* gave it an infusion, enough to fix the broken scopes?

I crept into a corner and waited until my latest invisibility expired. Then I approached Seth. "Excuse me," I said.

His eyes looked like diamond disks, an odd contrast to the sickly color of his skin. "Yes?"

"Uh, I notice your station needs to be refreshed."

He grunted. "You noticed, eh? Very observant of you."

"If I wanted to give your station a radia infusion, how would I do it?" I tried to sound nonchalant.

Seth wiggled his green ears. "You? Give us radia?"

"How much would you need?"

He chewed his lip. "To get the lenses in working order, a full degree of orange."

"A hundred radia? How much to mend everything?"

The genie snorted. "Another hundred."

"What's the spell? And what level?"

He chuckled. "Spell was set forth long ago by the Ancients. Simple infusion is all it takes to refresh." He turned to the wall behind him and gave it a pat. "Infusion port."

I looked closely. One of the malachite bricks was carved into the image of a crown. It held a notch for the tip of a wand.

So this was an infusion port. I drew my wand.

When Seth saw my stylus, he swung himself in front of me, blocking the port. "A newfangled wand. Unchanged. You're a Red. Can't allow a Red to give up any radia. Besides, you're too young to be here at all."

"I'm not Red. I haven't changed my wand, but I'm—" I stopped. I had almost said it: *I'm Violet.*

"Can't let you do this." The genie set his feet a little farther apart.

The brown-winged fairy called out. "Seth, help me with this worthless scope!"

Seth shook a finger at me before going to help the fairy. The instant his back was turned, I pressed the tip of my wand into the notch on the wall. It was easy enough. A small square window next to the port lit up, showing the number of radia I was giving. The numbers spun faster and faster as I poured two hundred radia out of my wand.

The change in the station was instantaneous. Cracks in the doors vanished, and scopes shone flawlessly. The floor tiles became as smooth and clean as if they'd been laid the day before. Chips and pocks disappeared from the walls.

I can't describe the elation I felt. At last, my magic had done something good, something that would last longer than a day, something many could enjoy.

Astonished shouts erupted. "Trolls and pixies, who turned up the radia?"

Seth whirled around and gaped at me. Smiling, I rushed past him into a vacant booth. The door had a heavy latch, which I fastened behind me before squinting into the eyepiece of the newly repaired scope.

"Show me Michael Seabolt," I said eagerly.

Chapter Thirty-nine

FAIRIES AND GENIES WHOSE LIVES ARE DRAWING TO A CLOSE MAY DECIDE TO TRANSFER THE REMAINDER OF THEIR RADIA RESERVES TO ANOTHER. IF THIS IS NOT DONE, THE AMOUNT OF RADIA LEFT UNUSED AT THE TIME OF DEATH DISAPPEARS FOREVER.

—*Orville Gold, genie historian of Feyland*

The man I saw through the scope had fiery red hair plastered to his head in lank strands. His eyes were dark hazel, his skin sunburned and freckled. He was walking through a moonlit landscape, looking into the distance. Rocks and sand and a few scrubby plants were his only companions.

A gash on his forehead was covered with crusted blood.

When I reached out to read Michael Seabolt's nature, I didn't think about the strict laws against using magic on behalf of a grown person. I thought only of Sam and Jenna, of how they missed their father and wanted him to come home.

And I made a startling discovery. Michael Seabolt had forgotten who he was. He'd forgotten his wife and his children and the place where he lived.

My first thought was that he might have stumbled upon a crowd of genies who had put him under a strong enchantment to keep him from remembering what he'd seen. But the longer I viewed Sam's father, the less I believed it was magic that had deprived him of memory.

I stared at the wound on his head and then noticed that one of his arms hung stiffly, the elbow twisted. He looked overly thin. How long had he been missing? I didn't know.

How had Michael Seabolt come to be alone in such desolate country? And how could I tell Sam his father was injured, unable to remember him?

At least this man was alive.

He probably needed to eat. And if I had known how to find an Earth portal close to where he was, I could have found some human food and taken it to him.

But I didn't know how to find other portals. In fact, I was discovering just how little I knew about everything. I thought of Meteor, studying in the library. He had always understood how much there was to learn. I wished I could ask for his help now.

I heard raps on the door to the booth but didn't look away from Earth. I had to do something for Michael Seabolt, but what?

There were spells to make a human forget. Maybe I could cast a spell to help a human remember.

Why had he lost his memory in the first place? If it was

because of the wound on his head, I would not be able to help him. No spells could heal a physical injury. But what if his memory loss were due to something else?

Looking at his sunburned face, I began to feel as if I walked beside him. I could almost hear his feet on the barren ground, almost smell the quiet night around him. I sensed the confusion in his mind and the pain in his heart.

He had seen something. Something terrible. What if he had lost his memory, not because of the gash on his head but because of what he had seen?

When my parents and Jett disappeared, the pain had been so great I'd shoved it far down in my heart and never let any of it out until the day I turned fourteen. For years, I had refused to talk about my parents or my brother, avoided their rooms, turned them into vague memories I seldom saw and never tried to find.

Maybe Michael Seabolt had pushed his good memories into a place far inside himself along with the terrible memory of what he'd witnessed.

I had to try to help him. The scope I was using had a port for sending gifts to human children. I could use it to send a spell to Sam's father.

Not knowing what level would be needed, I infused my wand all the way to the end, and then slid the narrow tip of my stylus into the sending port.

"Remember yourself," I said. "Remember your family."

The rapping on the booth became loud knocking.

I leaned into the viewer and saw Sam's father fall to the ground.

I snatched my wand out of the port. What had I done? Had I sent too much magic?

Knocking changed to pounding. It seemed the booth would shatter, but I wouldn't turn away. I watched the red-haired man get slowly to his knees. He clasped his hands and bowed his head. His lips moved silently. Tears stood in his eyes, but he was smiling.

I faced the door. A small crowd of fairies and genies hovered behind Seth, who was beating on the glass.

I hurried to unlatch the booth. Seth threw open the door.

"Who are you?" he asked. "And who sent you?"

Without thinking I held up my stylus, and Seth backed away.

"No one sent me," I answered.

I didn't have to push through the crowd; everyone made way. As I glided toward the exit, they all looked at me as if I were Queen Velleron herself.

"But who are you?" Seth called after me.

"No one," I called back, and dashed out of the viewing station.

Before Seth or anyone else could gather their wits to follow me, I laid another invisibility spell on myself. Then I took to the air, flying low toward the Golden Station.

I wanted to see Sam's face when I told him about his father.

Emerging through the Cornfield Portal, I breathed in the cool, dark air of Earth, the sweet scent of corn plants with their dusky crowns of silk, faintly golden in the moonlight.

But I had not come back to Earth to look at corn. I glanced at my watch. Close to midnight! How fast the time had gone.

"*Transera nos,*" I said, visualizing Sam's house.

He was sitting on the steps of his porch, head buried in his arms. An old blanket draped his shoulders. Seeing him that way reminded me of how I'd felt when my parents had first disappeared.

"Sam," I whispered as I approached.

He lifted his head. "Zaria?"

"You can't see me, but I'm here."

He stood. A small breeze touched his hair.

I drew close to him. "I found your father. He had lost his memory, but I gave it back. He's on his way home."

I didn't know that for sure, but where else would Michael Seabolt be going, now that he had his memory again?

"On his way home?" The blanket fell from Sam's shoulders as he stood straighter. "Are you sure?" He put out a hand, and I took it.

The porch light flickered. The door of Sam's house opened, and he let go of my hand.

His mother stood framed in the doorway. "Sam? What are you doing?"

It took him a moment to answer. "Nothing," he said.

"Jenna's awake and won't stop crying. She's asking for you. Will you calm her down?"

"Be right there." Sam stooped to pick up the blanket. When he straightened, he looked at the spot where I stood, his eyes focused on a point just slightly to my left. "Thank you," he said.

His mother held the door wide. I reached out and brushed Sam's face. "Good-bye," I whispered, so lightly it was little more than a tremor in the air.

Chapter Forty

TROLLS ARE THE MOST FEARED CREATURES OF TIRFEYNE, DESPITE THE FACT THAT THEY ARE SAID TO BE GREGARIOUS AND FUN–LOVING WHEN THEY ARE TOGETHER.

TALLER THAN THE TALLEST OF GENIES, TROLLS HAVE STRENGTH TO MATCH THEIR STATURE. THEY EAT THE *PUTCH* THAT GROWS PLENTIFULLY IN THE SWAMP OF SWILLICH, A VAST TERRITORY WITHIN TROLL COUNTRY. IT HAS ALSO BEEN REPORTED THAT THEY HAVE NO OBJECTION TO EATING OTHER LIVING THINGS. IT HAS EVEN BEEN RUMORED THAT TROLLS WILL CONSUME THE FLESH OF HUMANS, BUT THIS IS UNVERIFIED.

VISITORS TO TROLL COUNTRY ARE NOT WELCOME, AND THEREFORE IT IS DIFFICULT TO LEARN MUCH ABOUT THEM FIRSTHAND.

THE MOST FRIGHTENING CHARACTERISTIC OF TROLLS IS THAT THEY ARE UTTERLY UNPREDICTABLE. THEY ARE ALSO EXTRAVAGANTLY RICH IN MAGIC AND VERY SECRETIVE ABOUT THEIR MAGICAL METHODS.

—Orville Gold, genie historian of Feyland

$\mathcal{I}$ sped through the Zinnia Portal into Galena at the stroke of midnight, just as my invisibility expired. I looked around for Leona.

"Zaria?" someone said.

It was not the voice I expected.

I peered through the night at a looming shadow floating toward me. "Meteor?"

"It's me." Starlight gave his eyes a strange gleam and shone on the stripes in his hair.

The last time I had seen Meteor, he had been so angry I'd doubted we could stay friends. What was he doing here?

"They've caught Leona," he said. "And they're looking for you."

I felt unable to speak. Caught Leona? How?

I remembered the rush of genie feet when Leona and I were talking. "You," I said. "*You* were the spy!" I drew my wand, unfurling my wings and lifting into the air.

"Wait!" Meteor cried, rising with me.

I tapped my head. *"Verita—"*

Lightning quick, his hand shot out and grabbed my wand.

My heart burned, and my throat seemed stuffed with ashes. Meteor, my friend since childhood, had taken my wand!

I didn't even try to fight him. I sank downward, barely catching myself before landing on the ground.

Meteor followed. "Zaria," he said huskily.

I wouldn't look at him.

"It's true that I eavesdropped on you and Leona."

I ventured a glance at his face. His dark skin blended with the night, and I couldn't see his expression.

He talked faster. "When you told Leona I was under a layered enchantment, I didn't believe you. But because we'd been friends for so long . . ." His chest rose in a heavy sigh. "I went to my mentor, and he told me how to overcome layered enchantments. That's how I know it wasn't you who put a spell on me."

Then Meteor Zircon did something I would never have expected. He went down on his knees. "Take back your wand," he said. "I took it to make you stay and listen."

My hand closed around the simple stylus, the slender key to my power. As the glow of my magic filled me again, I wanted to cry. I didn't, though. I swallowed the ashy lump in my throat.

"Get up, Meteor," I said.

He got to his feet. "Zaria, the drink Beryl served had layers dissolved in it. I'm not enchanted anymore. I'm sorry. I didn't know a spell could make me—" He stopped.

"Make you hate me?" I asked softly.

He sighed again. "On my way to see my mentor, I thought you were nothing but a liar and a sneak. And when I was asking him about layers, I felt as if something had hold of my mind; it was like trying to talk while asleep."

I remembered the sticky haze that had covered me the day I fled from Lily's apartment, and I sympathized.

Meteor's voice dropped. "But when I found the layers and reversed them, I understood. I hope you never have to find layered magic in yourself, Zaria. There's great pain when it's revealed." He sounded sickened. "I'm so sorry."

I shuddered. "But if it could happen to you, it could happen to any of us." I grabbed his arm. "When layered magic is revealed, do you know who cast it?"

"Yes," he said. "Lily Morganite was behind the spells laced in the tea Beryl served."

Now I knew for sure. "Did Lily ask you to spy, too?"

Meteor paused. "No one asked me to spy. I believed you had enchanted me, and I came here on my own because I wanted to get you back. I knew this was your favorite place," he said remorsefully. "Then when you and Leona started talking, I thought the best revenge would be to eavesdrop and hear your secrets." He hung his head. "Please forgive me. I wasn't myself."

"Of course, I forgive you. If you hadn't eavesdropped, you would still be under a layered enchantment." I tried to smile at him, but deep uneasiness gripped my heart. "How did they catch Leona?"

"A snare in the Gateway of Galena."

I asked myself why Leona would have tried to go through the gateway, when she was supposed to meet me at the Zinnia Portal.

"Her wand shrieked loud enough to wake all Feyland until it was locked in an iron box," Meteor continued. "I heard that it's being guarded by gnomes, somewhere in Oberon City."

"And Leona?"

Meteor stared at his hands. "Layered sleep spell, I believe. After they caught her, they carted her off to the Iron Lands."

"The *Leprechaun Colony*?" I couldn't bear to think of Leona, separated from her wand and shut away in a place where magic was useless.

"Zaria, as soon as she wakes up, they'll make her tell them everything she knows. Everything!"

"No," I said. "Leona would never tell them *anything* without a compulsion spell, and spells have no power in the Iron Lands." My wings trembled. "I wonder why they would take her there?"

Meteor's voice was full of sadness. "Leona has powerful friends." He gave me a quick bow. "Maybe they were making sure no one could help her by using magic. And she has so much natural magic of her own, just being in the Iron Lands could take the heart right out of her."

I wouldn't think about that. I couldn't. If I did, I would pull my wings around my head and do nothing but cry.

"We were going to seal the portal," I said. "She was so afraid it would be found. She was going to ask her mother how to do it." I stared at the lumpy sandstone boulder a few wingspans away among the shadowy zinnias.

"You can still seal it," Meteor said. "I know how it's done."

• • •

When Meteor had heard the news of Leona's capture, he had gone to Doreen Bloodstone. He persuaded her to tell him all about the portal in Galena: where it was and how to seal it. But sealing it would take Level 75. As a Level 50 genie, Meteor wasn't capable. It would have to be me.

"How much radia?" I asked.

"A thousand."

One degree of Yellow. Less than I would have guessed. "Tell me what to do," I said.

To my surprise, Meteor reached into his genie robes and produced a tall bottle of indigo-colored glass. Starlight reflected eerily off its surface.

"What's that?"

"Water from the Azurite Springs in the heart of Troll Country," he said. "Mixed with honey made by bees on Earth."

Troll Country? I didn't like the sound of that.

"It's an elixir," said Meteor. "Doreen gave it to me. The portal can't be sealed without it."

"But what do I do with it?" I hefted the bottle. It felt peculiar—as if it were much bigger than its actual dimensions.

He held up a crystal goblet. "You drink a cup, and pour a cup on the portal."

I almost dropped the bottle. "Drink? Why would I drink?"

"I don't know why. I only know the spell won't work unless you do."

I eyed the indigo bottle suspiciously. "What will it do to me?"

"Troll magic affects everyone differently."

Chapter Forty-one

FORTUNATELY FOR FEY FOLK, TROLLS MOST OFTEN KEEP THEIR MAGIC TO THEMSELVES. BUT EVERY NOW AND THEN, TROLL MAGIC ENTERS FEYLAND.

TROLL MAGIC, LIKE TROLLS THEMSELVES, IS DANGEROUSLY UNPREDICTABLE. EVIDENTLY, TROLLS CAN EASILY ADAPT THEIR SPELLS TO CLING TO OBJECTS. THEIR MAGIC ALSO HAS AN AFFINITY FOR LIQUID, MAKING IT WELL SUITED TO ENCHANTMENTS THAT ARE DISSOLVED INTO BEVERAGES.

SOMETIMES THE EFFECTS OF TROLL MAGIC ARE FLEETING, SOMETIMES THEY ARE LASTING, BUT ALWAYS THE EFFECTS OF TROLL MAGIC ARE POWERFUL.

—Orville Gold, genie historian of Feyland

I didn't want any part of drinking something from Troll Country. Their magic was too different from that of fey folk. I had no confidence that my new spell of protection would apply to harmful troll enchantments.

"I hope sealing this portal is worth doing," I said. "I'd rather go after Leona and try to get her out."

"Out of the Iron Lands?" Meteor lifted his white eyebrows. "You'd have better luck rescuing her from a tribe of trolls. Without your magic, what could you do?"

My voice rose. "You want her to rot in the Leprechaun Colony?"

"No." He put out a hand. "Give me the bottle. I'll open it, you'll seal the portal, and once it's closed, nothing can be proven against Doreen Bloodstone. We'll be helping Leona that way."

"Fine." I handed him the indigo bottle. "I'll do it for Leona."

When Meteor opened the bottle, the lid exploded into little pieces. He staggered back. The elixir overflowed, fizzing into tiny bubbles that ran down the sides of the bottle.

Meteor regained his balance and poured foamy elixir into the goblet.

"What if it turns me into a trog?" I asked.

"I'll watch you," Meteor said. "I'll stay with you until the effects wear off."

I took the full goblet from his hand. "Don't let me do anything troggish."

"I won't."

I raised it to my lips. The elixir fizzed down my throat, making me cough. I stood waiting a few moments to see what would happen. At first I didn't notice anything, but then I felt a sensation in my feet, as if something heavy had been pumped into them. They seemed to weigh twice as much as usual, while my head felt like a large soap bubble, ready to float away. It was a very unpleasant feeling, and yet I wanted to laugh.

"Zaria?" Meteor sounded so solemn! "Hold out the goblet, so I can fill it again."

I did.

"Pour it on the boulder, then speak the spell," he told me. *"Chantmentum sealerum resvera."*

I felt clumsy. It took more effort than it should have to hold the full goblet in one hand and my wand in the other. As I tried to keep them steady, Meteor reached out and took back the goblet.

"Wait," he said. "We should go through to the other side of the portal. If we seal it from this side, you'll be stuck."

"Stuck?" I said, and giggled uncomfortably. My feet felt even heavier.

"There are no other portals in Galena, and the Gateway is enchanted with snares," he went on. "They were looking for Leona, which means they're also looking for you. You said you want to try to rescue Leona, but you can't do it from Galena."

He was right. I didn't want to test my protection spell on the Gateway. Who knew what devious enchantments the Council or the Radia Guard might have laid down?

For no reason at all, I snickered. It must have been the troll magic.

Slipping the bottle of elixir into a pocket of his robe, Meteor grabbed my hand. I found it hilarious that his palm was bigger than my whole hand. Not only that, but the careful way he moved looked completely ridiculous. He was only trying to keep from spilling the open bottle inside his robe or the full goblet in his other hand, but to me it all seemed funny.

I was laughing out loud when he pulled me through the portal.

Something hit my wrist, knocking my wand out of my hand. I stumbled, spinning sideways, as an object struck my wing. Unable to gain my balance, I fell awkwardly on the ground of Earth.

"*Ooph,*" I cried, spitting out a dry stalk of grass.

A squat shape hurtled at me, slamming me between the eyes. Whatever it was, it was squishy and bounced away again as if alive.

"No," I gasped. "Meteor, it's—"

A toad.

This time the toad flung itself right at my mouth, slamming into my lips. Ugh! I tried to grab its leg but it leaped out of reach. It snatched my stylus from the ground with its mouth before hopping away in the moonlight.

"Catch it!" I wailed, scrambling to get up. "Meteor, that toad has my wand." I reeled forward and then tripped. My wings caught me, but not very well. I flew crookedly, my feet not quite leaving the ground. Blast that troll elixir! It wouldn't let me fly.

Meteor turned in circles, holding up the full goblet, looking for a safe place to set it down.

"Oberon's Crown, Meteor. Get the toad!"

He hesitated. I swooped toward him clumsily. I planned to hold the goblet for him, but I bumped into him instead, and knocked the brimming goblet from his hand. Though we both tried to catch it, it fell, spilling the elixir.

"Sorry!" I cried. "But that toad's a human in disguise. A human with a grudge."

"*You* turned a human into a *toad*?"

"It wasn't me. He got into a fight with Leona."

Meteor drew his wand. *"Leona?"*

He was scowling so hard, his eyebrows overlapped at the bridge of his nose. The sight was too much for me, and I lost myself in laughter. I tried to stop, tried to follow the path of the toad as it hopped below us toward the grove of trees—covering quite a bit of ground very fast—but I couldn't help myself. Spluttering and gasping, it was all I could do not to fall over.

Throwing me a pitying look, Meteor rushed after the toad, leaving me to catch my breath and settle my wings. The bright moon showed his flight, but the toad, with my wand, seemed to have vanished.

Meteor floated back and forth over the tussocks of grass and the hollows in the hillside. I flapped toward him, still unable to get off the ground.

"We'll never find him without magic," I called.

"The quickest way would be to release him from Leona's spell," Meteor answered. He pointed his wand at the ground. *"Chantmentum pellex,"* he said.

Jason Court appeared in the grass, crouching with my wand in his mouth. Jumping up, he held the wand in both hands as if he would snap it in two.

"I know what this is!" he shouted. "You called it a wand."

How small and fragile the stylus looked in his hands. I wasn't laughing anymore.

"Obliv trau," Meteor said.

Jason fell, sound asleep.

I flapped over to him, fell at his side, and pried my wand from his grasp. It was a little slimy; I wiped it on my gown.

Staggering up, I rapped Meteor's head. *"Verita sil nos mertos elemen."* He disappeared and I repeated the invisibility on myself.

"Thank you," Meteor said. "I forgot it would be easy to spy on us with scopes, now that we're on Earth."

That's when I realized this was Meteor's first trip through a portal!

"How do you like Earth?" I swept my arm in a gesture meant to be grand, before remembering he couldn't see me.

"I would probably like it better if I weren't chasing down toads and watching over fairies full of troll magic." I thought I heard a chuckle in his voice.

Jason Court chose that moment to groan in his sleep. "What'll we do with *him*?" I asked.

"A forgetting spell," Meteor said. "That way he can wake up and remember nothing of us—or of Leona."

For a moment, I was tempted to turn Jason back into a toad. It didn't seem fair to let him completely forget. He was such a horrible human—exactly the type Beryl was always warning me about. In only a few days, he had stolen two fey wands and badly injured Leona and her mother. Who knew what other nefarious schemes he was plotting?

"You know I'm right," Meteor said.

"Yes," I answered grudgingly. It was true that a forgetting spell would solve the problem of Jason. "I'll do it," I said. "I know everything that he needs to forget. Tell me the spell."

"*Obleth nor vis elemen.* Level Thirty. Focus on removing every memory of Leona or you or me."

Or the portal, I thought.

"*Obleth* what?"

He repeated it twice.

My wand didn't cooperate when I infused it; the seam of light wavered and danced. I hoped the troll magic in the elixir would wear off soon. At last I succeeded in holding the infusion steady. Pointing at Jason, I spoke the forgetting spell and focused on every memory connected to me—or Leona, Doreen, Meteor, the portal, wands, wings, exploding houses . . .

Jason's body relaxed and his face grew peaceful.

I pointed my wand at him again. "*Transera nos,*" I said, visualizing his backyard. The night was only slightly chilly; he would be all right. "I sent him home," I told Meteor. I saw no reason to let Jason wake up on this beautiful quiet land. I didn't want him to remember this place even existed.

"Let's go seal the portal," Meteor said, and I heard him swish past me on his powerful magic feet.

With Meteor out of earshot, I decided to take the opportunity to perform another spell—this time to keep others from touching my wand. In the past hour, it had been seized by a genie and a toad! So much for the wonderful protection I had cast earlier that evening.

I concentrated carefully as I infused again. "No one and nothing but myself may touch this wand unless I allow it," I said. *"Ad eternum."*

There! That should do it. *Now* I could seal the portal.

I tried to get aloft but couldn't. And what I saw next surprised me so much that my wings gave out completely.

Chapter Forty-two

HUMANS WHO POSSESS ENOUGH MAGIC TO TRAVEL
THROUGH PORTALS SOMETIMES FIND THEIR WAY INTO
FEYLAND. WHEN THEY DO, THEY CARRY TALES TO
EARTH, TALES OF UNIMAGINABLE RICHES. THEY SPEAK
OF THE CITIES OF GOLD, THE FOUNTAIN OF YOUTH,
THE SHANGRI-LA. THOSE WHO GET A GLIMPSE OF
FEYLAND WILL SPEND THE REST OF THEIR LIVES
TRYING TO FIND IT AGAIN UNLESS PLACED UNDER A
FORGETTING SPELL.

—*Orville Gold, genie historian of Feyland*

Someone was walking through the wild grass toward the sandstone boulder—a human someone with a quick stride and a head of unruly curls. Moonlight darkened his hair, but I knew him anyway.

Sam.

He could be here at this hour of night for only one purpose: to see me. Our conversation about his father had been interrupted. He must have questions.

But the timing was all wrong. I was about to do an important spell to seal the portal. And Meteor was here.

Meteor must not find out about my friendship with a human! He'd never understand.

Desperate to catch up to Sam, I moved in hopping leaps, more like a toad than a fairy. Sam stopped when he got to the boulder, and I reached it seconds later. As he stood there contemplating the rock leading to another world, he didn't know he was being watched, not only by me but also by a tall dark-faced genie with white eyebrows.

"Zaria?" Sam said. "Are you here?"

Trolls and pixies, did he have to use my name in front of Meteor? Should I answer him or wait for him to go away?

Then Sam put his hand into the boulder.

"Wow," he murmured. "Wow." He stepped through the portal!

I darted after him only to smack into Meteor. We had both dived for the portal at the same instant. When we crashed into each other, we fell through the portal into Feyland. I heard the glug of liquid running out of a bottle, and Meteor's startled yell.

Just then our invisibility ran out. I saw Meteor jump up. He brought out the elixir bottle, fizzing and dripping. He shook the bottle gently, and a feeble sloshing sound reached my ears. The bottle was almost empty.

Dragging myself upright, I confronted Meteor's frown.

"That human knew your name," he said quietly.

I had no answer to give.

Peering anxiously ahead, I could see Sam's outline on the

rock overlooking Galena Falls. My wings opened up and carried me over to him, but not very gracefully. My toes still scraped along the ground.

As I stood beside him, Sam turned slowly to look at me, and then turned back to stare over the waterfall. Starlight splashed down the falls and glimmered on the gemstones lining the pool below.

"I dreamed my dad had amnesia but you gave him back his memory," he said. "What a dream. And I'm still in it."

"You're not dreaming. It's true, all of it." He looked so sad that I stepped close to him and put my arms around him. "Your father's alive. You'll see him again."

When Sam hugged me back, I lost my balance and slipped off the rock.

My wings unfurled, but they didn't slow us down very much. Arms wrapped around each other, surrounded by the soft roar of the falls, Sam and I plunged through the spray.

When we hit the water, Sam let go of me. My wings kept me afloat but he sank beneath the surface.

Only for a moment. Then his head burst out of the pool. He laughed aloud, spinning in the water, stirring a circle of spray. I laughed, too, our laughter mingling like mist.

Sam started swimming toward the sloping sand with long strokes. He waded out, then looked around with a dazzled expression. My dripping wings slowed me, and my feet felt like boulders, but I made it to the bank and struggled up beside him.

"We have to get you back to Earth," I said. "Now."

"Back to Earth." He sounded awed.

"This way. Follow me."

His shoes squelched as I led him along the path made for children too young to fly. Shallow steps were carved into the rock; it should have been an easy climb but I kept tripping.

Sam didn't miss a single step. A couple of times, he caught me when I was about to fall.

"Here's the way home," I whispered when we got to the portal.

Sam's wet hair clung to his head. His eyes shone.

I heard a rush of air, and Meteor wedged himself between us. He shoved Sam through the portal.

"Meteor!"

"No time, Zaree." He gestured upward.

Dazed, I saw a cloud of moving lights in the sky. Fey searchlights, roaming purposefully. I wasted no time drawing my wand.

I cast invisibility on Meteor first, and then myself an instant later. We hurried through the portal. Sam stood a few paces away, staring at the boulder.

"*Obliv trau,*" said Meteor, and Sam sank to the ground, fast asleep.

"Send him home, Zaria," Meteor ordered. "Whatever he means to you, he cannot stay here now."

I knelt beside Sam. *"Transera nos,"* I whispered, visualizing his bedroom.

As soon as he was gone, I asked Meteor if we had enough elixir left to seal the portal.

"I don't know," he answered. "If not, we have no time to find more. Do you remember the spell to seal it?"

"Tell me again."

He told me, and I felt the sticky elixir bottle pressed into my hands. I splattered the dregs over the sandstone boulder. Throwing down the bottle, I infused my wand to 75.

"Chantmentum sealerum resvera," I said loudly. Then under my breath I muttered, "Seal this portal. *Ad eternum.*"

If Meteor noticed that I'd echoed the spell with normal words, he said nothing about it. I heard him knocking on the boulder. "Sealed," he said.

Sealed. Just like that. Forever and always.

"The searchers in Galena . . . ," I said breathlessly.

". . . Won't find any portal," Meteor answered. "It's a wonder you sealed it in time."

I was afraid he would bring up Sam, but he didn't.

"Will you go with me into Oberon City?" I asked.

Meteor's hand found mine. "Of course. I promised to stay with you."

Chapter Forty-three

LAYERED MAGIC IS AN INSIDIOUS FORM AND REQUIRES LARGE AMOUNTS OF RADIA TO PRODUCE. SPELLS ARE CAST ON TOP OF EACH OTHER; EACH ONE LEADS TO THE NEXT. CUES ARE EMBEDDED, TO SET OFF EACH LAYER. CUES MAY BE DIRECTED AT ONE PARTICULAR INDIVIDUAL OR THEY MAY BE DIRECTED TO ANYONE WHO HAPPENS TO ENTER THE VICINITY OF THE SPELL.

—*Orville Gold, genie historian of Feyland*

From the hillside, I transported both Meteor and myself to the cornfield portal. But before we went through to the Golden Station, he insisted on doing a protection spell against layered magic for me.

"Fendus altus prehenden nos elemen."

"Thank you," I said, though I doubted I needed it. My own spells had been effective against layered magic so far. "I wish you could help me throw off the troll elixir." I gave an experimental hop. "I can jump a little higher, but I still can't fly."

Meteor was quiet for a moment. "We need a plan," he said. "We have to find a place to think about what to do next.

But as long as we stay on Earth, we'll have to keep doing invisibility spells to stay out of sight of the scopes. Let's go into Feyland."

He astonished me by asking if we could hold hands through the Golden Station, a place he'd never been. "We don't want to lose each other."

I was very glad of Meteor's hand. The Golden Station was a scene of chaos, more so than I had ever seen it. The noise was deafening. Fairies and genies were crammed in so densely that even if I had been able to fly, we couldn't have gotten through them. All of them seemed to be yelling and screaming, but I couldn't hear what they were saying because their words were lost in one continuous roar. The floor space was crawling with gnomes.

"Hang on!" I shouted into Meteor's ear. I transported us both to the first familiar place I thought of: the courtyard of the FOOM dome.

More chaos. Dozens of searchlights, some positioned on the ground and others beaming from domes and towers, flooded the air. Fairies and genies zoomed back and forth in a formless swarm. A voice, amplified by magic, boomed out:

"All fey folk are called upon to find Zaria Tourmaline, a purple-winged fairy who carries a plain black stylus wand. Reward: ten thousand radia delivered tip to tip. If you find her, notify a Council member. She has committed high crimes against Feyland. All fey folk are called upon to find . . ."

"This—for me?" I murmured, appalled. High crimes? A reward—to be paid in *radia*?

I was horrified to see Meteor become visible. In the flicker of an instant, I recast the spell, renewing invisibility for us both.

Meteor's voice rumbled in my ear. "Put your hands on my shoulders."

The announcement kept blasting the air over and over as I locked my arms around Meteor's neck. He flew straight up, dodging hundreds of searching fey folk while I clung to him and tried not to look down. When he had a clearer flight path, he headed out of the center of the city. He kept moving until the crowds thinned and then dwindled to nothing.

In a silent neighborhood, he landed on an empty balcony in a dilapidated tower. I slid from his back onto a ledge. He settled next to me, and I leaned against his shoulder. We sat, breathing hard.

A dim fey globe shone above us. The balcony had once been polished granite, but now it was notched and cracked, covered with dust and dirt. My wet skirt would soak up the grime, but what did it matter? Far worse things had happened.

"Thank you for rescuing my wand from the toad, and helping with the portal," I said when I got my breath. *And for not despising me for being friends with a human,* I wanted to say.

"Thank you for trusting me again," Meteor answered, just as his invisibility lapsed. He looked worried and tired, his eyes like submerged emeralds worn down by many waves.

"Let's stay visible," I said. "No one will look for us here."

He nodded. "Zaria, you know you have to put a forgetting spell on the human who went into Feyland."

I shrank from him. "But . . . he'd never harm us."

"For *his* sake," Meteor answered. "He'll never get over seeing Feyland."

I remembered the awe and delight in Sam's face. "You're right," I said, desperately wishing to change the subject.

Fortunately, there was plenty to talk about. "I've never heard of the Council offering a radia reward," I muttered. "I've broken laws. But what have I done against *Feyland*? Why would they denounce me to everyone?"

"You're Violet," Metoer said hoarsely. "You're Leona's friend. Obviously, Lily Morganite does *not* want you to be free."

I gazed at the crumbling balcony. "Maybe we could find Leona's wand and take it back. Then, once we get her out of the Iron Lands, we could give it to her."

Meteor frowned. "Even if we knew where it was, even if we were invisible, we would never get past all the gnomes guarding it."

Ideas spun through my weary mind. "Maybe we could *bribe* the gnomes."

"Bribe them?" Meteor got a strange expression on his face. Earlier, it would have made me laugh, but not now. The troll elixir must be wearing off a little. I swung my feet against the edge of the balcony. They still felt heavy.

"What do gnomes love best?" I asked.

Meteor put his arms around his knees. "They don't love anything," he said. He rested his head on his arms, looking exhausted.

I went back to staring at the balcony and thought for a while. "How do you reverse layered magic?" I asked.

Meteor raised his head. When he spoke, he sounded like he was reading from a book. "There are two spells. One reveals the layers. The other banishes them. To reveal takes Level Forty magic and a minimum of one hundred radia. You have to be close enough to touch a subject with your wand. The spell is *'Extred rev dolehr.'* It reveals the enchantment, and who put it there." He shuddered. "To banish layered magic, you say, *'Banjan ex lomel.'* It takes the same level and the same amount of radia."

It had cost Meteor two hundred radia to become my friend again!

"Layered enchantments are rare, my mentor said, because they use so many radia," he continued. "And Zaria, those who try to use *chantmentum pellex* to reverse a layered spell find that the layers have landed on them, too."

"She wants you in her clutches," Beryl had said. I remembered Beryl's terror when I had offered to reverse the spells on her. She must have been trying to protect me.

I folded my wings close and took a deep breath. "Meteor, will you do something for me?"

"Besides sit on an old balcony waiting until you can fly again?" He gave me a wry smile.

"Will you go back to Galena and reverse the layers on Beryl?"

"Galena? But I promised to stay with you until—"

"Please. It's important. I don't want Beryl to suffer any longer, but you'll be much safer without me: I can't fly, and everyone's looking for me. Besides, once Beryl's free, she might help us. She might know something about the Iron Lands. She might even know what gnomes love best."

He looked doubtful. "What if someone finds you here?"

I waved at the deserted towers. "If someone comes looking for me, I'll become invisible. Please, Meteor. I'll give you five hundred radia if you go."

He scowled at me.

"I owe you at least that much—although you'll have to teach me how a transfer is done."

"You owe me nothing," he said. "I'll go."

"Don't be angry." I touched his arm.

"I'm not angry," he said, but his eyebrows met at the bridge of his nose. He floated up.

"What's wrong?" I rose, too.

"Nothing's wrong."

I flipped open my watch face. Almost three in the morning. "When you come back, I might have a plan," I said a little hesitantly. Maybe he wouldn't like to return. Maybe he'd had enough of me.

"You sure you want me to come back?" The scowl left his face.

"Of course. I'll wait for you."

Meteor nodded. He gave my shoulder a quick squeeze, then flew away with his usual silent power.

Leaving me alone.

Chapter Forty-four

"ANY FAIRY, GENIE, OR LEPRECHAUN WHO IS SEEN BY
A HUMAN MUST INSTANTLY CAST A FORGETTING SPELL
UPON THAT HUMAN. THE SPELL SHALL SPECIFY THAT
THE HUMAN IN QUESTION WILL FORGET SEEING THE
FEY PERSONAGE."

—*excerpt from the Edict of the Unseen*

Time seemed to be rushing away from me like sand from a broken hourglass.

I was so tired, yet terribly restless. I wanted to *do* something, but what? My thoughts bounced between Leona and Sam.

Meteor's words beat at my heart: "*. . . put a forgetting spell on the human who went into Feyland.*"

Unfair! If Sam had been a genie, we could have had many meetings in the skies over Oberon City, exploring Feyland together. No one would have thought it was wrong.

But Sam was not a genie. Sam would never fly. His Level 5 magic, high for a human, would mean little in Feyland.

And I, Earth-struck though I was, could never live in Sam's world for even a day. My wings alone would proclaim me an outsider, a permanent stranger with no chance of belonging.

Meteor was right. When Sam woke, he must not remember where he had been. And if I was going to make him forget me, I might as well do it now, while my resolve was strong.

I had told Meteor I would wait for him, but just then it seemed that anything would be better than sitting there alone with no idea how long it would take him to come back.

I stood on the grimy balcony and made myself invisible again. I transported into the small viewing station where I had located Michael Seabolt.

In less than a blink I found myself in the lap of a startled genie who jumped as if a swarm of beetles had landed on him. I turned to see a white face, black eyes, and gaudy pink hair. His mouth opened so wide I could have fit my head inside it, but before he could let out a yell, I infused my wand.

"Sleep," I commanded, and he immediately slumped forward. Unfortunately, he wedged me between his chest and the scope. I squirmed until I could reach the lever and bring the eyepiece in range. Just as I managed to put my forehead against the fitting, I heard heavy pounding on the booth's door.

"Oberon's Crown," I muttered, craning my neck to see another group of fairies and genies writhing in a knot outside the viewing booth.

Had someone announced that I'd visited this place

earlier? Were all these fey folk crowding the door in hopes of catching me on Earth, and getting the reward for my capture?

A short round genie had his orange nose squished against the glass and he banged the door with a pudgy fist.

"Let me in," he shouted.

Ignoring them all as best I could, I looked through the scope and asked for Sam. The scope showed him asleep in a soft pool of light from the streetlamp outside. His hair looked like a banked fire against the pillow.

The yelling and pounding on the door accelerated.

I had forgotten the exact words of the formal forgetting spell. I would have to use one of my own. Infusing, I poked the tip of my wand into the sending port. "Forget me," I said. "Forget me, and Leona, and Meteor. Forget the portal and Feyland. Forget everything about us." I hesitated and then added. "*Ad eternum*. Forever and always."

There. It was done.

With a loud crack the door to the booth burst open. I didn't have time to see if Sam's face changed when the spell took hold. Disentangling myself from the sleeping genie, I ducked under the scope and dodged against the wall.

"*Transera nos,*" I said, and pictured the lonely, decrepit balcony.

What would my parents say if they could see me now? Bedraggled and exhausted on the edge of a seedy balcony in a filthy and wrinkled gown, hunted for a reward of ten thousand radia. A Violet, unable to fly, a sad, Earth-struck fairy whose best friend was locked away in the Iron Lands.

Waiting for Meteor, I kept testing my wings. I still couldn't fly, but my leaps were gradually getting higher. Maybe the troll elixir would turn me into a leprechaun.

Thinking of leprechauns made me think of the genie Laz. And thinking of Laz gave me an idea.

Chapter Forty-five

THE CODE OF THE FEY ENJOINS FEY FOLK TO BE KIND
AND CAREFUL OF ONE ANOTHER. GREAT CARE IS TAKEN
TO PREVENT INJURY. THIS IS TRUE OF FAIRIES, GENIES,
AND LEPRECHAUNS, AND ALSO EXTENDS TO GNOMES.

—*Orville Gold, genie historian of Feyland*

I pictured the sign for The Ugly Mug and transported to it.

The sign still hung in ramshackle glory outside the one-story building beside the wall of the Leprechaun Colony. I didn't want to be there, especially in the wee hours, but I figured that if anyone could tell me how to get into the Iron Lands—and out again with Leona—it would be Banburus Lazuli.

I hoped to find him inside.

Sounds of hooting laughter and banging drums leaked from The Ugly Mug into the night. I watched the tarnished door, and when a fairy bounced out I used the opportunity to slip past her.

The place was lit with plentiful candles; apparently no one here wanted to spend even minimal radia on fey globes. Flickering flames showed a room even longer than I remembered, cluttered with tables overflowing with raucous genies and loudmouthed leprechauns drinking from steaming mugs. Shrill giggles of fairies mingled with the rumble of male laughter while the rich, heady aroma I remembered from before hung in the air.

I tried to flatten myself against the wall, which seemed to be the only unoccupied space. At the far end of the room, a band of leprechauns played fiddles and drums, their music adding a throbbing wail to the rest of the noise.

I strained to see. It took several minutes to locate Laz, at a table in the corner near the musicians. He sat with his long legs tucked under a chair, dealing cards to a motley group.

Beryl had warned me repeatedly about Earth cards. They were used for gambling, she said, and gambling led to ruin as surely as ingesting coffee and chocolate, according to Beryl.

I moved along the wall. It wasn't possible to keep from bumping a number of rowdy patrons. If someone had been watching for traces of an invisible fairy, my trail would probably have been obvious. But everyone seemed to be completely caught up in the conversations they were having, and so I continued unnoticed until I stood behind Laz's gray-blue head.

The other players around the heavy brass table were studying their cards with intent expressions. Infusing my wand, I pointed at the table. "This game is finished," I said very softly.

The table tipped. A dozen mugs slid across its top, dumping into the laps of the genies on one side. The table itself quickly followed the drinks, crashing to the floor, pinning a few of the players while the others threw down their cards and jumped up.

"Why'd'ja do that?" asked a short genie with bumpy skin. He bopped a hairless genie next to him with a fist.

"Wasn't me, you trog," the hairless one shouted, punching back.

Soon a brawl had taken the place of the card game, but Laz kept aloof from the fray. His murky eyes slid from side to side as he backed through a curtain behind the toppled table.

I followed him. "Speak privately?" I said in his ear.

Laz wasn't startled at being spoken to by an invisible fairy. He turned and led the way behind the stage. I followed him through a tarnished silver door into a small room packed with crates. The lock snicked as he closed the door, which shut out most of the noise, though I could still hear the drums booming in the background.

When my invisibility expired, Laz showed no surprise. "Well, well," he said. "To what do I owe the honor of this visit?"

I wondered what his age was. His blue-black skin was smooth except for two grooves that bracketed his mouth, but his eyes seemed very old.

"Do you live here?" I blurted out, knowing instantly it was a silly thing to say.

He shrugged calmly. "I own the place, so yes, I'm here most often. And you? Why are *you* here?"

"I need your help."

"You need more help than I can give you." Laz's delicate cough sounded mocking. "You fit the description of the one all Feyland is out looking for."

"*You're* not out looking for me." I gripped my puny wand, feeling uneasy.

He snorted. "Only because I've been a gambler long enough to know when my odds are bad." His arm shot out. He grabbed my wrist. "Have you now, though, don't I?"

The wrist he'd chosen belonged to the hand holding my wand. His grip was like steel. He pressed so hard, my fingers let go and my wand clattered to the floor.

Laz chuckled. "Haven't altered your wand yet, I see." Still clamping my wrist, he bent to pick up my stylus.

A roaring hum filled the air, and Laz fell backward against the door. Yelping, he let go of me. I scooped up my wand and waved it wildly.

"Powerful protection," he muttered, rubbing his ears. "Stupid of me. I shouldn't have touched your wand."

"You shouldn't have touched me, either." I was happy that my spell had worked, but angry at the genie.

He clicked his tongue. "Now you know the importance of protecting yourself not only against enchantments but also against what humans call 'brute force.'"

"Why would you try to capture me?" I snapped.

"Nothing personal, but ten thousand radia is quite a reward. Most of the gambling pots in this fine establishment don't amount to more than a few degrees of Red."

"You gamble for twenty radia?"

He shrugged. "We're not all as lucky as you. If rumors are real, you're not just a pretty little thing—you're also a Violet fairy, quite rich in reserves. I hear you fixed a broken-down viewing station by *donating* a bundle of radia."

"You know about that?" I wanted to take the words back as soon as they were out.

He chuckled again. "Sooner or later, I hear about everything that happens in Feyland."

"Please don't tell anyone I'm here." I held my wand higher.

"Don't worry, Zaria Tourmaline," he said. "I've regained my senses. I know where to place my bets, and they're on you." He combed his fingers through his stringy hair. "Now what is it you need?"

I watched him warily. "I need to get into the Iron Lands and bring my friend out."

He threw back his head and laughed. He made quite a show of blowing his nose and mopping his brow. Fuming, I waited until he quit sniggering.

"Friend?" he said. "Is that *friend* the other Violet fairy who was captured earlier tonight?"

Evidently he *did* hear about everything that happened in Feyland. "Do you know where she is?" I asked.

His bleary eyes opened a fraction more than normal. "You want to rescue Leona Bloodstone from the Iron Lands? That's a tall order," he said. "A very tall order. The question is, what's it worth to you? Because it's going to cost you." His eyes darted back and forth. "One hundred thousand radia, to be exact."

I gasped. "What!" One hundred thousand was a full degree of Blue!

"Let me explain." Laz sat on a crate. "Living as I do carries high costs. Half my merchandise is lost to bribes, and the Forcier keeps raising my radia tax. I could use a sizable infusion. Besides, it's a reasonable asking price. If I'm caught aiding you, I risk going to the Iron Lands myself on a *permanent* basis."

Drumbeats shook the room so hard I felt like a bug in a can. "Have you been to the Colony before?" I asked. "Do you *know* you can help me?"

"Been there many times on business. As to whether I *know* I can help you, I don't. But I'm your best bet." He flipped his wand in an arc and then caught it. "So? Do you accept my offer?"

I felt horribly tired. I knew this sleazy genie was taking advantage of my love for my friend. But if we could rescue Leona, it would be well worth paying what he asked. "All right," I said. "Once we're safely out of the

Iron Lands, I'll pay you one hundred thousand radia."

"No, no, my fine fairy. That's not how it's done. Half now, and the rest when we come back."

I glared at him, weighing the risks. Fifty thousand radia was probably more than he'd ever seen at one time. Once he had it, maybe he would decide it wasn't worth endangering himself to help me. How did I know I could trust him?

Beryl had. And Beryl always said she could smell a liar from one hundred wingspans.

"I've never transferred radia before," I said.

Laz grinned. "I can teach you."

Chapter Forty-six

THE TRANSFER OF RADIA IS THE PREFERRED CURRENCY
OF SMUGGLERS.

—*Orville Gold, genie historian of Feyland*

*P*aying Laz was much like putting radia into the durable-spell port at the viewing station. When we were done, he was fifty thousand radia richer, and I was eager to enter the Iron Lands.

Laz told me to wait while he assembled the supplies we would need. I sat tiredly on one of the crates and wondered whether the walls to this room were made of aluminum. They vibrated with every beat of the drums.

I peeked at the radia hand on my crystal watch. It had moved again. It pointed to a spot about two-tenths of the way toward the first notch within Violet. I was down about two hundred thousand radia from where I had begun.

I wasn't surprised. Since I had last checked, I had not only sealed a portal, but I had performed several transports, a good many invisibility spells, a memory spell for Michael Seabolt, and a forgetting spell for his son.

I had also placed enduring spells of protection on myself

and my wand, as well as on the ground beneath the spruce tree on Earth. At least I would never have to do those spells again. I could slow down and conserve the radia I had left.

Laz came back wearing a long cloak with a hood. Thick gloves covered his hands and extended up to his elbows. He carried another cloak, which he threw over me.

That cloak was so heavy, it felt as if several tons of rock had been pressed into its fabric. It was crushing my wings! Immediately, I tried to throw it off.

I may as well have tried to get out from under a slag heap.

I grabbed desperately for my wand, but even though my fingers found it, no magic flowed. The pressure on my wings seemed to be increasing.

"Resvera den." I spoke the breaking spell, hoping to tear the cloak apart.

The spell didn't work.

"What have you done?" I tried to cry out, but my voice was terribly faint.

"Sorry," said Laz, his tone brisk. "The reward for locating you has been raised to fifty thousand radia. By turning you in, I'll get another fortune without any risk."

"You lied to me." All I could manage was a whisper.

Laz shrugged. "Just business."

He moved in. He obviously expected no resistance from me as he fastened a button at my throat. I tried to punch him, but my arms and legs were growing heavier by the second. Laz belted the cloak, strapping my wings and arms against my body. He fastened the belt with a tight buckle.

"Please," I whispered. "Take it off. It's killing me."

"You won't die. You're wanted alive." He opened the door. "I won that cloak at a card game from a leprechaun very much down on his luck. He was a prince before the Lep Edict, and that cloak was handed down in his family from the time of the Troll Wars. It's made with a rare blend of troll magic."

Troll magic? Not again! I hadn't even recovered from the elixir.

Laz sighed. "While you wear that cloak, Zaria, all your magic is extinguished."

Extinguished? I was finding it hard to breathe.

"There is a small consolation," he went on. "No enchantments can land on you, either." He went through the door and then leaned his head back in. "A word of advice: don't fight it. Accept that you have less power than a Level One Red."

The lock clicked behind him.

I took one shuddering step and collapsed. I lay on my side. When I tried to get up, heavy spikes of pain nailed me to the floor.

Abruptly, the stomping beat of the drums died. I heard protesting shouts, and then Laz's voice raised above the rest. "Clear out! Council members on their way."

Howls and running feet and banging doors answered him.

• • •

I discovered that if I didn't move at all, the pressure from the cloak stopped intensifying. Was this what Laz had meant about accepting it?

By the time he opened the door again, I cared for nothing except the importance of keeping still.

Laz stepped aside for Lily Morganite. Opals glittered in her hair. Strands of pearls hung over the neckline of her soft pink gown, and the scent of lilies drifted around her.

I coughed, setting off a grinding wave of pressure.

"There," said Laz. "The one you're looking for."

Lily gazed down at me. No doubt I was a satisfying sight: bound and powerless, weary, grief-stricken, and afraid. I tried to look defiant but probably looked more pathetic than brave.

"It did not have to be this way, Zaria," Lily said. "You have made some very unfortunate choices."

I didn't try to answer. Even if my voice had been working, what could I say?

"Did you get her wand?" Lily asked Laz.

"Tried. Couldn't," he grumbled. "It attacked me. But under that cloak, it's useless to her."

Lily narrowed her pearly eyes.

Laz shuffled his feet. "I don't care about the bonus. I've had enough trouble just capturing her."

A bonus for turning over my wand?

"In what way did the wand attack you?" Lily asked.

Laz tapped both ears with his long fingers. "A sound. Thought my ears would break."

She looked sharply at me and frowned. Avoiding her gaze, I focused on Laz's shabby boots.

Out of the corner of my eye, I saw Lily crook a finger at a band of gnomes crowding the doorway. They began marching in. They wore helmets and armored plates over their chests. Clubs hung from their belts, hard black clubs that looked as if they'd been formed from iron.

Could I be seeing straight? Could gnomes be carrying iron clubs?

"Wait," Laz said to Lily. "You owe me fifty thousand radia. Before you take her, pay what you owe."

She put a hand to her heart. "Really, Mr. Lazuli, your greed is shameful. What about doing your part for Feyland?"

Laz thrust out his chin. "Don't try to get out of this."

She waved a graceful hand. "You will receive your reward in due time. I cannot arrange payment this very minute."

The genie drew his wand. "You think I don't know how much radia you carry? You're the Forcier! How many times have you taken a tax transfer from *me*?"

Laz's words acted like a spell on my mind, a spell of sudden understanding. In that moment, a dozen clues about Lily fell into place, and as they did I wondered how I could have missed them before.

I had distrusted her, yes. I'd felt bewildered and angry,

overwhelmed, sad, afraid. I had wished I could take away her power. But all those feelings had only distracted me from the truth.

Now I saw.

No wonder she didn't worry about using radia. No wonder she had offered to do the spell of disclosure on my wand herself without help from Zircon or Wolframite. Twice she had done that spell, without hesitation—and then a third time the following day for a total of 150 radia. She'd also performed one to search me and my home. Expensive enchantments, but she had done them casually.

How smug and disdainful she had been as she lectured me on wasting radia—and then used her own stores whenever it suited her.

I thought of Seth, the attendant from the viewing station near the Malachite Towers. His words echoed painfully in my thoughts: *". . . gave us an infusion of fifty radia. The scopes didn't improve one jot."* Of course the viewing station in the Malachite Towers had shown no improvement after a visit from *"that high and mighty Morganite."*

She had given nothing.

For ten years, Lily Morganite had been entrusted with the duty of collecting radia taxes and caring for the durable spells. What if, instead of doing what she was supposed to do, she had been accumulating radia for herself?

"Layered enchantments are rare, my mentor said, because they use so many radia," Meteor had told me.

But Lily had strewn layered spells all over my home. Obviously, she had plenty of radia to spare.

And now that I was finally beginning to see the truth about her, I lay trussed inside a cloak that extinguished my magic. I had no way to fight.

Chapter Forty-seven

GNOMES ARE KNOWN TO BE DRAB AND UNINTERESTING.
HOWEVER, THEY HAVE REDEEMING QUALITIES. NOT
ONLY ARE THEY HARD WORKERS, BUT THEY ARE ALSO
INCAPABLE OF LYING. THEIR WORD, ONCE GIVEN, IS
ALWAYS HONORED.

—*Orville Gold, genie historian of Feyland*

I wanted to signal Laz somehow. He had betrayed me
for radia, but he was my only hope. He might be a mercenary,
but I doubted he knew that Lily could be completely *diabolical*.
If he would just get me out of this cloak, maybe together we
could escape.

But the instant I tried to lift my head from the floor, the
cloak got heavier, pressing down so hard I could barely breathe.

I looked up at Lily berating Laz. "How dare you draw
your wand?" she said.

"It's to receive my reward!" He looked nervously at the
crowd of gnomes. "Where are the other councilors?"

But Lily's wand was already infused. *"Desmar poteris!"*

Laz dropped his wand. While he fumbled to pick it up,
Lily struck again.

"Obleth nor vis elemen."

The forgetting spell!

I listened to Lily thanking Laz for his selfless work on behalf of the Council. I heard his stammering, confused replies. She had made him forget that she owed him!

Then she turned to the gnomes again. "Take the criminal's wand," she commanded.

No! Gnomes would be impervious to the protection spells on my wand. They could take it and put it into an iron box for Lily.

Was this how things had gone with Leona?

I tried to struggle, but pain from the cloak hammered my wings. I couldn't breathe. Forcing myself to lie still again, I could feel tears leaking down my face. I had vowed upon my family's honor never to give up my wand. What did that matter now? Lily always got what she wanted.

I looked imploringly at Laz, but he was staring at the gnomes.

And the gnomes were actually shaking their heads at Lily.

"What is the trouble?" she asked quietly.

One of them appeared to be the leader of the rest. "Troll magic," he answered in a gravelly voice. "We gnomes are sworn never to interfere."

For a second I locked eyes with him, and his features engraved themselves on my mind. I saw wiry tufts of hair growing on his forehead and a deep cleft in his chin. It was the same gnome who had stood guard outside my window at home in Galena.

Lily tilted her head at him. "Do you mean to say that *all* gnomes have an agreement with *all* trolls never to interfere with their magic?" She spoke respectfully, much more respectfully than she had ever been with me.

"Correct," he answered.

"Fascinating," she said, and for a second she sounded both aggravated and scornful. But she quickly put on a charming smile and bowed to the gnome leader. "Is there anything that might persuade you to do this small favor for me?"

"No," he answered. "If we were to break our word with the trolls, then how could you trust our word with you?"

Still smiling, Lily bowed to him again.

Turning to Laz, she gave him an order. "*You* will take it."

The tall genie's reply was simple and brief. *"Transera nos,"* he said, and vanished. Apparently he'd had enough of Lily.

She shook her wand at the place where he'd been standing, then dropped her arm to her side. "We will meet again, Mr. Lazuli," she muttered.

She stood over me. "I had hoped, Zaria, to relieve you of the burden of that cloak. Wearing it must be quite uncomfortable. But for now, I am afraid it will be necessary to keep you under troll magic. Later, when I have adequately studied the situation, I will take your wand for safekeeping and remove the cloak."

I was surprised she didn't just reach under the cloak with

an iron box and take my wand herself. She must be afraid of troll magic! I remembered what Meteor had said about how it affected everyone differently. What might it do to Lily Morganite?

"It is time to take her to FOOM," Lily told the gnomes. "She must arrive there by nine in the morning."

Gnomes lifted me, jostling every nerve. They bore me out of the tavern and put me in a cart enclosed by brass bars. The shiny brass looked out of place, as if we were going to a party, but I was very glad the cart was not made of iron. Laz had said the cloak would not kill me, but I doubted I could survive it while inside an iron cart.

I supposed that criminals placed in carts would normally have been deprived of their wands; they'd be unable to do a breaking spell, so iron wouldn't be necessary to contain them. I, on the other hand, still had my wand. I gripped its slender handle underneath the horrid cloak.

But my wand felt less magical than the fake I had taken from Sam. Where could my magic have gone? How could the troll cloak have turned my wand into something so lifeless, as if it belonged to a dead fairy instead of to me?

Gnomes formed ranks around the cart. Lily hovered a minute or two, giving instructions before she flew off.

The cart began to move, and the cloak grew heavier again, the mass of a mountain laid over me.

I thought of Meteor. Had he returned to the empty balcony? What would he do when he heard about my capture?

Chapter Forty-eight

MEMBERS OF THE RADIA GUARD ARE SWORN TO OBEY
THE COUNCILORS WHO GOVERN FEYLAND.
 —*Orville Gold, genie historian of Feyland*

After an interminable time, the cart came to a stop just as the sun lifted fiercely above the horizon. Dawn had arrived.

A strange screeching and rumbling filled the air. Through the bars, I saw a tattered mob of fairies and genies swelling around the cart. They were chanting, *"Free Zaria! Free Zaria!"*

Gnomes still surrounded the cart, but the crowd was pushing in at them. I recognized the blue-faced fairy who had once scolded me outside the FOOM dome as we both waited for Leona. She dove in and out among the gnomes, snatching their helmets off. Some gnomes ducked, but she was very quick. Two burly genies, working together, picked up a gnome and floated off with him. In the gap they created, another genie got close enough to stick his hand through the bars.

Black hair, rather sickly green skin, and disklike eyes. It was Seth.

"I knew it must be you they were looking for," he shouted. "We'll get you out of there."

Behind him, another gnome was carried upward.

"Please," I whispered. "Get me out of this cloak."

He couldn't have heard me over the hooting and yelling but he seemed to understand. He stretched forward and grabbed the collar of the cloak. He let go at once, as if he'd seized a handful of stinging insects.

"Oberon's Crown," he shouted. "What *is* that?"

Troll magic. I wondered what it felt like to Seth.

Gritting his teeth, he thrust his hands back into the cart. Swearing upon trolls, pixies, and gremlins, he worked to push back the hood.

"Thank you," I mouthed, still unable to speak above a whisper.

He reached for the button at my throat and wrestled with it. Before it could open, his face contorted in pain, and his arms jerked out of the cart. He slipped to the ground and in his place a gnome appeared, shaking his club. It was Lily's lead gnome, the one with the cleft chin.

The blue-faced fairy darted in to attack him. He swung his club against her wings as if she were a giant moth. She wailed and reeled away. A genie zoomed downward, only to take a blow to the shins. He soared off, roaring.

Gnomes harming fairies and genies? *Trying* to inflict injury! How could this be true? How could it possibly be happening?

But now all the gnomes had clubs in their hands, crunching and smashing any who dared to come close.

Then above the sobbing moans and furious shouts, an amplified voice rang out: "The Radia Guard has arrived! Disperse or face the wrath of the High Council. . . ."

Staring up, I saw a tight group of fairies and genies approaching from the west, all wearing golden robes.

Radia Guard.

I heard the hum of wing-beats and the rush of flying genies as the rabble who wanted my freedom tore away.

The cart lurched forward again, and though I tried to see what had become of Seth, grim-faced gnomes surrounded me, blocking my view.

Battered by the jolting cart and tired beyond exhaustion, I slipped into a dark sleep.

Chapter Forty-nine

FEYLAND IS OSTENSIBLY RULED BY KING OBERON AND QUEEN VELLERON (SOMETIMES CALLED MAB). HOWEVER, THEY HAVE NEVER ENJOYED THE DEMANDS OF GOVERNANCE. THEY LIVE ON ANSHIELD, THE FABLED ISLAND WHERE TIME TAKES NO TOLL UPON THE LIVING.

FEYLAND IS ACTUALLY GOVERNED BY THE HIGH COUNCIL. THERE ARE TWELVE COUNCILORS—SIX FAIRIES AND SIX GENIES—WHO BEGIN THEIR SERVICE WITH RADIA RESERVES OF GREEN OR ABOVE. THE LEADER OF THE COUNCIL PRESIDES OVER MEETINGS.

THE NUMBER OF YEARS A COUNCILOR MAY SERVE DEPENDS UPON FACTORS TOO MANY TO LIST HERE. SUFFICE IT TO SAY THAT OUTGOING COUNCILORS SELECT THEIR OWN REPLACEMENTS. ONCE KING OBERON AND QUEEN VELLERON HAVE PUT THEIR SEAL UPON THE CHOICE, THE NEW COUNCILOR IS OFFICIALLY RECOGNIZED.

—*Orville Gold, genie historian of Feyland*

*H*ours later I woke to find myself propped against the bars of a brass cage. A gnome stood guard just outside the bars. Laz's infernal cloak still was securely fastened, but the hood had been allowed to fall back from my head. Clutching my useless wand, I focused on keeping perfectly still.

Two wingspans away in another cage stood Leona. Her silver wings were bound with thick rope; they hung limp and dull, the burn from Jason's laser gun standing out starkly. Her hair fell loose down her back, tangled and lackluster.

I tried to catch her eye but she gazed fixedly out across a cavernous chamber that echoed with the murmurs of ten thousand fey folk. We must be inside the great hall of the FOOM dome. Gnomes lined the edges of the entire chamber in orderly ranks.

"Leona," I said, but though I meant to shout, I barely whispered, and she didn't turn my way.

Across from us, on the dais where our cages stood, was a long granite table. Perched at the table were twelve fairies and genies wearing bracelets set with the rubies of Oberon. Magistria Lodestone presided, her ruby pendant glowing around her neck. On the table in reach of her was a long, narrow iron box wrapped with rusty chains fastened with an old-fashioned titanium padlock.

Leona's wand.

I recognized Councilor Zircon, his white hair like a crown of frost. And Wolframite, tweaking his bulbous nose, his orange skin blotchier than ever. I didn't know any of the others.

Behind the councilors stood a large squad of the Radia

Guard in shimmering gold robes, their faces cold, each holding an infused wand. There were perhaps a hundred of them—many more than there had been at our class ceremony to receive our watches and wands. The tall, gold-skinned leader stood apart from the others. His eyes were on me.

Behind the dais hung a deep blue curtain. I found myself admiring the soft, rich color. How different from the hideous troll magic draped over me!

Magistria Lodestone touched her throat with her wand. Her amplified voice carried across the sea of murmurs: "This tribunal will begin."

Silence in the great hall was instantaneous.

"All spectators, keep to your feet. Neither flying nor hovering will be tolerated."

A flurry of wings blurred the vast room before everyone settled to the floor. Uneasily, I searched the crowd for familiar faces.

I looked for Beryl but didn't find her. I noticed Laz standing well back near the far door, his lanky height making him easy to spot. He wore a puzzled frown.

A blue-haired genie close to the front bobbed and waved. It was Andalonus, the first friendly face in all that mob. Beside him was Meteor, staring at the Council, his white eyebrows drawn together, his striped hair disheveled. He wore the same plain robe upon which the elixir had spilled last night; I could see the stain.

As if he could feel my glance, Meteor looked ·up, and although we were separated by a brass cage, a dais, and several rows of fey folk, for a moment I felt as if he stood beside me.

Then a cloud of satin sailed across my vision, and the odious smell of lilies wafted past my nose. Lily Morganite stood gloatingly in front of my cage in another elegant gown, her hair now twined with fat rubies.

She signaled a gnome. Again I recognized the fellow with the deeply cleft chin who had clubbed Seth. He took out a large key, fitting it to the door of my prison. He beckoned me. When I didn't move, he reached in and hauled me out.

He set me on my feet, but I could no more walk than I could fly. I fell like a sack of sand onto the stone floor.

Chapter Fifty

THE HIGH COUNCIL OF FEYLAND HAS THE POWER TO
DECLARE A CRIMINAL WHO IS WITHOUT REMORSE AN
OUTCAST. AN OUTCAST IS SHUNNED BY OTHERS, AND
HIS OR HER WAND IS CONFISCATED.

—*Orville Gold, genie historian of Feyland*

*T*wo gnomes stood me up again. They dragged me to a spot closer to the table where the councilors perched. They fastened brass shackles around my ankles and neck, then chained me between two posts bolted to the floor.

I don't know why they bothered. The cloak made me perfectly helpless.

Next, they released Leona from her cage and brought her to a round platform in the center of the dais. I thought she would throw me a sympathetic smile as she passed, but she didn't. Her eyes were vacant. She climbed the short steps to the platform and stood quietly facing the Council, her back toward me.

What had they done to her? What evil enchantments could take away Leona's passion, her courage, her fury?

Lily touched her own throat and then Leona's with the tip of her wand. *"Augnere ros."*

After that, their voices were amplified. Lily's sickeningly sweet tones reverberated from every wall. "Leona Bloodstone, tell us what happened on Earth yesterday."

Leona mesmerized everyone in the dome with a tale of how she had followed me to Earth because she was afraid I would hurt a human boy. Apparently, I had a grudge against this poor human because he had slighted me somehow. She spun a story of how I had turned the boy into a toad and set his house on fire. Showing her hand and wing, she claimed I had burned her when she tried to stop me.

This could not be Leona. Never. I knew her. I knew her faults as well as her good points. She could be touchy and proud, but Leona gave loyalty in full measure. Blaming her closest friend for what she herself had done? She'd rather die.

I sought my other old friends in the crowd. Andalonus's coppery eyes were glazed, his lips clamped together, both hands pulling at his ears. Meteor stood with hunched shoulders, chin on his chest, eyes shut.

"Is there anything else?" Lily Morganite asked Leona.

Leona apologized for trying to cover up my crimes.

"Tell me, Leona, until yesterday, did you consider Zaria Tourmaline a friend?"

"Yes. We were friends."

"Thank you. Regrettably, I must ask that you be confined a little longer." Lily's tone implied she'd much rather set Leona free.

Without objection, Leona walked back to her cage and

let herself be locked in while the High Council of Feyland—including Leona's mentor, Magistria Lodestone—sat in judgment.

On the platform where Leona had given false witness, Boris Bloodstone now stood. I saw only his rigid back, his gray neck, his close-clipped hair.

Lily's sugary tones saturated the air. "Mr. Bloodstone, did you observe Zaria Tourmaline and Leona Bloodstone from a viewing booth during their ill-advised journey to Earth?"

"Yes, Councilor," Bloodstone answered.

"And you can verify Zaria's abuse of magic?"

"Yes."

Lily thanked him, while I tried to think of spells I would cast on him if I ever got free. He deserved a gag, at the very least. A long-lasting gag.

After Bloodstone, Meteor Zircon floated onto the dais. As he came toward the witness platform, he looked at me. All the brightness was gone from his eyes; they looked like dead stones.

Like the others, Meteor had to turn his back to me to face Lily. All I could see of him was the wrinkled robe stretched across his shoulders, and the stripes of his hair.

Lily asked if he had been to my dwelling very early that morning.

"Yes," Meteor answered, his amplified voice hoarse.

"And what did you find?"

"I found . . ." Meteor bowed his head.

"Please continue."

"I found Zaria's guardian, Beryl Danburite. So I summoned my father, Councilor Zircon."

"Yes?" Lily pivoted to face Meteor's father. "And?"

Councilor Zircon rose, touching his throat with his wand. "Beryl Danburite is dead. It appears that she died from the effects of layered magic," he said, glaring sternly at me.

A horrified gasp rose in the chamber. Lily turned, and I saw the triumphant scorn in her eyes.

She had won.

Whatever Lily had held over Beryl since my parents' disappearance must have been dire. It had come between my guardian and me for all the years we had lived in the same house. I had believed Beryl was naturally distant and cold, that she didn't care about me. But it seemed much more likely she had let her fear of Lily Morganite take over her heart, her mind, her life.

Two days ago, she had been ready to put that fear aside. For me.

Now she was gone, snuffed like a fey globe that had run out of time. I had sent Meteor to free her, but it had been too late. No amount of study, no quantity of radia, could bring her back. Whatever she had wanted to tell me, Lily would not allow me to know. Beryl was silenced. *Ad eternum.*

I stared into an abyss of pain, while memories of Beryl trickled through me like unshed tears.

"Thank you, Meteor," Lily said.

"Wait," Meteor said, his voice strengthening. "It wasn't Zaria who killed Miss Danburite."

"No one said she did," Lily answered smoothly.

"And Leona Bloodstone is lying about what happened on Earth," Meteor continued.

"Indeed?" Lily put on an indulgent smile. She turned to the chamber as if to say, *You see how it is? Zaria Tourmaline has enchanted this unfortunate genie.*

She faced Meteor again. "It is understandable you want to shield your friend from the fate that awaits her. But that fate is out of your hands, Meteor Zircon."

He bounded from the platform toward the councilors and stopped in front of his father. "You promised to perform the spell to reveal layered magic on yourself! Did you keep your promise?"

Councilor Zircon put up a hand. "We will discuss it when you are calm."

Lily crooked a finger, and seven gnomes rushed Meteor. I called a warning, but my whispered shriek was lost.

Meteor shouted. "I call on all Council members—"

If he'd lifted off the dais before the gnomes reached him, he might have had a chance to draw his wand. But in the first charge, they wrenched his arms behind his back and clapped manacles around his wrists.

"Brute force," Laz had called it. I knew Meteor would have prepared for this moment by casting a protection spell—but a

protection spell would work only against magic. Who among us was prepared for a physical attack within Feyland?

"You cannot let this happen!" Meteor shouted.

Behind him, the gnome with the cleft chin raised his iron bat.

"No!" I cried, a soundless scream no one noticed.

The bat struck Meteor's shoulder with a dull *thwack*.

"Agh!" His cry echoed through the great chamber. He dropped to the floor. Gnomes piled onto his legs and chest.

"She's enchanted all of you!" Meteor yelled. "Every one of you councilors. Reveal—"

The gnomes stopped his words with a cloth gag. They fastened more shackles around his ankles and threw him in the cage where I had been. The gnome leader turned the key on him. Meteor lay motionless, gazing at his father, the father who had merely watched as his son was silenced. Not only silenced but hurt. *Harmed.*

Harmed in the sight of many. Why didn't the onlookers rise up? But the fairies and genies in the chamber said nothing. They did nothing.

Lily spoke into the terrifying quiet. "I hold you blameless, Meteor Zircon. When this tribunal is concluded, I myself will free you from the spells that have clouded your judgment."

Meteor strained against his bonds.

Lily approached me, gliding with dramatic grace, her wand extended as if to ward off evil. "Zaria Tourmaline, for your crimes you should forfeit any right to speak."

Approving murmurs from the crowd.

"Even so," Lily continued, "King Oberon's law requires that you be heard. Therefore, please tell me what happened on Earth yesterday, and why you injured Leona Bloodstone. I regret that the garment you are wearing will make it impossible to amplify your voice, but I am willing to stand near you and listen."

So, she knew the cloak would not allow her to use magic on me.

I put all my strength into my answer, but it was no use—my voice was too weak to be heard by anyone but Lily. "Tell me why a gnome who battered a good genie stands by *you* with an iron club."

She paid no attention and went on to her next question. "Who taught you layered magic?"

As if it were established I had used it.

How confident she looked, hovering lightly, her elegant skirt swaying like a satin bell, the rubies in her hair tossing red sparkles, her wand like a scepter.

I looked past her to the crowd. Ten thousand pairs of eyes pierced me. What was I to them? Someone who would enchant and betray her friends. A murderer.

I saw a bobbing head with hair like blue suds—a genie who caught my eye and sent me a look of encouragement. Andalonus. I feared for him. What would they do to anyone who kept faith with me?

Painfully, I turned and saw Leona, locked not only in a cage but also in layers of enchantment.

S

And Meteor, also caged.

I turned back to Lily.

She tilted her head. "How many unlawful trips have you made to Earth, Zaria Tourmaline?"

I didn't answer.

"Why take such heavy vengeance on a human boy? What did he do to slight you?" she asked, her amplified voice echoing from floor to ceiling. "Or do you hate all humans for what they did to your family?"

That's when all my sorrow converged. Every grief, every searing sadness met in one great wave.

The shackles around my neck and ankles cracked and fell apart; the pieces dangled from their chains, and the chains clanked against the posts. The buckle on the cloak popped open. The next instant, the buckle itself was gone, and so was the cloak that had covered me.

It happened in the blink of an eye. The only thing left of Laz's cloak was a heap of fine dark powder at my feet.

294

Chapter Fifty-one

FEY FOLK ARE NOT ACCUSTOMED TO FIGHTING BAT-
TLES USING PHYSICAL WEAPONS. INDEED, MOST FAIRIES,
GENIES, AND LEPRECHAUNS ARE UNITED IN THEIR
ABHORRENCE FOR ACTS OF PHYSICAL VIOLENCE.

—*Orville Gold, genie historian of Feyland*

The little stylus in my palm pulsed with power. Strength poured into my hand, up my arms, and across my wings. My first impulse was to fly upward out of reach of the gnomes and their wicked clubs. Getting free of the cloak had also freed me from any last effects of the troll elixir. I soared.

But a satiny shadow flew with me. *"Reducto et eloquen!"* Lily cried at full voice.

When her gag spell bounced off the shield that appeared around me, her eyes lit with anger. Then I saw her own spell catch her by the throat.

The enchantment I had cast the night before had taken hold. Lily's spell had rebounded! Her jaw hung open, and her white wings rippled wildly. She looked purely astonished.

Then afraid.

In the moment it took me to get my bearings, Lily

Morganite flew at high speed through the blue curtains and disappeared.

I should have chased her—it would have been my best opportunity to catch her when she couldn't defend herself. But I didn't. I was still stunned by my own power, still grasping the fact that I'd overcome my deathly prison.

The dais erupted into motion. All the members of the Radia Guard except the gold-skinned leader pelted me with spells. The shield around me got thicker and brighter, and the hum of rebounding spells made the air ring.

They were falling prey to their own magic. Many hit the floor, soundly sleeping, their robes rumpling around them. Some gripped their throats. Several dropped their wands; one of the wands landed on the magistria's head and clattered on the granite table.

Their leader yelled, "Stop! She is turning our magic against us!"

At this, quite a few of the Radia Guard fled through the curtain.

Council members rushed from their perches, then hovered uncertainly, wands poised. Magistria Lodestone held on to the ruby pendant around her neck as if it could tell her what to do. Zircon scowled wrathfully but came no closer to me. Wolframite's nose wiggled as if he'd inhaled a buzzing bee, but he, too, stayed back. Not a single councilor did anything but hover.

The crowd, like a great banner torn into scraps, began to

rip apart. Half of it pushed toward the doors at the rear; the other half scrambled toward the dais. Wings became tangled with other wings, and genies collided with each other. A high-pitched whine rose to the ceiling as fairies cried out; the whine blended with thunderous roars from genies.

I spotted Andalonus weaving hurriedly toward the dais. Not far behind him was Boris Bloodstone. Far to the back, battered by fey folk hurtling through the doors, I saw Laz. For once, his eyes were wide open.

A stream of gnomes began flowing up the steps onto the dais. Andalonus flew faster now, with Bloodstone only a length behind him.

I flicked my wand at the turbulent crowd. "A wall holds you back," I said. No one could hear me speak the improvised spell; I couldn't even hear myself in the pandemonium. And then I turned to the blue curtain behind me. "No one leaves or enters through the curtain."

A wall of granite bricks slammed into place at the edge of the dais from floor to ceiling, cutting off all who had not yet reached it. The last one to make it through was Bloodstone.

My wall shut out the screeching roar of the mob, and I clearly heard Magistria Lodestone shriek, "She will kill us all!"

Ignoring her, I swooped to Meteor's cage. *"Resvera den!"* I screeched.

The cage shattered, the brass bars rolling and bouncing,

and the manacles on Meteor rattled to the floor. Gnomes sprang at him, but Meteor shot up, too quick for them.

He smiled at me, a smile I'll keep next to my heart to brighten dark days.

"Your shoulder?" I asked.

He rotated it, and though it looked a bit stiff, he didn't lose his smile. Then he zoomed to the row of hovering councilors.

"I have a protection spell just as Zaria does," Meteor said. I expected he was bluffing, but who would dare call his bluff? The councilors obediently kept their magic to themselves.

The tip of Meteor's wand made contact with his father's head. *"Extred rev dolehr,"* he said, the spell to expose layered magic.

Councilor Zircon's stern face crumpled. He doubled over, groaning as if he'd taken poison. "It can't be," he moaned.

"It can," Meteor said, and then spoke the spell to banish layered magic: *"Banjan ex lomel."*

I didn't wait to see its effects. I turned to Leona.

The gnomes below followed my glance, rushing Leona's cage to surround it on all sides, the one with the cleft chin climbing on top.

I couldn't understand it. Why were these gnomes still behaving as if Lily had given them orders? She wasn't here. She was under a gag spell of her own making, and she had left them to themselves. What had she ever done for them, to engender such loyalty?

Leona stood silent and empty-eyed, as if she didn't see the strange tableau playing out in front of her. Her rope-bound wings hung straight and calm despite the burn on one of them, and her hands were humbly folded.

"She's enchanted," said a voice at my shoulder.

"Andalonus!"

He grinned beside me. "What now?"

"Now, look out."

Bloodstone, frowning contemptuously, was bearing down on us. He held up his wand, a copper rod with a bloodstone tip. "You will pay for your crimes, Zaria," he said.

The sound of his voice, so cold and gray, took me back to the classroom, and for a moment I was his student again, the timid small fairy who feared his authority and his dislike. I froze, completely forgetting that my protection would make any spell Bloodstone cast at me rebound on him.

Andalonus swooped in and snatched Bloodstone's wand, then darted back and forth, flourishing it. Bloodstone shouted and attacked but he couldn't catch the agile Andalonus, who threw the wand into Leona's cage.

Bloodstone hovered, sputtering, but only for a second, and then charged the gnomes below. "Leona, I will save you," he called, kicking at the nearest gnome.

Andalonus winked. "I'll get the gnome off the top of the cage while our good friend Bloodstone creates a diversion."

He dived toward the gnome with the cleft chin and seized both his arms, lifting him away from the cage. Below,

Bloodstone was fending off three more gnomes.

Holding my stylus like a dagger, I zoomed close to Leona's cage and put my hand through the bars on the top, barely touching her head.

"Extred rev dolehr," I cried.

Chapter Fifty-two

TIRFEYNE IS A WORLD RICH IN INSECT LIFE AND
BIRDS. HOWEVER, THERE ARE NO BEASTS LIVING UPON
TIRFEYNE—UNLESS GREMLINS OR TROLLS WERE TO BE
COUNTED AS BEASTS.

—*Orville Gold, genie historian of Feyland*

*L*eona screamed, a long shrill wail of pain. Even Lily's
gnomes stopped waving their clubs to stare at her. Bloodstone
took the opportunity to grab his wand—and shake it at *me*.

"Haven't you done enough?" he shouted.

I plunged toward the cage again and tapped Leona's head
a second time. *"Banjan ex lomel."*

Her screams stopped. Three gnomes leaped on top of the
cage, forcing me to retreat as they lunged for me.

"Resvera den!" I yelled, aiming at the rope binding Leona's
wings. I dared not break the cage itself for fear the gnomes
would mangle her.

"My wand, Zaree," Leona called. "They took my wand."

I looked down at the granite table. The padlocked iron
box was gone.

Behind the table, Meteor was struggling to get his wand

within striking distance of Magistria Lodestone. I knew what he was thinking: *If the leader of the Council understands she's been under layered magic, she will make the rest of the Council reveal the presence of layered magic in themselves.* But Wolframite and seven other councilors had ranged themselves in front of the magistria. Each time Meteor darted forward, they flew at him, forcing him back.

Meanwhile, Councilor Zircon, wand upraised, was holding two more councilors at bay. One was a pink-haired fairy with stalk-like arms that looked as if they could barely support the ruby on her wrist. The other was a portly genie with lilac curls.

Why didn't Zircon act to reveal the layers on his fellow councilors? Why didn't he show them that they, too, had been ensnared by Lily? Surely he could do a Level 40 spell? Or was he too stingy to part with any radia?

I had to help Meteor! I rushed toward the magistria, but a cry from Leona made me stop and spin around. Gnomes had opened her cage. They were wrestling her out, one of them twisting her injured wing.

I streaked toward her. Bloodstone lay on the floor, unmoving. Gnomes thrashed the air with their clubs, eyes on me as I hovered just out of their reach.

"Meteor!" a voice yelled.

It was Andalonus, still carrying the gnome leader, who kicked in fury.

Meteor looked up. Andalonus let go. The angry, clawing

gnome plummeted, taking two councilors down with him. The rest rushed to get out of the way.

Meteor rammed into Magistria Lodestone and his wand made contact. *"Extred rev dolehr,"* he shouted.

Her screams said that now she knew she had been duped by Lily Morganite.

Meteor turned his back on her to join Andalonus. The two genies hurtled toward Leona's captors. I'd never seen either one of them use force except during games. Now, working together, they seized helmets and threw them in the faces of the gnomes, then swiped two clubs. When they first grasped the iron, they flinched, but they thumped heads and whacked arms until the gnomes holding Leona let her go.

Flinging away his club, Andalonus put his shoulder under Leona's and helped her fly. And Leona, proud Leona, leaned on him gratefully as he rose up to meet me.

I looked to the Council, still hovering in a knot, wrangling with one another. I heard Zircon's rumbling voice and the magistria's measured tones. She must have spent enough radia to free herself from the layered spells, for she was no longer screaming. Her wings were far from calm, however.

Who among them had Leona's wand?

"Zaree," Leona said. "I'm sorry. You know I wouldn't—"

"Of course, Leona. I know. I'm sorry I couldn't get to you sooner. I tried—"

"The portal," Leona whispered, her eyes flicking back and forth. "I—"

"Sealed," I said, and tapped my lips with my forefinger.

She brightened, her eyes widening. I nodded.

"We'll find your wand," I said.

"Is this what you're looking for?" asked Andalonus. He reached into a pocket of his robe, bringing out the iron box. "I'd love to get rid of it; it's wickedly cold."

"Allow me," I said, aiming my wand at the titanium lock. *"Resvera den."*

The lock broke, the rusty chain slid away, and the box fell open. There lay Leona Bloodstone's wand, a thing of beauty emitting a horrendous screech. Leona snatched it up, and it fell silent. Andalonus dropped the box, which jangled against the stone floor.

Leona gave Andalonus a brilliant smile. "You are the best of genies!"

His coppery eyes glowed and he looked complacently at Meteor. "Remember this moment!"

"I doubt any of us will forget," Meteor said, smiling, too.

"Look." Andalonus gestured at the floor.

Below, the gnome with the cleft chin was leading the entire group of gnomes past the mess of broken cages toward the blue curtain. Some of them were limping, but they marched with precision, as if they had never used clubs against fey folk, as if they were simply going out to patrol Oberon City as usual.

I thought the councilors might call them back or at least ask where they were going, but the councilors were too busy arguing.

Surreptitiously, I infused my wand and waved it at the curtain, trying to look as if I wasn't doing anything purposeful. "Gnomes can leave," I said, "but they can't come back."

The gnomes marched out, the curtain closing quietly behind them.

Leona knelt by her uncle. Andalonus helped her roll him over. He was breathing, but though Leona snapped her fingers near his ear, he didn't respond. A bruise darkened the gray skin at his temple.

"I believe he'll wake up," Meteor said. "Later."

"I hope so," Leona said. "Poor Uncle Boris. He tried to help."

He's a trog, Leona. But seeing Bloodstone helpless and injured, my heart softened—just enough so that I no longer felt like putting a long-lasting gag spell on him.

Leona looked from one to another of us. "Thank you all for rescuing me. Especially you, Zaria."

"And especially me," Andalonus said. "Best of genies, remember?"

"Yes! Especially you." Leona's silver eyes shone. "And especially you, Meteor."

We all smiled.

"Now what?" asked Andalonus.

"Now," she said, "we meet with the High Council of Feyland."

Magistria Lodestone, flanked by Zircon, was facing an agitated clump of her fellow councilors.

"Every one of you," she was saying, "perform the spell to reveal layered magic in yourselves. Now! Or feel my wrath."

"But Magistria," Wolframite complained, "you do not know for certain that the rest of us are enchanted."

"True," agreed another councilor, the genie with lilac curls. "If you are wrong, we will waste one hundred radia!"

The pink-haired fairy piped up. "Zaria Tourmaline may have enchanted *you* so you would think her accuser was in the wrong. But Lily Morganite has an excellent reputation, while Zaria is a known criminal."

A flapping blur went past me. Leona's wing might be damaged but apparently she could still fly very fast. Even so, she didn't quite beat Meteor to the councilors.

"Criminal?" Leona said. "Let me show you criminal." She leaned toward Meteor. "What's the spell?"

With the tip of his wand, Meteor batted Wolframite's nose. *"Extred rev dolehr,"* he said.

Wolframite sank to the floor weeping.

Leona bopped the pink-haired fairy on the head. *"Extred rev dolehr."*

The fairy wilted completely. I thought for a moment she would shrivel. "Please," I heard her whimper. "Please, no."

Leona and Meteor had moved on, leaving Wolframite and the pink-haired fairy to their misery.

I knew I should force these councilors to spend their own radia to free themselves from the painful knowledge that they had fallen under layered magic. After all, they had proclaimed me a criminal.

But they had been enchanted. They had not known what they were doing. And they were suffering.

"Banjan ex lomel," I said, brushing first the pink-haired fairy and then Wolframite with my wand.

Both of them sighed deeply and stopped crying.

Ahead of me, Leona and Meteor were pouncing on one councilor after another, as if competing about who could reveal more enchantments in the eight remaining.

I followed after. As the councilors began to weep and moan, I gave them the second spell. I felt I was setting things right, things Lily had put wrong.

When all twelve councilors were freed, we stepped back, ready to receive our thanks. We had just donated hundreds of radia, enough to repair several durable spells. We had restored the High Councilors of Feyland to their senses.

But not a smile did they give.

Chapter Fifty-three

TOO MUCH POWER OVER OTHERS HAS A CORRUPTING
INFLUENCE.

—*Orville Gold, genie historian of Feyland*

The councilors lined up behind the granite table.

"Zaria Tourmaline," said the magistria in a grave tone, "reverse the spells on the members of the Radia Guard at once."

In the commotion, I had forgotten the Radia Guard. Most were still sprawled on the floor asleep—the spells they had thrown at me must have been strong. The few who weren't sleeping were huddled like rumpled golden patches in the folds of the blue curtain, watching warily, clutching their wands.

When their gold-skinned leader heard his squad mentioned, he floated forward. "The penalties for attacking any member of the Radia Guard are severe," he said, giving me a cold stare.

"As they should be," put in Magistria Lodestone. "Anyone who presumes to interfere with the Radia Guard undermines the entire order of Feyland." She nodded at the leader. "Thank you, Renclair." Then she frowned at me. "Because you are young, Zaria, we will assess fines instead of imprisoning you. Now, reverse the spells on—"

"Fines?" interrupted Meteor. "Why would you fine Zaria? She just spent *eight hundred* radia helping you!"

"She will be fined for performing unlawful spells," the magistria snapped. "Fines payable in radia should be no hardship to a Violet fairy. As for the eight hundred radia—it certainly is not enough to cover what she will owe." She lifted the chain at her neck, spinning the ruby pendant between a finger and thumb.

Meteor's frown could have frightened a troll. "And what about *you*?" he demanded. "You failed to uphold your position as leader of the Council. What is the penalty for *that*?"

"Yes," Leona chimed in. "How many radia do *you* owe, Magistria?"

Andalonus's blue head bobbed in indignation. "The whole Council should pay *Zaria*!"

Wolframite's blotches stood out like a bad rash. "How dare you? You upstart youngsters have less than fifty years among you! You have nothing to say!"

"Yes, we do," Leona answered, her silver eyes shining like blades. "If not for us, you would still be under Lily Morganite's spells."

"Silence!" Magistria Lodestone twirled her pendant faster. "Zaria, you must release the Guard *at once*." She waved a hand at the wall that shut off the dais from the great chamber beyond. "And I assume this granite monstrosity is also your doing? I command you to restore the hall to its former proportions. Now!"

The entire Council nodded, glaring at me.

"I don't understand," I said.

"It is quite simple," the magistria answered. "You have committed many crimes, Zaria, and you are not demonstrating proper remorse. By rights, you should be named an outcast. But we will allow you to regain your good name by undoing your brazen spells and then paying whatever fines we assign you."

"I don't understand," I said again. "You're not enchanted anymore. Why are you treating me like a terrible criminal? All I've done is make a few unlawful visits to Earth. I haven't been a smuggler. I haven't hurt anyone. I tried to help you!"

The magistria leaned forward on her perch, scowling. "You should become an outcast for your impertinence alone. I order you to release the Guard immediately and to restore the hall!"

Anger poured through me. "You're not being fair."

"And who are you to decide what is fair and what is not?" she asked scornfully. "I will give you one last chance. Reverse the spells on the Guard. Take down the wall."

I wished my wings wouldn't tremble. I wanted to be strong and steady. I was grateful when Meteor moved closer to me. So did Leona on my other side, while Andalonus stood behind me.

Surrounded by my friends, I looked from one councilor to another. "No," I told them. "I won't." My voice quavered, but I kept going. "I did not attack the Radia Guard. Their spells were cast *against* me, not *by* me. And if I take down that wall, we could be mobbed by thousands of fey folk. Thanks to you, they believe I've committed dire crimes against Feyland."

The magistria looked like a furious trog. "You have admitted you went to Earth unlawfully. Do you expect us to absolve you?"

"I—"

She rose from her perch, her black wings unfurling. "All four of you have committed crimes, and yet you show no remorse. Therefore, remove yourselves to the other end of this dais while we councilors decide your punishment."

Meteor's whole face tightened as he looked at his father, who refused to meet his gaze.

Andalonus yelled out, "Rotten trogs!"

But Leona began to laugh. "Punishment!" she cried. "They want to punish *us*."

Looking at her wide smile, I suddenly felt as if I were a bottle of troll elixir, as if a million tiny bubbles were rising from my toes to my head. Each bubble held a hundred painful giggles, and every bubble was erupting at once. I exploded in laughter.

Leona and I held on to each other as peal after peal shook us. It took a few minutes before I noticed that no one else seemed to find the situation funny. Meteor's worried face was bending toward me, and Andalonus was tugging my arm.

Tears streamed from my eyes, and my chest heaved. They must think I was crying! That's why they looked so concerned. I needed to tell them it was only laughter, but I could not stop long enough to speak.

Then Leona was shaking me gently by the shoulders. "It's all right, Zaree. It's all right," she kept repeating.

That's when I realized I *was* crying. Crying for Beryl, and all we had never said to each other. Crying for Seth, and wondering if he had lived. Crying for Sam, who would not remember me.

Crying for my family, whose story I would never know.

Chapter Fifty-four

In the distant past, certain spells were concocted by wicked fairies and genies. It is unfortunate that such spells have been meticulously preserved in spellbooks handed down by family members.

The following spells are unlawful: the compulsion spell, the statue spell, and the spell to diminish a person's height.

Other spells are also unlawful, but I shall not name them, hoping instead that they will fall into permanent obscurity.

—*Orville Gold, genie historian of Feyland*

I heard Meteor's voice, low and urgent. "Zaree," he said. "Leona."

Mopping my eyes with my hand, I became aware that Meteor was gripping his wand intently, his face taut, his gaze fixed on the councilors. Andalonus was standing straight and still, his hands bunched into fists, also watching them.

Leona lifted her hands from my shoulders. "What is it?" she asked. "What's wrong?"

The councilors and Renclair, leader of the Radia Guard, had gathered into a hovering semicircle with Magistria Lodestone at the apex. All of them held their wands so the tips were touching.

Leona gasped, and then her wand flashed out, pointed and infused. *"Frio stas im elemen!"* she said in a terrible voice.

Everyone in the semicircle froze, then crashed to the floor. They landed like thrown statues. Not even their eyes blinked; they seemed to have quit breathing.

"What's happening?" I asked.

"They were going to combine their powers," Leona answered, her eyes on the councilors.

"Against us," Meteor said. "With a combination spell, together they could overcome any enchantment—including that strange rebounding protection on you, Zaria."

"But what did Leona *do*?" Andalonus asked, sounding shaken.

"Statue spell," Meteor told him.

"Get their wands," Leona said icily. "And don't worry. It's not as if we'll keep their wands forever—unless they keep acting like trogs."

"But—" Andalonus began.

"Oberon's Crown," Leona exclaimed. "We can't let the councilors squander their radia by using it against us!"

"But a statue spell?" I asked.

"Do you have a better plan?" Leona sounded as if she really would like to know.

I heard Meteor inhale a very long breath and then blow it out. "Leona's right," he said gloomily.

Then Meteor, the most upstanding member of our class, began collecting wands from Feyland's High Councilors. He moved with care, his deft fingers coaxing each one from its owner. Some of the wands yelped or squawked when they were taken but quickly subsided. Apparently not much radia had been spent on alarms.

When he came to Zircon, Meteor paused. I saw the muscles in his shoulders bunching, but I couldn't see his face. Then he slipped the wand from his father's grasp.

A movement next to the curtain caught my eye. It was one of the genies in the Radia Guard.

"*Obliv trau,*" Leona cried, and shook her wand at all the members of the Guard crouching by the curtain. They slumped into sleep.

Meteor set the bundle of councilors' wands on the floor, and the four of us gathered around them.

Leona asked Meteor to explain how she had been captured. "I had a protection on myself." Anger sparked in her eyes. "What went wrong?"

"Layered magic," Meteor answered. "A normal protection won't work against layers." He turned to me. "How did they catch *you*, Zaria? I thought you were protected. When I saw you in the cage . . ." His green eyes looked misty.

"It was the cloak," I answered. "More troll magic."

All three of my friends spoke at once. "Troll magic?"

"Laz said it would take away my power."

"Who's Laz?" Andalonus asked.

Then I remembered none of them knew that part of my story.

"You undid *troll* magic?" Meteor looked at me as if I had ridden a comet and lived to tell the tale.

"I was upset," I mumbled.

He snorted. "I'll try not to upset you."

I glanced at the dark little heap of powder on the floor between the posts where I'd been chained.

Meteor followed my gaze. "You should gather the residue," he said. "It could have valuable magical properties."

I felt sick and weak at the thought. "I don't want it."

"Zaree," he said gently. "None of us knows how big this is, or how long it will last."

"This?"

He gestured at the frozen Council. "All of this. Don't turn your back on something that might help you one day."

I gulped. He was right, of course. Lily Morganite might have left the chamber when she lost her powers of speech, but a gag spell was temporary. She would be back.

"I don't suppose you know a spell for gathering *residue*?" I asked Meteor.

"*Wispera ve,*" he said. "Level Ten." He reached into his robe and pulled forth the empty elixir bottle. "Perfect for holding the dust of troll magic." He held it out to me.

The indigo bottle was faintly sticky. "You kept this?"

"Souvenir." He smiled at me, and for some reason my face felt hot.

I glided to the spot where the powder left over from the torturous cloak was lying. The powder was very dark, and yet it had an ominous shimmer, as if it absorbed light.

It didn't seem wise to keep such a substance. It would never create happy moments. But if I didn't take it, someone else could pick it up and use it against me and those I loved.

It took only an instant to gather the powder into the indigo bottle. Once full, the bottle felt strangely heavy. I glanced over at Meteor. He was talking with Andalonus. I turned away so no one would see me tap the top of the bottle with my wand. "Seal this bottle so none may open it or break it but me," I whispered.

A cap appeared along with a seamless band that fit snugly around the top. Hastily, I wedged the bottle into the largest pocket of my gown and returned to my friends.

Leona was worried that Lily could return at any moment, invisible. "We need to protect ourselves. Meteor, what's the spell against layered magic?"

"*Fendus altus prehenden nos elemen,*" Meteor said. "Level Thirty. Three hundred radia will last a month."

I infused to Level 30. "Allow me."

"No need," Meteor said. "I've already cast it on myself."

I turned to Leona, but she was in the midst of doing the spell.

"Andalonus?" I said.

He shook his head. "Don't waste your radia. No one would bother putting layers on a common Red."

Leona rounded on him. "Common?"

"Who overcame those gnomes?" I said.

"And who took back my wand?" Leona added.

"And who threw a gnome at the councilors?" Meteor put in, grinning.

Andalonus bobbed his head. "Well, yes, brilliant of me. However, that Lily fairy won't spend her radia on me. I have none to oppose her. I doubt she even knows my name."

I cast the spell anyway. "We'll take no chances," I told him.

"You don't need loads of radia to be the best of genies," Leona said.

Chapter Fifty-five

To dote upon one is to be blind to another.
—*Orville Gold, genie historian of Feyland*

*G*asping groans made us turn around.

Bloodstone was struggling to a sitting position. "Leona?" he said, sounding dazed.

Leona hurried to his side. The rest of us trailed after her more slowly.

"The gnomes?" he asked.

"They're gone, Uncle." She gave him a tight-lipped smile. "Thank you for helping Zaria rescue me."

His face pinched. "I was not helping *Zaria*!"

Sighing, Leona touched his shoulder with her wand. "*Extred rev dolehr.*"

I waited for Bloodstone's wails, but they did not come. Instead, he frowned. "What are you doing?"

Leona rose up, staring at him, her silver eyes snapping. "I was trying to help you," she said, her voice thick with anger. "But you weren't impaired, were you?"

His hand gingerly prodded the bruise on his head. "Not impaired? But—"

"Can you stand?" Leona interrupted.

Meteor moved forward and helped Bloodstone up.

"Can you float?" Leona demanded.

Bloodstone demonstrated that he could, but then he stopped short, hovering unsteadily. He pointed at the councilors, who lay like tipped-over statues. "What in Oberon's name has happened here? Leona, your so-called friend has put statue spells on the High Council of Feyland! *Statue spells.* Unlawful!"

"*I* did it." She held her wand high. "And no, Uncle, I am not taking the blame for Zaria. *She* would never cast such a spell."

Bloodstone's face seemed to be made of chalk. His lips moved but only a small whine came out.

"Leave," said Leona. "And if you tell any more lies about Zaria, I will make your wand disappear. *Ad eternum.*"

Bloodstone's chin was quivering. "I wanted to help you. I never meant—"

"Good-bye," Leona answered.

Bloodstone didn't look at any of us as he floated toward the curtain with jerky movements.

"Let him leave," I murmured, flicking my wand just enough.

The curtain parted around him like rain falling past gray rock.

With Andalonus guarding the batch of wands, Meteor and I

hovered like Leona's personal guard as she lifted the statue spell.

"Chantmentum pellex."

Renclair, the leader of the Radia Guard, was the only one of the group who wasn't completely disoriented when the enchantment fell away. I wondered if he'd been under a statue spell before, because he immediately began to shake out his hands.

"What has happened here?" the magistria demanded, her black wings fluttering as she tried to get up.

"Statue spell," Renclair answered grimly, shrugging his shoulders and swinging his arms.

"More crimes!" Wolframite blustered. He pushed to his feet, then toppled over.

Zircon fixed Meteor with a glare. "What is the meaning of this?"

"My wand!" squeaked the pink-haired councilor, sitting up with slow, clumsy movements. Her wings flapped awkwardly and batted against the lilac-headed genie sprawled beside her. "Where is my wand?"

Pandemonium, as all the councilors realized they were without their wands. They shrieked and roared. They called down imprecations on our heads. Renclair alone kept quiet, carefully easing himself to his feet.

"Stop, all of you!" Leona screeched. "You have not been hurt. Your wands are safe. They will be returned when you're ready to use them wisely!"

Shocked exclamations. Indignant mutterings.

"We have no time for this." Something in Leona's tone—or maybe it was the way she waved her Level 200 wand—seemed to get through to the councilors. They shut their mouths and stared at her.

Leona gave a disgruntled nod. "There are important things to discuss, things that have nothing to do with you councilors passing judgment on *us*."

Chapter Fifty-six

MANY BELIEVE THE LEADER OF THE COUNCIL HOLDS
THE MOST POWERFUL POSITION IN THE LAND. THIS IS
FALSE.

THE MOST POWERFUL POSITION IS THAT OF THE
FORCIER.

—*Orville Gold, genie historian of Feyland*

There was a long pause as Leona stared down the High
Council of Feyland. Then they all got up, copying Renclair
and shaking out their hands and feet.

When they could move more freely again, they returned
to their perches behind the table and settled in sullenly.

"You have us at a disadvantage," the magistria said. "What
is it you wish to discuss?"

Leona huffed impatiently. "Tell them, Zaria."

"Me?"

"Yes, you. Of course, you. You drove Lily Morganite away.
Tell them."

How could I begin? "Well," I said. "Um." The councilors'
deepening frowns flustered me.

"Speak up, child," Wolframite urged.

VICTORIA HANLEY

I tried not to focus on their wrathful faces. "Uh, Lily Morganite has been the Forcier for ten years?" I asked.

Wolframite and Zircon looked at each other. Magistria Lodestone shifted and looked up at the ceiling. "About ten years, yes," she answered resentfully.

"And when did the durable spells first show signs of weakening?" I asked.

"Perhaps five years ago. Maybe a bit more."

Five years. A number I associated with my parents' disappearance.

"And Lily," I went on shakily, "was responsible for adding enough radia to the durable spells to keep them strong during that time?"

"Yes," Wolframite answered.

Beside me, I heard Meteor gasp. He bounded toward his father. "That's it!" he roared.

All the councilors, including Zircon, had vacant stares on their faces.

Meteor pointed back at me. "Zaria figured it out! *That's* what Lily Morganite was up to!"

"Figured out *what*, son?"

"That Lily Morganite was stealing radia from Feyland and keeping it for herself," Meteor shouted.

Zircon tumbled from his perch and then bounded up again. "By Oberon, what a foul situation!"

"What are you nattering about?" the magistria asked.

Zircon's white head wagged from side to side as he looked

from one to another of his fellow councilors. "Do you not see what these children are getting at?"

"Explain," the magistria answered.

"Lily Morganite said she could not keep up with the durable spells because there were too many Reds," Zircon boomed. "She said there was not enough radia available from taxes. But what if she did not even *try* to keep up?"

Wolframite looked as if someone had strung his beady eyes on a wire and then pulled. "By Velleron's wings," he breathed. "She's been hoarding Feyland's radia?"

"It explains everything," Zircon answered. "She probably used the stolen radia to enchant us into believing she could do no wrong."

Andalonus seemed stunned. "She was stealing radia?" he whispered.

Leona was glaring at the magistria distrustfully, as if she suspected her mentor of conspiring with Lily Morganite.

But the magistria was clearly shaken. Her black wings began to spasm, and her white face got even whiter. "Stealing radia?" she repeated. "The Forcier of Feyland was *stealing*?"

The pink-haired fairy sagged like a wilting stalk. As for Renclair, his face settled into rocklike fury.

Renclair. How could we have forgotten to reveal layered magic on the leader of the Radia Guard?

I flew at him and slapped his shoulder with my wand. *"Extred rev dolehr!"*

But he shook his head calmly and met my eyes. "I am not enchanted."

Puzzled, I peered at him, searching for signs he was hiding tears.

"I think Zircon is right," he said. "By now Lily Morganite has vast reserves of radia. But she is not wasteful. Since I am sworn to obey the Council, all she needed to do was command the Council: that way she would command me and all whom I lead."

The magistria had recovered enough to look disgusted. "She did, indeed, command us—as we now know."

"How many radia do you suppose she may have amassed?" Zircon asked.

Wolframite spoke drearily. "Many millions. She calls herself a Blue fairy, but no doubt her reserves are now well beyond blue."

"And she is *free!*" Magistria Lodestone gripped her pendant. "Free to roam invisible, casting spells, wreaking havoc."

Zircon nodded bleakly. "And she has armed gnomes at her beck and call."

"As Forcier, she would have inspected the crystal watches of everyone who registered Orange or beyond," the magistria fumed, "while her own reserves were never questioned." Her fury seemed to be increasing. "Lies! Morganite lied about everything—even telling us the cloak Zaria wore was made by trolls." Her eyes twitched scornfully. "She said it would *extinguish* Zaria's magic. Ha!"

What? She didn't believe it was really a troll cloak? I looked from one councilor to the next, waiting for someone to contradict the magistria, but all were nodding their heads sagely.

"Troll magic would be impossible for any lone fairy to overcome," the magistria went on. "And if, by some unknown means, it *had* been overcome, it would have left a residue." She flapped her hand at the empty spot on the floor where I had gathered the dark powder into the indigo bottle. "There is nothing there."

The bottle in my pocket felt suddenly heavier. My friends and I all faced forward, not looking at one another. I tried not to tremble. Surely, at least one of the councilors would have noticed that the dust of the cloak had been there before?

Apparently not.

"Morganite must have enchanted the cloak herself," Zircon said, "but she made a mistake in allowing Zaria to keep her wand."

"Lucky for all of us," Wolframite rasped, "Morganite overestimated herself and underestimated a Violet fairy."

A Violet fairy. That was who I was to them—who I was and always would be. Not Zaria Tourmaline, who loved both Earth and Feyland, a fairy with friends she would die for, a unique being with a full heart.

Good. I found myself glad I didn't have to explain how

I overcame troll magic. I had done it. For now, that was all I knew about it anyway.

"The question is," Renclair was saying, "what does Lily Morganite want?"

While they paused to think, Leona spoke up. "Now that you know Lily Morganite is the *real* criminal," she said in a ringing voice, "you should stop using your radia against me and my friends."

They were silent. Silent, and very grim-faced.

Finally Zircon spoke. "Quite right," he rumbled. "You youngsters have helped uncover a malevolent plot."

"And," Leona continued, brandishing her wand, "there will be no more talk of how Violet fairies should not be friends with other Violet fairies."

The magistria looked flustered. "I suppose if you are friends, you are friends," she mumbled.

Leona and I exchanged smiles.

"Good," Leona said. "So, what is the Council going to do about Lily Morganite?"

Chapter Fifty-seven

IF THE DURABLE SPELLS WERE TO FAIL, IMPORTANT
STRUCTURES WOULD DEGENERATE. FOR EXAMPLE,
WITHOUT THE ALARMS EMBEDDED IN THE GATEWAY
OF GALENA, YOUNG FAIRIES AND GENIES WOULD NOT
HAVE THE CHANCE TO GROW UP INSIDE PROTECTED
TERRITORY.

IMPORTANT LINKS BETWEEN FEY FOLK AND
HUMANS WOULD BE UNDONE. IT WOULD NO LONGER
BE POSSIBLE TO SEND GIFTS TO HUMAN CHILDREN
THROUGH THE SENDING PORTS OF SCOPES, NOR
WOULD IT BE POSSIBLE TO WATCH OVER THEIR WEL-
FARE.

PERHAPS EVEN THE NECESSARY AND EVER-PRESENT
FLOW OF THE ENERGY OF HAPPINESS MADE BY HUMANS
WOULD BE DISRUPTED, THOUGH MOST SCHOLARS DIS-
PUTE THAT IDEA.

—Orville Gold, genie historian of Feyland

Everyone seemed to be talking at once. Leona, the
councilors, Meteor . . . they were asking and answering,
discussing and exclaiming, arguing and persuading. Their

words jumbled together in my ears. I hovered silent, immersed in my own thoughts.

Five years ago the durable spells had begun to show signs of wear, and five years ago my brother had told me Feyland was about to change. *"For good,"* he had said confidently. *"For good."*

Then he was gone. And so, a short time later, were my parents.

Wolframite had reported that they had traveled to Earth. Bloodstone had often sneered about my "foolhardy" family. And Beryl had always assured me they died at the hands of humans.

But the more I thought about it, the more those stories seemed like nursery tales, made up to explain a disaster to an orphaned child.

Why would my father, a genie even Lily had called resourceful—and my mother, a Blue fairy with a spellbook full of advanced magic—fall prey to vicious humans on Earth? My brother was no fool, either!

What if laying the blame on humans was totally wrong? What if Jett, Gilead, and Cinna Tourmaline had discovered Lily Morganite was stealing radia and tried to stop her?

Lily's pearly eyes appeared in my memory, and I heard her sweet voice goading me: *"You want to hear about your family. Naturally, you do. And I can tell you, Zaria. The whole story."*

I stood lost to the scene around me, my anguished mind beating the same idea up and down, around and through, over and over: it was Lily who had made my family disappear.

Leona had said I drove Lily away. It was true, but only because I had been lucky enough to catch her off her guard. But what now? How many radia did she have in reserve? *"Many millions,"* Wolframite had said.

I opened my watch-face cover to check my own reserves. What I saw horrified me. The tiny golden hand had moved a full notch. It pointed to the mark just under nine million radia.

In less than one day, I had used a million radia!

Frantically, I thought back. Since I had last checked the radia hand on my watch, I had thrown up the wall to block the chamber from the dais and tampered with the blue curtain. That might have used as much as five hundred radia. The spells to banish layered magic on Leona and then the councilors . . . a protection spell against layered magic for Andalonus . . .

Even added together, the amount would not make the golden hand on my watch drop so far.

What else had I done?

The indigo bottle in my pocket felt suddenly heavier. With a jolt, I realized it must have taken great quantities of magic to make the troll cloak disintegrate. Close to a million radia.

I had summoned all that magic *involuntarily,* and without the use of my wand.

How?

My head was beginning to hurt, and then suddenly Meteor was hugging me, his smile deep and warm, his emerald eyes sparkling.

"We did it," he said. "We did it!"

Puzzled, I pulled back. He bent his head down, and his smile faded. "Aren't you happy? We'll be exonerated. And the Council will proclaim Lily Morganite an outcast."

"Of course I'm happy," I said dully.

I watched Leona and Andalonus passing out wands to the councilors, their movements bouncy and joyful.

The councilors seemed less enthusiastic.

Meteor put a finger under my chin. "You're exhausted," he said.

I sighed. Later, I would tell him my thoughts. Later, when I could grasp the meaning.

"Well," Magistria Lodestone declared, "this has been a productive meeting. But now we councilors have more work to do—and you youngsters should get some rest."

She rose loftily from her perch. As she sailed toward the curtain, followed by the other councilors and Renclair, I waved my wand.

"The exit is open," I muttered.

None of them took any more notice of me than they took of the sleeping members of the Radia Guard, but Meteor stared, his green eyes full of curiosity.

Andalonus gave a mighty yawn. "Let's go home."

Home. The word tolled in my heart. How could I go back to my empty dwelling alone? No Beryl to greet me. No Beryl ever again. Now, when I understood how much she had cared about me, she was dead. Murdered. Sobs threatened to engulf me again. I choked them back.

Andalonus looked stricken. "I'm sorry, Zaria. I didn't think about Miss Danburite."

Meteor patted my shoulder. "They took her body away," he said. "I wish I could have revived her, Zaree. I did all I could, but she was gone."

"Thank you," I whispered.

"I'll stay with you tonight," Leona said, her silver eyes soft. "You shouldn't be alone."

Chapter Fifty-eight

WHEN FAIRIES AND GENIES REACH THE AGE OF
EIGHTEEN, THEY LEAVE GALENA FOR OBERON CITY
OR ONE OF THE PROVINCES.

— *Orville Gold, genie historian of Feyland*

I lifted the spell on the curtain but left the wall of granite where it was. If the councilors wanted it removed, they could do it themselves.

The heavy bottle of powder weighed me down as I flew toward the Gateway of Galena with my friends. I flapped almost as much as Leona did with her injured wing. As usual, she refused help. "I'm learning to adapt," she said when Andalonus offered his support. "But thank you."

I looked covertly at Meteor, wondering how many bruises he was hiding as he floated beside me.

I dreaded passing through the gateway, but the councilors must have done something to quell any crowds; it was almost deserted. Leona hesitated, but when she saw me go past the pillars, she followed.

The genies asked whether they could come over later to keep Leona and me company for a while. I said,

"Of course," and watched them race away.

Leona showed no desire to go home. "My father will be there, taking care of my mother. If he doesn't see me today, he'll shout at me tomorrow. But if I go home now, he'll shout at me today. He says it was my mother's fault she got burned by a human; I'm sure he'll say I became a criminal to spite him."

After Leona and I landed outside my door, it took me a few minutes to get up the courage to enter. The hush inside covered every surface and stuck to me like cobwebs. Without Leona, I would have felt paralyzed.

"We should go through this place and get rid of any lurking enchantments," she said, drawing her wand.

"I don't want to come across the spell that killed Beryl," I said, my voice rasping.

"We don't have to see the spells. We can banish them without revealing them."

I dragged forth my stylus. "I'll do it. You should start conserving your radia."

She wouldn't listen, running her wand across walls and floors, calling out, *"Banjan ex lomel!"*

I joined her, and together we finished the rooms downstairs. I paid special attention to all the jars of tea.

Leona cleared Beryl's room so I wouldn't have to look at my guardian's silent nest or the neat rows of baskets where she had kept her things.

I went slowly up to my mother's room. As I cleared it of hidden enchantments, I began to feel a sense of peace. At last, this room could be a haven again. I touched the trees in the painting and let myself remember how good it felt to be near real trees on Earth.

"Zaria?" Leona called.

She was in the hallway by the last door. It was made of a sheet of raw copper, dark green. "I'll clear your father's room," she said.

How well she knew me. Soon, I would let myself remember my father and all the ways I missed him. Soon, I would explore the room he'd called his own.

Soon, but not now.

"Thank you," I told Leona, and drifted downstairs.

I pulled the bottle of powder from my pocket and set it on the granite shelf next to the stove. It had a sinister air of waiting.

Waiting for what? Or whom?

"What are you good for?" I asked the bottle uneasily.

I doubted it was *good* for anything. Or anyone. It was probably extremely dangerous, something I should guard with great care.

I lifted my wand and spoke quietly. "Only those who love me may enter this house as long as I'm alive; no one and nothing else may come into this house in any form. Without my permission, no spell may cross the threshold."

Magic flowed through my wand, and into the stones and metal from which the house was built. The spell would use a lot of radia, but it was worth it to have a refuge.

• • •

Leona nestled among the patched pillows of Beryl's perch, looking tired and in pain.

"How bad is your wing?" I asked.

She sighed. "Better than it was. If that troggy gnome hadn't twisted it . . ."

Silence began to build as I wished in vain for a way to drive away her suffering.

"Have you ever wanted to enchant yourself with a forgetting spell?" she asked.

I took the perch opposite her and thought for a while. "No," I answered. "I've tried to forget many things. But in the end, I would rather remember."

"We'll all remember Beryl," she said.

"Yes," I whispered.

"But remembering some things is terrible. Being caged. Layered magic. Telling lies about my best friend." Leona looked haunted. "I've done so many things I regret."

"Me, too," I said.

"I let being a Violet go to my head. I went too far, Zaree. Putting a compulsion spell on my own mother! And I should never have blown up that human's house." She bit her lip. "I wish I could forget."

I thought of Michael Seabolt and the way he had fallen to the ground when his memory was restored.

"I keep thinking of Beryl the last time I saw her," I said. "So worn and tired, because of me."

"We could do a forgetting spell on each other," Leona said.

I shook my head. "If we couldn't remember, we might make the same mistakes."

She was quiet for a while. "At first, I thought it would be fun to be Violet," she said. "But now, I feel horribly responsible. I know I should use my powers with wisdom. Wisdom I don't have."

"Maybe," I said, "we can help each other be more wise."

In the evening, Andalonus and Meteor arrived with an enormous bowl of freshly picked sonnia. We gobbled the scarlet flowers and told one another the stories of our separate adventures.

Leona's time in the Iron Lands had been short. "It's a hideous place," she said. "A desert, without magic of any kind. No one can even fly there." Gnomes had tried to get her to talk by threatening her wings. She had pretended to be unable to speak. Then they had moved her back into Feyland and taken her to Lily Morganite.

"She laid layers and layers of magic on me, including a compulsion spell." Leona's silver wings flared out angrily. "Now she knows everything that I know." She gave me a meaningful look. "I'm sorry."

"No one blames you," I said, shivering. "I can't imagine anything worse than being under a compulsion to Lily."

Leona shook back her hair. "It's lucky the transfer of radia can't be compelled. If it could, Lily would be much richer, and my reserves would be zero."

It turned out that Leona had been looking for me when the gateway snared her.

"But why?" I asked. It wasn't like her to wait for someone.

She made a face. "I was afraid of the troll elixir for sealing the portal. I was hoping *you* would drink it, Zaree."

Andalonus's smile reached his ears. "Afraid? *You?*" he said.

"Troll magic," Leona answered. "Unpredictable! What if I lost control?" She took another sonnia flower. "Where *were* you?" she asked me.

"Sidetracked," I answered, pushing Sam to the back of my mind. "I'm very sorry."

Before Leona could pursue it, Meteor launched into our side of the tale. When he got to what I did after drinking the elixir, Andalonus laughed long and loud, but Leona cringed.

Meteor described how we'd sent Jason home unharmed. "Sorry we undid your spell, Leona," he said. "But it seemed best."

She didn't argue.

Fright tingled along my wings as I realized what came next in Meteor's tale. Sam had walked through the boulder right after I transported Jason away. I shot Meteor what I hoped was an eloquent glance.

"You should tell the rest, Zaree," he said. "I want to hear about the cloak."

I smiled at him. When I took up the story, there was no word of Sam in anything I said. I skipped ahead to how Meteor and I had gone through the Golden Station and discovered that all Feyland was searching for *Zaria Tourmaline.*

Meteor didn't correct me about Sam. But he wasn't satisfied with my report of how the troll cloak had turned to powder.

"What you did was impossible," he insisted. "The councilors might have decided you weren't really wrapped in troll magic, but *I* think you were."

"If it was impossible, then how did I do it?"

"I don't know." His white eyebrows came together in a frown of concentration. "I'm beginning to believe there's something very different about you, Zaria. You seem to have unusual talents. How did you put up that wall? And how did you seal the indigo bottle?" His eyes gleamed. "And why did you act like you were giving permission to anyone who left FOOM through the blue curtain?"

I shrugged uncomfortably. I didn't feel ready to talk about making up spells.

"And," Meteor went on, "what sort of enchantment made all those spells rebound off you?"

I sighed. Sometimes Meteor was too observant. "I'll tell you another time," I said, "if I ever understand it myself."

Chapter Fifty-nine

THE CREATION OF GLACIER CLOTH SHOWCASES FEY COMPREHENSION OF THE PRINCIPLES UNDERLYING TIME ITSELF, AND REQUIRES LEVEL 100 MAGIC. GLACIER CLOTH IS A FABRIC THAT FREEZES WHATEVER IT TOUCHES, THOUGH NOT AS ICE FREEZES—IT FREEZES IN *TIME*.

THE PRINCESS WHO BECAME KNOWN AS "SLEEPING BEAUTY" WAS WRAPPED IN GLACIER CLOTH. SHE DID NOT FIND THE EXPERIENCE UNPLEASANT, BUT SHE WAS A HUMAN, AFTER ALL. SHE DID NOT HAVE MAGIC OF HER OWN, ONLY THE MANY GIFTS HEAPED ON HER BY COMPETING GODMOTHERS. FOR HER, THE YEARS SPENT FROZEN WOULD HAVE SEEMED MUCH LIKE A DREAM.

BUT GLACIER CLOTH IS NOT SO KIND TO FEY FOLK. A FAIRY OR GENIE IN GLACIER CLOTH DOES NOT SLEEP BUT IS PRESERVED, AWAKE BUT UNABLE TO MOVE. IT IS A LIVING DEATH, AN EXISTENCE OUTSIDE OF TIME. ANY WHO TRY TO FIGHT THE EFFECTS BECOME DRAINED OF THEIR RADIA RESERVES.

—Orville Gold, genie historian of Feyland

*I*n the morning, I was barely aware of Leona nudging me to say good-bye before she left. We'd both gone to sleep in the main room on the perches where we'd been resting. I muttered something and fell back to sleep.

I woke in the afternoon and stretched my cramped wings.

There was so much to do.

Several things gave me the strength to seek out Banburus Lazuli again. First, I was well protected. Second, I doubted that Laz had any more enchanted cloaks—or if he did, he wouldn't waste them on me. Third, he didn't seem to be friendly with gnomes. If he'd had a private legion to serve him, I would have seen them before.

Last, and most important, I was desperate.

The Ugly Mug had not changed. I don't know why I expected it would have. Though it was afternoon, plenty of tables were filled with energetic patrons swilling various aromatic brews. In the back of the room, a card game was happening. On the makeshift stage, a band of genies was setting up drums and tuning fiddles, blowing a few notes on silver flutes.

I discovered that entering the place while visible was quite different from slinking along the walls unseen. Young as I was, before I was a wingspan past the door, I received many invitations to share a drink—everything from coffee to cocoa.

The stir I caused drew Laz's attention. He slapped his cards facedown and left the game. He ambled toward me, lank and unhurried, a large cup in one hand. I turned and left the tavern, knowing he would follow—and he did, around the side of his disreputable building.

We faced each other. He shuffled his feet and then floated a few inches off the ground. I matched him, rising until our eyes were on a level.

"Impressive bit of magic making that cloak disappear," he said, as if discussing the weather. "And what a moment you chose for it." His eyes shifted back and forth before settling on me. "It's good to know I can still be swindled now and again."

"Swindled?" I asked.

"Clearly the cloak was not as powerful as I was led to believe." His expression said, *Or you would never have freed yourself.*

My pride was a little stung, and I remembered that destroying the cloak had cost me a fortune in radia. But I had no wish to discuss troll magic with Laz, so I didn't deny what he'd said.

He took a drink, wiping his mouth with his hand. "What brings you here?"

"Curiosity," I said, hoping I sounded calm.

"Oh?"

"Do you know a spell for restoring lost memory?"

Eyeing me blearily, he took another drink. "What's it worth to you?"

"Nothing. But it may be worth something to *you.*"

He snorted. "I'm not under a forgetting spell."

I drew my stylus. "I'm betting you are. Tell me the spell, so I can test my bet."

He blinked warily. "You believe I'm enchanted?"

"Definitely."

Laz seemed to lose some of his swagger. "If you want to throw away ten radia, I won't stop you."

"No, no, my fine genie," I said sarcastically. "That's not how it's done. First we decide on the stakes. If it turns out you're under a forgetting spell, I get to ask you two questions that you will truthfully answer."

He chuckled, but his eyes shifted back and forth. "Sorry. Can't agree."

"I paid you fifty thousand radia for nothing," I said. "You owe me."

"And these questions you want to ask would be worth fifty thousand?"

"To me." *They would be worth a million.*

"Hmm." He drank again and smacked his lips. "And if I'm *not* enchanted?"

"We'll call it even."

Laz didn't hesitate. "Deal." He strummed his fingers through his gray-blue hair. "The spell to recover lost memories is *storen los moro.* Level Thirty. You don't have to be near the subject."

I infused to Level 30 and pointed my wand at him. *"Storen los moro."*

Laz's expression went from startled to enraged. He let loose a blast of frightening curses. He finished by calling Lily Morganite a wretched gremlin.

"You'll never collect that reward now," I said, keeping my voice light.

Calm again, Laz rubbed his chin against the edge of the cup. "Yes, I hear she's in disgrace, and those other councilors can also be counted on to go back on their word."

I took a deep breath. "You said sooner or later you hear about everything that happens in Feyland."

"True."

Now that the moment had come to ask my questions, my tongue felt dry. I swallowed. "What have you heard about Gilead and Cinna Tourmaline—and how they disappeared?"

He took a long drink, the cocoa gurgling in his throat until the cup was empty. Then he looked at me. "You should let bygones be bygones."

"You agreed to the stakes."

"Yes, but you cheated. You knew the outcome."

"I won the bet."

He glanced around as if afraid of being overheard. But we were alone. "There was a rumor," he said. "Unverified, you understand?"

"What rumor?"

"That your family was bound in glacier cloth."

My wings suddenly collapsed, and I fell forward. When Laz caught me by the shoulders, I allowed him to prop me up.

He shook me a little. "Do you want some coffee? On the house," he said. "It might help."

Breathing deeply, I waited for my strength to come back. "Glacier cloth," I said. "My family could be frozen in time?"

He let go of me and stepped back. "That's my understanding of the effects, yes."

"They could be alive?" I felt a tiny spot of hope in the center of my chest.

"Could be."

"My family could be *alive*? All I have to do is find them?"

Laz cleared his throat. "If the rumor is true."

"Did the rumor say where they might be?"

He shook his head. "Nothing about that. And like I said, unverified."

"Who told you?"

"Traveling genie, years ago. Never saw him again. That's the whole story, Zaria—such as it is." He folded his arms.

"Thank you," I said, and spread my shaky wings. I wanted to be alone now—alone to nurture the small bright hope in my heart, alone to think about what to do next. "Maybe I'll see you again someday."

"Wait," he said, before I lifted off. "What was the second question?"

The stunning rumor about my family had driven it from my mind, but I remembered then. "Oh, yes. Do you know what gnomes love best?"

Laz clicked his tongue. "Gnomes, eh? That's easy, Zaria

Tourmaline. What gnomes love best, what they want most, what they'll do almost anything to get—is respect."

I looked hard at him. "Respect? But if you know that's all it takes, why don't you have gangs of gnomes helping *you*?"

"Me?" He gave his coughing laugh. "I don't respect anyone."

He turned his back and glided into The Ugly Mug.

Chapter Sixty

MORE AND MORE ITEMS ARE BEING SMUGGLED ONTO TIRFEYNE FROM EARTH. A FEW ARE JUSTIFIABLE— FOR EXAMPLE, PENS AND PAPER. BUT MOST ARE MERE FRIPPERY AND HAVE NO PLACE IN FEYLAND. SUCH ITEMS INCLUDE A WIDE VARIETY OF PLASTICS, MOLDED INTO EVERYTHING FROM BUTTONS TO UMBRELLAS TO TOYS.

IN ADDITION, THE SMUGGLING OF CHOCOLATES AND COFFEES HAS INCREASED A HUNDREDFOLD. DETERMINED RESIDENTS OF FEYLAND MAY HAVE A CHOICE OF UN-HEALTHY CONFECTIONS AND DEGENERATE BREWS, ALL OF WHICH OVERSTIMULATE FEY PHYSIOLOGY.

UNFORTUNATELY, THE BAN UPON LEPRECHAUN TRAVEL TO EARTH HAS NOT BEEN EFFECTIVE IN HALTING THE FLOW OF SMUGGLED ITEMS.

—Orville Gold, genie historian of Feyland

I flew in joyous turmoil high over the seedy side of Oberon City. My father, my mother, my brother—might be alive, might one day come home.

Would come home. Because I would look until I found

them, and then I would free them. Somehow.

If the rumor was true.

It had to be true. Banburus Lazuli had heard about it. His sources might be shady, but I believed they were accurate.

I soared, picturing myself with my parents and brother. *Alive* was the word singing through my wings as I flew. *Alive, alive, alive!*

My plan? I would read my mother's spellbook at long last. Maybe it would contain clues about my family, clues that could lead me to where they were.

To go to Earth, I would have to be invisible. Although Lily Morganite had not shown herself, she was surely out there somewhere. She might be wearing a disguise. She could be in a viewing booth at this very moment, watching for my appearance on Earth.

I was just about to cast the invisibility spell, but I stopped. Somehow, the thought of hiding myself again seemed unbearable. I didn't want to do it anymore.

What could I do instead?

As I buzzed past a crumbling tower, it occurred to me that I could create a spell to keep the fey scopes from finding me. Then I wouldn't have to wonder if Lily Morganite—or anyone else—was watching me during my visits to Earth. I didn't know how many radia it would cost, but it couldn't be more expensive than repeated invisibility, every ten minutes, every time I went to Earth.

For I *would* go back to Earth. Many times. The law

prohibiting journeys to the human world for underage fairies was a law I intended to keep on breaking.

Hovering in midair, I scanned the sky around me. Nothing and no one crossed my view, so I infused my wand halfway. I tapped my head and improvised a spell: "For the next month," I whispered, "I cannot be perceived by any magical means, no matter where I am."

The grove where I'd buried the spellbook was aglow with sunlight as I began scooping handfuls of dirt from under the blue spruce. Soon my mother's spellbook was in my hands. Dirt smudged the cover, but the book felt as light as ever.

Holding it in my lap, I sat leaning against the trunk of the tree, my wings comfortably folded. First I planned to skim every page, and then go back and read all of it, word by word. Even if my *unusual talents* meant that I didn't need to memorize specific spells in the ancient language, reading the book would be a way to get closer to my mother.

I turned each page lovingly, admiring the careful, even script. The spells were perfectly organized, but occasionally there were sections of scribbled notes that made no sense.

Translation of transfers, I read. *Invisible theft?*

And on another page: *J & G delve, unoccupied tower*

There were many similar notes, all of them incomprehensible.

After the last spell, there were about ten more leaves left in the book. I turned the empty pages slowly and then stopped when I saw that one of them was full of writing.

It was a letter, with my own name at the top.

My wings began to quiver as I started reading.

My dearest Zaria,

If you are reading this, your father and I have not come home. This means you are under the care of our friend, Beryl Danburite, who is one of the few fairies we trust completely. It also means that it is likely that years have passed between the last time we saw each other and now. For all I know, you are a full grown fairy.

Then again, you have always been curious, and I think it is possible that you have found this book while you are still quite young, perhaps as young as fourteen.

Tears flooded my eyes, making it impossible to read. A letter from my mother! It had been in the book for five years. Had Beryl known it was there? Had she kept the spellbook hidden away, and then put it into the copper cupboard on the day I got my watch and wand? Had she known I would look for it when I turned fourteen?

I wiped my eyes and began reading again.

I am so sorry that you had to grow up without me. You are one of the great joys of my life, and it is a terrible hardship even to consider the possibility that you are reading these words. And yet, I must write them. If the worst happens, and we do not return, I cannot leave you without an explanation.

Before he disappeared, your brother Jett believed he had found proof of vast smuggling rings operating between Earth and Tirfeyne. Humans crave our gold and jewels, and we crave their paper, their pens, their books, and other things.

On Earth, the smugglers are often unwitting participants, finding payment in diamonds and gold under their pillows—or not at all. Fey smugglers learn to be sly, and they help themselves to the goods they want when humans are not looking.

In itself, Jett's discovery is not surprising, for goods have flowed back and forth between Earth and Tirfeyne for centuries, though always on a limited basis and never with official approval. The High Council has always condemned smuggling, although in nearly every home in Feyland, at least one item from Earth may now be found.

We believe that unless the flow of goods is limited, the balance between worlds will be disrupted, a balance the Ancients urged us to keep. We do not know the cost of disrupting that balance; we suspect that it will be high.

What has made Jett's discovery so dangerous is that he found evidence that the smugglers in Feyland were paying certain Council members kickbacks in radia, for allowing unregistered portals to stay open so smuggling could continue unchecked.

To make matters worse, your father and I suspect that one of the councilors involved in smuggling may also be somehow diverting radia from the durable spells that need to be refreshed and hoarding that radia for herself. I am sorry to mention the possibility of such corruption within the High Council. And I dare not name those whom we suspect, for I do not wish any of this to harm you one day.

Your father and I are going after Jett. He has been missing for three days, and we are very uneasy. We hope our mission will be swiftly concluded, that we may return to you soon. If we are successful, I will destroy this letter. If we are not, then you are reading it, and we are gone.

Remember, my darling Zaria, that love does not disappear with time. My love, and your father's, and your brother's, will be with you always.

I stayed for several hours, rereading my mother's letter over and over. It didn't explain what Lily had held over Beryl; maybe my mother didn't know about that. But Beryl had spoken the truth when she called Lily diabolical.

Had Cinna and Gilead confronted Lily Morganite? Or had someone else told Lily they were on her trail?

She had taken her vengeance on my parents. Then she had ignored their small, forgettable daughter until she knew I possessed the power of a Violet.

Her radia reserves surpassed mine now. She was far more cunning than I. But I had something she didn't. I could improvise spells.

She must never know I could.

"I will overcome you," I said aloud. "Somehow, I will."

Wherever the quest took me, whatever it showed me—whether I went alone or with companions—I would overcome Lily Morganite and free Gilead, Cinna, and Jett Tourmaline. Leaning against the blue spruce tree in the grove on Earth, I vowed upon my family's honor.

Chapter Sixty-one

TRUE FRIENDS GIVE NOT ONLY AFFECTION BUT ALSO
UNDERSTANDING. LONG LIFE MEANS NOTHING WITH-
OUT THE PRESENCE OF SUCH FRIENDSHIPS—AND IF
A GOOD FRIEND IS ALSO AN EXCELLENT SCHOLAR, SO
MUCH THE BETTER.

—*Orville Gold, genie historian of Feyland*

The viewing station near the Malachite Towers was bustling. Each booth had a line, and the fey folk waiting jostled each other and traded insults freely. The mood seemed cheerful. Green streamers decked the walls, and collections of fey lights twinkled over the clean tiles.

Looking for Seth, I hovered behind a fairy who waited for a turn. It was none other than Shirelle, the grouch I'd seen during my first visit.

"Do you know what happened to Seth?" I asked her.

"Seth! Didn't you hear? Bashed on the head by a gnome!" She gestured around at the decorations. "Quite the celebration," she said caustically. "We finally got an infusion! And those highfalutin councilors had nothing to do with it. It was a donation. A Violet fairy flew in and fixed everything."

I drifted back from her, ready to leave.

"Zaria Tourmaline," said a pleased voice nearby.

I whirled to see Seth beside me, a green bandage wrapping his head.

"Seth!" I squealed. "You're alive."

"What's a knock on the head to someone with a granite skull?" he said, chuckling. "And *you* look a bit better than the last time we met."

I had to persuade him not to make an announcement that I was in the station; he wanted to publicly thank me for my donation of radia. When he finally agreed to keep quiet, I led up to the reason for my visit.

"Do you suppose you could let me into a booth?"

A few minutes later, I was secure inside a viewing booth. Seth told me I could have as much time as I liked.

I didn't hurry as I adjusted the eyepiece and made my request. "Jett Tourmaline," I said.

Blank. And the scope stayed blank when I asked to see my father and mother.

I sighed. Stubborn hope had urged me to look, though I had been almost sure of the outcome. The councilors and Beryl would have looked in viewing scopes, of course, long ago when my family had taken their last journey.

"Well," I muttered, "I know two places I won't find them. Earth—unless they're underground. And the Iron Lands— because magic doesn't work in the Iron Lands, and glacier cloth is magical." If only the scopes could be turned upon Feyland, I might learn more.

I sighed. I should leave the booth. There was nothing left to do here.

And yet, I felt a tug on my heart, as if a slender ribbon stretched between me and Earth. "It can't do any harm to *look*," I whispered.

The eyepiece fit snugly as I opened the lens. "Show me Samuel Seabolt," I said.

Instantly an image appeared, so clear I felt as if I hovered close beside the people shown in the scope.

Michael Seabolt reclined in a hospital bed, propped comfortably against pillows. His head was bandaged, and his arm was in a cast.

I would have liked to ask him what had happened to him while he was gone. I would never hear the full story, now, and yet I was happy just knowing that he had come back to his family. His eyes, alert and bright, were on them: a slender woman, a little girl with red braids, and a tall boy with gold-toned eyes.

Sam's hair was slightly rumpled, his smile eager. "Jenna made you a picture, Dad," he said.

Jenna held up a drawing. "For you, Daddy."

Michael Seabolt took the paper from her. "Thank you, sweetie."

She beamed. "It's a fairy."

Their father examined the drawing solemnly. "Beautiful," he said.

"Her fairies always have purple wings," said Sam, lifting one of Jenna's braids.

I allowed myself a full ten minutes watching them. Sam reported that Jason's house had blown up in a mysterious explosion but no one was hurt. Jenna blithely announced that a fairy with purple eyes and wings had come to see her. Her parents smiled indulgently.

Studying Sam, I tried to find an absence in his eyes, something to tell me he missed me without knowing what he missed. But no shadows clouded his face. He looked at ease and healthy, talking with his father.

When the ten minutes were over, I lowered the lever on the scope. "Good-bye," I whispered.

When I left the viewing station, Meteor was outside, hovering patiently, his striped hair waving a little in the night breeze. I didn't ask him how he had known where I would be. As we rose into the velvet air, I was simply grateful to see his smile.

Acknowledgments

Thank you, Zaria Tourmaline, for visiting me, introducing your friends, and letting me know about your travels.

Thank you to the people at Egmont USA, for all their work and kindness on behalf of this story. Regina Griffin and Nico Medina believed in Zaria's adventures while those adventures were still in the form of a raw manuscript. Editor Ruth Katcher provided deep insights and a gentle guiding hand. Sammy Yuen created the shining cover illustration. Mary Albi and Rob Guzman and their marvelous team brought the word of Zaria's world to Earth. And many more people behind the scenes did so much for the love of books in general and for this one in particular. Thank you all!

Rebecca Rowley and Lisa Pere are my wonderful critique partners. I'm grateful for all the Saturday meetings, the laughs, the caffeinated conversations, and the keen comments. Thanks also to the members of the Weekly Writers Workshop who saw some of the early chapters of *Violet Wings* and cheered for Zaria. And other dear friends—they know who they are—actively urged me on and put up with my disappearing for weeklong stretches many times during the course of writing.

My husband Tim has been, as usual, full of smiles and love. Thanks, Tim! And my delightfully honest and perceptive children read the final draft and made important suggestions for improvement. I overflow with gratitude for you, Emrys and Rose!

My sisters Peggy and Bridget gave unstinting encouragement—one from the far-flung reaches of Florida, and the other from the coast of California; so did Sophie Hicks, my agent, from across the ocean in London.

Victoria Hanley
Foothills of the
Rocky Mountains, Colorado

Victoria Hanley has done a lot of traveling in search of fairy hotspots. She's made long journeys by car, plane, bus, train, and bicycle, not to mention plenty of hiking. Along the way, she has lived in California, Massachusetts, Wisconsin, New Mexico, Oregon, and Colorado, and her novels have been published in ten languages. Her fantasy headquarters are now located in Loveland, Colorado, at the foot of the Rocky Mountains, a place where fairies and genies, along with pixies, trolls, gremlins, and assorted humans, are always welcome to gather. You can visit the author at www.victoriahanley.com.

Lake Zurich MS North
LIBRARY
95 Hubbard Lane
Hawthorn Woods, IL 60047